THE EDEN STORIES

Saturn:
The Eden Experiment

Terry Toler

Saturn: The Eden Experiment

Published by: BeHoldings Publishing

Copyright @2020, **BeHoldings, LLC**
Terrytoler.com,
All Rights Reserved

Cover and interior designs: BeHoldings Publishing
For information, address support@terrytoler.com.

Our books can be purchased in bulk for promotional, educational and business use. Please contact your bookseller or the BeHoldings Publishing Sales department at: sales@terrytoler.com

For booking information email: booking@terrytoler.com
First U.S. Edition: January, 2021
Printed in the United States of America
ISBN 978-1-7352243-3-6

OTHER BOOKS BY TERRY TOLER

Fiction

The Longest Day
The Reformation of Mars
The Great Wall of Ven-Us
Saturn: The Eden Experiment
The Late, Great Planet Jupiter
Save The Girls
The Ingenue
The Blue Rose
Saving Sara
Save The Queen
No Girl Left Behind
The Launch
Body Count
Mercury Protocols

Non-Fiction

How to Make More Than a Million Dollars
The Heart Attacked
Seven Years of Promise
Mission Possible
Marriage Made in Heaven
21 Days to Physical Healing
21 Days to Spiritual Fitness
21 Days to Divine Health
21 Days to a Great Marriage
21 Days to Financial Freedom
21 Days to Sharing Your Faith
21 Days to Mission Possible
7 Days to Emotional Freedom
Uncommon Finances
Uncommon Marriage

Uncommon Health
Suddenly Free
Feeling Free

For more information on these books and other resources
visit TerryToler.com.

PRAISE FOR THE EDEN STORIES

"I love this new style of writing you've invented. It's telling the story in the most interesting way."

"These books are riveting."

"Ground-breaking."

"These books left me with something important. A feeling that we were there and witnessed something great."

"Your cliffhangers are the most compelling I've seen in a long time."

"Great writing style! You capture me from the first chapter."

"The endings are the usual Terry Toler style. Leaving ones with their mouth hanging open."

"Oh man! These are definitely Terry Toler books."

"Very intense. You tackle subjects most dare not touch."

"Every story gives me a lot to think about."

"What a great premise!"

"You've created a new genre of speculative fiction."

"Wow! That's all I can say."

"As soon as I finish one, I have to start the next one."

THE EDEN EXPERIMENT

1

Saturn, 4013 Sat Year

What the First Minister of Saturn had asked me to do was unthinkable. Barbaric. Deplorable. Unspeakable.

I can't believe I agreed to do it.

As the head of SR&MDA, the Scientific Research and Medical Development Agency, I had devoted my life to new discoveries and the advancement of medical knowledge. As the foremost medical physician on Saturn, the oath I signed upon graduating from medical class stated my first responsibility above all else was to do no harm.

An oath I was about to violate for the first time in my long and distinguished career.

Mark Sandifer lay on the table in my research laboratory, breathing on his own. A thin white sheet covered his body. A thirty-five-year-old male, Mark was six foot, a hundred and ninety-five pounds. A former athlete, he should've been in the prime of his life. Five minutes from now, he'd be breathing through a ventilator controlled by me. Right after I did him considerable harm. Right after I killed him.

Necessary, I'm told. Evil really. A necessary evil. The first of two I had to kill.

I took no consolation in the fact that it was Mark's choice. He signed up for it. The twelve pages of medical waivers prepared by the best legal minds on the planet, signed and initialed and witnessed by a notaria, made it very clear that Mark was submitting to the experiment voluntarily, without coercion, and with a sound mind. The one million rings paid to his family was more than poor

Mark would've made in his entire life, had he lived to the average lifespan of eighty-eight. The sum was more than he could make in two lifetimes.

Tomorrow, another subject would be brought in to meet the same fate. A Satite.

No payment would be made to him. He wasn't doing it voluntarily. A prisoner of war recently captured in the battlefield, the Satite was locked safely in confinement where he'd be brought to me tomorrow, and I'd repeat the process.

I felt a little better about that one. Not much, but a little. Knowing he'd kill me first if he had the chance. Mark, on the other hand, was someone I'd grown to like. I told myself I wouldn't allow myself to get close to him or emotionally attached. I couldn't help it. He was such a genuinely nice guy.

When Mark said his tearful goodbyes to his family, I refused to be there. Made up some excuse about needing to prepare the laboratory. I knew it would be too hard. I'd been at the bedside of many patients who passed away and had consoled countless grieving families. This was different. I needed consolation as much as they did.

Mark let out a light cough which brought me back to reality. He was slowly drifting asleep from the light sedative given to calm his nerves. I'd take one myself, but I needed all my faculties and all the skills I possessed to make sure this experiment worked. One slip-up on my part, and Mark would have died in vain.

A few minutes before, Mark and I had discussed it again at length.

"Are you sure you want to do this?" I asked him. "It's not too late to back out."

"I'm sure, Dr. Forrester," he said confidently.

"Call me Roger. I think we're good enough friends to be on a first name basis."

"I really appreciate everything you've done for me and my family... Roger," he said, smiling.

Those were his last words. He seemed at peace with it. I wished I was. Someone once said that death was harder on the living than the one who died. No truer words were ever spoken, at least as it pertained to how I felt at that exact moment.

I placed a needle in Mark's arm and shot a drug into his bloodstream so he wouldn't feel any pain. A few seconds later his eyes drooped, his breathing slowed, and he fell asleep. For good. A machine monitored his vital signs. I stared at them. For some reason I couldn't bring myself to look at him. The numbers showed everything was normal.

I took the surgical knife off of the table and stood over him, torn, a debate raging in my head. Still not willing to look at his face. Would God approve of what I was about to do? The First Minister could not answer that question.

I had no answer for myself. I'd stayed awake many nights contemplating this very scenario. Praying. Wanting to talk to someone but sworn to secrecy.

My hand shook.

The room was empty. No one could know what was about to happen, other than the handful who already knew. My assistant knew some details but not many. Just as well. I'd tell her after the fact and give her a chance to participate.

The National Security Council consisting of the First Minister and a select few of his advisors had been briefed by me earlier in the day. They were excited to get the experiment going. I resented them. They had a cold callous to loss of life. Probably from ordering many young men and women into battle knowing they would die. For the greater good was their only consideration.

I'd spent my life battling to keep people alive. My war was with death. Making people's lives better. Not taking their lives from them.

The Eden Experiment.

As if somehow, giving it a biblical name justified it.

So highly classified, no one would tell. The program was not sanctioned by any governmental agency. If it got out, we'd all go to confinement and spend the rest of our lives locked in a ten by ten room.

The temperature in the laboratory was set at a blistery cold thirty-three degrees. Yet sweat crystals formed on my forehead. I wiped them off with my sleeve. I took a deep breath. Exhaled. Tried to calm my own nerves. I needed a steady hand.

"God forgive me," I said aloud, as I took the knife and cut open Mark's chest, exposing his heart. I waited for two minutes. His breathing became labored. His heartbeat slowed. Blood pressure dropped. The machine would notify me when he was clinically dead.

The alarm from the machine sounded. A loud blaring flatline. Normally, an alarm to warn me something was wrong. Everything was actually going as planned. Mark was dead.

I had to hurry.

2

The Satite was brought to my lab early the next morning, flanked by four soldiers. One on each arm and two from behind. His arms were bound in front of him and leg irons were locked around his ankles, forcing him to shuffle his feet in small steps. The two from behind were each holding thick ropes tethered to a belt around the man's waist.

When I learned four soldiers were accompanying him, my first thought was why so many? After seeing the man, my first thought was four might not be enough. The Satite was at least six foot, six inches tall. I estimated two hundred eighty-five pounds. Solid muscle. One of the soldiers had blood trickling from his nose, likely from a fight the man put up as they tried to restrain him.

His sandy blond hair was mussed slightly but laid almost neatly with a slight part to the left side. Perfect features. The only thing out of place in the picture was his eyes. They were filled with hate. Evil almost. Darting back and forth. Looking for an opportunity to escape. His hands were in a fist, looking for someone to strike. His jaw clenched. Shoulders raised. Like a warrior ready to kill someone. A frightening sight even though well restrained.

I shuddered. Not sure if from fear or regret. I almost regretted having to kill such a perfect specimen. The only consolation was knowing he wasn't really a man in the sense that he wasn't made in the image of God. And until he was dead, he would be a considerable risk to me and everyone else in the room.

The operating table was prepared, but I was certain it wasn't long enough. His legs would hang off the end. A specially constructed table, it was bolted securely to the floor with restraints attached to it, but the restraints would not likely reach his legs.

That might be the least of my worries. How was I going to shoot his arm with a sedative even if his arms were restrained? And would the restraints hold? I'm not sure they anticipated someone of his size and strength when they constructed the table.

Surprisingly, the man got on to the table voluntarily. Before he did, he looked at me with a sly and mischievous grin as if he had a plan only he knew about. Perhaps, he thought the odds were better with him against me rather than him against the four soldiers. Something I wouldn't disagree with.

The soldiers secured his arms, but, as I suspected, his legs hung off the end of the table so they couldn't restrain them. They left the leg irons around his ankles and used some steel cuffs designed for hands and secured his legs to the table. I wasn't confident they'd hold if he really applied his strength to them. The soldiers thought the same thing because they began talking among themselves, trying to come up with a plan for how to restrain him better.

"Dr. Forrester, would you like us to stay and guard him until you get him sedated?" one of them asked.

That was not an option. As far as they knew, the man was having routine surgery. They could never know what was happening in that lab.

"No. I'll be fine. Can you restrain him at the waist? He needs to be immobile while I prep him for surgery."

The Satite continued to look at me with an evil grin, never taking his eyes off me. Eerie as they followed me around. I could tell he was using all his strength to restrain himself. He was biding his time, waiting for the right moment.

I was distracted and didn't notice one of the soldiers wandering around the lab.

"Stop! Don't go back there," I yelled at the top of my lungs.

"I'm just looking for something to restrain him with," he said.

Mark was in the corner of the room, a partition hiding him from view of the soldiers. I couldn't let the soldier see the ghastly site behind the curtains. He stopped in his tracks, not realizing he was doing something wrong.

"That area has some infectious chemicals," I explained. "Don't go near it. I wouldn't want you to get infected. You could die."

The soldier got a worried look on his face and immediately turned and walked away looking back at the area. The other soldiers seemed concerned as well and started hurrying to complete their task and get out of there.

"This will have to do," I said. "You can go now."

They couldn't get out fast enough.

I looked around the room and then back at the Satite, wondering how I got myself into this situation. I figured my best course of action was to get him under sedation as quickly as possible.

I scanned his wrist for an ID chip. It worked from a distance up to a foot, so I stayed a safe distance away from him. The chip read MC-43. A low number. One of the first in the Satite program to survive. I was amazed at the advancements they had made in such a short period of time. The scientist in me was anxious to explore him and see what I could learn.

I had to live long enough.

No way could I get him to take an oral sedative, so I readied the syringe filled with the anesthesia that would put him to sleep. I added more to the dose. A man that big wouldn't fall asleep easily. I also suspected he would not go quietly.

How was I going to shoot it into his arm? It was restrained but the buckle had about a foot of lag. He could move his arm a foot in any direction.

I approached cautiously. The syringe in my right hand, my left hand free so I could use it to hold him down, if necessary.

My heart was beating so hard I could hear it in my ears. My breathing was shallow.

He laid on the table calm and emotionless.

"This will help you to relax," I said nervously, trying to say it reassuringly. "It's going to put you to sleep. You need this so you don't feel any pain."

I met no resistance. His arm relaxed on the table. I relaxed a little as well. Maybe he was resigned to his fate. As far as he knew, the surgery was necessary to save his life. He probably had no idea what I was about to do.

Suddenly, his arm twitched.

I felt the movement but reacted too late.

He grabbed my lab coat and pulled me violently toward him. He released the grip on my coat and grabbed my right wrist.

I couldn't drop the syringe because he'd grasped my hand with a firm grip, like a vise.

I couldn't move it.

He brought my hand straight up in a motion toward my face—straight toward my eye.

I turned my head just as the needle gashed the right side of my face

Pain shot through me like a lightning bolt. The syringe fell to the floor, my blood dripping off my face onto the bed where the man lay. His shirt was now stained with my blood.

He released the grip on my hand and thrashed around. Pulling on the restraints.

I instinctively raised my hand to my face. I touched my cheek and then looked at my fingers which were covered with blood.

The man pulled against the restraints with all his might, but they were holding. The table made cracking and groaning sounds from the force his power was bringing against the bolts holding it in place. He kicked his legs back and forth against the cuffs. The table rocked like a boat battling the waves. Still bolted to the ground. Holding, but I didn't know for how long.

My first instinct was to run. But I couldn't. I looked over at the partition where Mark was laying.

I've come too far. Mark can't die in vain.

I had to do something quickly or he was going to get free. I wanted to shout out for help. But no one was there to hear me. I couldn't leave the man. He'd eventually break the chains and escape. I had to do something.

Whatever it was, I had to hurry.

3

Now I wanted to kill the Satite.

Before, I felt a certain level of regret having to take his life, even if for the greater good. All I felt now was anger, rage, and an intense desire for revenge. The pain in my face fed my outrage with adrenaline like gasoline stoking a fire. I wanted to tend to the wound, which was throbbing, but I had to focus on finding something to kill him with. Before he broke free and killed me.

The noise in the lab was deafening. The Satite had managed to break the bolts on one corner of the table from its foundation. He would alternate between straining with all of his might against the chains and then bouncing up and down, banging the corner loudly against the floor trying to break the rest of the table from its foundation. He was contributing to the din with intermittent loud screams. Sometimes the screams were high-pitched and piercing. Other times they were like the roar of a caged lion trying to escape a trap.

I was racked with indecision. Confused. Not sure what to do.

My caller was nearby. I could use it to call for help. Not an option. That would mean the project would be discovered, and I'd be arrested. The Eden Experiment would be exposed. The First Minister of Saturn would be removed from office and put on trial. It would become a national scandal of epic proportions.

That alternative was better than death I reasoned for a moment. But then I thought of Mark. I had his death to consider. I owed it to him to keep fighting and to not give up.

No one could get to me in time anyway. The building was empty, and help was too far away to do me any good.

I ran over to the cabinets against the far wall searching for anything that might work as a weapon. I grabbed a surgical knife and started to run back toward him but stopped after a couple steps. That small a knife would barely phase him. If I somehow managed to wound him enough to kill him, it might do so much damage I wouldn't be able to bring him back to life for the experiments.

He stopped struggling and turned and stared at me.

I had the knife in my right hand, staring back. For a moment, we were at a stalemate. No one moved. I don't think I took a breath for a full minute.

No words came out of either of our mouths. Blood was dripping from his wrists from where the chains had cut into them. He seemed oblivious to the pain. His anger, rage, and intense desire for revenge seemed stronger than mine. I could see how he'd killed so many Christians on the battlefield.

My blood on his shirt and the thought of the people he killed caused my resolve to return—stronger than before. Not only did I need to save my life but killing him would save the lives of many people. I needed that justification. A rationalization for what I was contemplating doing.

It gave me an idea. I went to a closet in the corner of the room, as the Satite went back to trying to free himself with renewed energy and effort. His resolve seemed to have grown as well. He probably realized he was running out of time. The screams became louder and more menacing as if maybe they'd scare me away.

I opened the door to the closet but then paused, thinking. Inside was a mask connected to a tank of oxygen. In another closet was a deadly gas, a nerve agent, that would kill a man almost instantly. In the next room, we had another lab full of monkeys used for other scientific and medical research. We used the gas to humanely euthanize them after they had served their purposes. I hadn't realized it before, but I could now hear the monkeys making noise, screaming, adding to the commotion in our room.

If I could connect the mask to the deadly gas and somehow get the mask over the man's face, it would kill him within a couple minutes. I quickly assessed the damage the gas would cause. What would the effect be on his body? Could I still do the experiment? I wasn't sure, but I was out of options.

I disconnected the mask from the oxygen tank and quickly ran to the closet to get the tank of deadly gas.

He tried even harder to break his chains, seemingly doubling his efforts as the din grew louder and his screams more intense. A quick glance, and I could see him foaming at the mouth, spewing saliva mixed with curse words.

"I'm going to kill you. I'm going to cut out your heart. You're going to die a slow and painful death," he said as he slammed the table against the floor again and again. I could hear the floor creaking and the table cracking as it started to give way. One of the cuffs on his legs had broken free. The other was still holding, but barely.

My hands were shaking so much I could barely attach the tank of gas to the mask. I tried to take a deep breath, but all I could manage were short, shallow pants. Once connected, I formulated a plan and approached the table from behind. He paused momentarily to try and look behind, straining to see what I was doing. As soon as he saw me with the mask in my hand, he let out a loud yelp and started thrashing his legs up and down wildly as he thrust his upper body from side to side.

I had the mask in one hand and the tank in the other. Cautiously I inched up behind him as he frantically started thrashing around even harder, now violently using all his strength against the table and chains. A loud bang and the opposite corner of the table gave way. Fortunately, not on the same side as the other or the entire table would have tipped over, ripping itself from the floor.

I wasn't a small man, but not athletic and not fit. Six foot, two hundred pounds. Most of the unwanted weight was in my belly which hung over my pants slightly. I came upon him and sat the tank on the floor. He tried to reach for me but couldn't. The chains didn't allow him to move his arms in that direction.

A jolt of panic went through me as I wondered if the line would reach from the floor to his face. A wave of relief came over me as I discovered I had just enough slack. I turned on the valve to the gas as it released the deadly agent into the line running to the mask.

I took the mask in both hands. The gas formed as the line became cloudy. Another valve on the mask could start and stop the gas on that end. I'd closed it to prevent the gas from escaping into the air where I might breathe it.

The Satite started straining, pulling, bouncing up and down with all his might. Probably realizing his dire situation.

I turned on the valve and with one motion I brought the mask down strongly over his nose and mouth and held it tightly, pressing his head against the table. A battle of wills ensued. He was stronger, bigger, more experienced at combat. I had the angle, the leverage, and a lethal weapon.

Though he was strong, his neck muscles were the weakest muscles in his body. I could hold him down with all my weight pinning his head against the table.

He tried to thrash his head from side to side but wasn't strong enough to break my grip. He was breathing hard from all the exertion and took in a huge gulp of the gas. Realizing what was happening, he started holding his breath. I heard a chain break. His other leg was now free. He started thrashing his legs up and down. Banging them against the side of the table.

My grip was too strong. Eventually, he had to take a breath. He tried to make it a short and shallow breath. But any amount of gas was lethal. It started working as he took more breaths. I could see the strength fading out of him.

He let out a loud moan. His efforts waned, and his eyes rolled back in his head.

A sudden calm came over the room. An eerie silence. I maintained my grip. Not necessary, but more out of fear and hatred than anything.

I heard him take his last breath. One deep gasp. His body convulsed, then went still. I finally loosened my grip and shut off the valve. The mask fell to the floor.

I collapsed to the floor as well. Exhausted. Trying to catch my breath and slow my heartbeat. My ears were ringing from the loud noises and from my heart I could feel pulsing in my ears.

Suddenly, I could hear the words of Jesus echoing through my mind. "If you have anger in your heart, it's the same as if you have committed murder in your heart."

Did I just murder him? Before it seemed justified. A duty and obligation, for the greater good. Now it was, in part, out of anger, malice, and revenge. What did that mean?

I quickly put the thoughts out of my mind. Time for self-reflection would come.

Later.

I stood and went up to the motionless body and checked for a pulse. The Satite was dead.

I had to hurry.

4

Now that I killed the Satite, I had to revive him, and quickly. The brain could only withstand three-to-six minutes without oxygen before permanent brain damage occurs. With Mark, I'd spent hours preparing. He was hooked to the proper machines. The environment was sterile to minimize the risks of infections. His body hadn't been pumped full of deadly gases—only light anesthetic to put him to sleep.

In this case, there wasn't enough time to hook up the machines. I was covered with blood and so was the Satite. In the fight, he'd sent the instruments next to the operating table flying across the room, including the syringe I needed to shoot into his brain. They laid scattered across the floor, no longer sterile and no longer available for me to access quickly.

When I put Mark to sleep, I shot a substance into his heart that stopped it. I then took a long needle and accessed his brain through the orbital socket. I shot a neurotoxin into the primary sensory cortex in the frontal lobe. The part of the brain that controls consciousness. The substance killed all of the neurotransmitters in the localized area and effectively rendered that part of his brain useless, leaving him without the ability to ever wake up again.

I needed Mark's body to be fully functional, but without him conscious. So, I restarted his heart, which was easy to do because I was prepared. The problem was that the primary sensory cortex also controls movement and breathing, so I hooked Mark to a heart/lung machine before I began. After the toxin was shot into his brain, he was unable to breathe on his own power. That part of the frontal lobe also told the heart to keep beating, so the machine acted like a pacemaker and kept his heart beating at a steady seventy-two beats per minute.

I accomplished all that in less than four minutes. No way I'd be able to do the same with the Satite.

Time to improvise.

"Okay, Clooney, we have to hurry," I said aloud. "We're cutting it close here. It's your fault, but I think I can do it." Clooney was the nickname I gave the Satite in my file. John Clooney was the name of a kid who bullied me in grade school. My way of having a little revenge humor at the Satite's expense.

I didn't have to do everything in the four minutes, but I did have to get his heart restarted. Mark's heart was restarted with an internal defibrillator. Paddles touched his heart and sent a current through, shocking it back to action. Clooney's heart would have to be started externally. I ran to the cabinet and took out a defibrillator and put it on the counter. I switched it to battery mode and prayed the batteries were charged. Not enough time to plug it into an electrical current.

I carried it back to the table and sat it on Clooney's lap. His face was already turning blue. Because of the gas, I didn't have four minutes. I was almost out of time. Surprisingly, my hand was steady. No wasted movements and no fumbling around with the controls. My training as an emergency room doctor was kicking in... almost second nature in times of crises.

I ripped open his shirt which was half torn anyway. I turned the machine on, and a loud hum filled the room. The machine took several seconds to warm up and the electrical current to start flowing to the handles. I gripped the handles and put them on his chest, waiting for the light on the side to turn green, signifying it was charged and ready to activate.

I paused for a moment. My thoughts swirling like a wind funnel in my mind. What will happen when I bring Clooney back to life?

Will he attack me again?

If he did wake up, I presumed the gas did enough damage that I could control him. He'd certainly be woozy. It's possible the gas had already produced permanent brain damage, and everything I was doing was in vain. It's also possible he could wake up and be at full strength, resume his attack, and I'd have to figure out how to kill him again.

A chance I had to take.

I placed one paddle to the left and slightly above his heart and one to the right slightly below the heart. I had no time to prep the skin for possible burns. The machine would send three hundred joules of electrical energy through his heart and jolt it back to life, assuming everything went right.

I instinctively yelled out, "Stop!" The term which I'd used in the emergency room hundreds of times. Different doctors used different terms. Some said, "Clear!" Others said, "Stop," the term I liked better. It meant stop what you're doing and get away from the machine. Not that it was really necessary. The amount of electricity was equivalent to the amount of current needed to power a light bulb. If you weren't in direct contact with the paddles, you couldn't be shocked anyway. I think doctors said clear or stop because it made them feel important at the moment. And what was more important than restarting a man's heart who was on the verge of death. Or in this case, already dead.

A button on the right handle activated the current. I gripped it tightly because they could create quite a jolt for the person holding them. I separated my legs, so they were farther apart and pushed them into the ground to get a more solid footing. I pushed the button. Clooney's chest contorted upward from the shock. Because I had no time to hook him to a monitor, I had to check his pulse manually.

Nothing.

I checked the settings. Clooney was a big man, probably with an oversized heart. I turned the knob on the settings to the right so more current would flow. I had to be careful not to give him too much of a shock that could cause permanent damage to his heart. Placing the paddles back in position, I pushed the button again, this time sending a stronger jolt. I had to hold on even more tightly to keep the paddles in place.

Still nothing.

I began manual compressions on his chest. For almost a minute, I furiously pressed up and down. I felt an adrenaline surge almost to the same level as when we were in the midst of our fight. I was in a fight. A fight for his life. A fight for Mark. This had to work. We had no other option. I wasn't going through this again with another Satite, even if they somehow managed to capture one.

I turned the machine up to its highest setting. What difference did it make if it damaged his heart? This was the last chance. If this didn't work, I would have to give up.

I muttered under my breath, "Stop," barely above a whisper.

"God help this to work," I prayed.

The machine screeched from the power of the current flowing through it. So strong it almost knocked me backward. A small cloud of smoke rose from the paddles. I could smell burning flesh from where the electrical current had singed Clooney's skin.

I didn't bother checking a pulse. Instead, I put my hand on his chest.

A heartbeat!

It worked.

I ran to the closet and got the oxygen tank and a different mask. I rushed back and put the mask over Clooney's face and manually pumped air into his lungs. I saw his body convulse as his heart sent much needed oxygen through his body and to his brain. A wave of fear washed through me.

What would happen next?

Would Clooney wake up?

I watched his eyes closely. They began to flutter.

What do I do if he opens them?

5

Clooney's eyes fluttered, his head tilted upwards slightly, and he let out a weak moan.

I didn't think my body could muster up any more adrenaline, but I felt a shot of it speed my heart as it started racing again at the thought of Clooney waking up. I balled my fists and braced my feet against the ground. Still behind him, I would have every advantage if he woke up. Restraints were still on both his arms and legs although his legs were no longer attached to the table.

His body convulsed in a jerking motion. His right hand lifted off the table and fell back down. His right eye opened and closed. Twice. Then he went limp.

I knew from experience that he was out and not likely to ever wake up again. Perhaps he was even in a vegetative state. I wasn't sure how that would affect the experiments. I thought about options, and wondered if there was anything, I could do about it. Nothing came to mind.

I checked his breathing and pulse which were shallow and weak. That told me two things. The primary sensory of the cortex was still working, so there was a possibility he could wake up at some point. It also told me that it was medically unlikely. The gas had done obvious damage to his brain. I had to hurry, or I would lose him altogether.

Clooney was near death again.

I leapt into action, ignoring the wound on my face I desperately wanted to tend to. It wasn't life threatening, so I put the pain out of my mind and went to work, organizing everything I would need to stabilize Clooney. Before Clooney had arrived, I'd prepared everything I needed and organized it on a tray next to the operating table. The tray and its contents had been sent flying in the struggle.

I got down on my knees and gathered up the various surgical tools, syringes, and gauze and placed them back on the tray. The fight was a blur, so I didn't know if I hit it or Clooney did. At that point it didn't matter. Time was of the essence.

There was no time to sanitize the instruments, but I wiped each one off with a piece of gauze. The best I could do under the circumstances. Clooney wouldn't be suing me for medical malpractice any time soon, I thought to myself with a chuckle, releasing some of the built-up tension while trying to maintain my sense of urgency. If he were able to sue me, the un-sanitized instruments would be the least of my malfeasance as it came to his care.

I was renowned as the foremost physician in all of Saturn. People came from miles to be under my care. Ironically, Clooney was getting the best medical attention from the best surgeon on the planet. Unfortunately, our goals didn't intersect, and my many skills were being used for my ends not his and he certainly would not be happy if he had any say in it.

The defibrillator that a few minutes before had brought him back to life, lay on the floor still humming. I turned it off and kicked it to the side. I rolled the heart and lung machine up to the side of his bed. Fortunately, it was far enough away from the operating table that it did not get caught up in the struggle.

I checked again for a pulse which seemed slightly stronger, but I could hear Clooney fighting to maintain his breath which had become more labored. I was glad he was in such good shape. Big and strong. A fighter by nature. That had helped him stay alive on the battlefield and would help him stay alive now.

Even then, I was running out of time and faced with a critical decision.

I removed his shirt. I picked up a syringe to sedate him. I sat the syringe back down, torn. If I gave it to him, I would assure myself he wouldn't feel any pain during the surgery. However, the sedative would slow his heart further and probably relax the cortex of his brain to the point that he would stop breathing. I decided to give him a much lighter dose. Enough to dull the pain if his brain was capable of feeling it, but not too much to stop his heart.

I commended myself. I was now thinking like a physician and not as an enemy combatant, no longer driven by rage or the need for revenge, I was considering my patient's best interests. Sort of. His untimely end would not have been his choice, but at least, I was considering making him as comfortable through the process as possible.

That's a good thing.

I haven't lost all my morals.

* * *

Everything went well with Clooney. He was stable and breathing normally through the ventilator. The toxin was in his frontal lobe so he would never wake up again. Mark and Clooney were now ready for the experiments.

I was driving in my airmobile, a new ride with all the latest technological advances in automotion. It had four wheels like the old mobiles but was equipped with air propulsion underneath that lifted it off the ground and allowed me to travel at faster speeds with increased maneuverability. It could actually steer itself, but I was enjoying operating it, testing it out to see what all it could do.

The upper flap on the driver's side had a mirror. I lowered it and checked my bandage to make sure the bleeding had stopped. The syringe had cut a path of almost two inches down the side of my face. While not deep, it was a long cut and required a bandage that covered the entire right side of my face. I would have to come up with a suitable explanation for my wife.

The mobile had voice activation features and I told it to call my assistant, Becca Holmes.

She answered on the first ring.

"Hello, Becca, sorry to bother you at home," I said. "Did I catch you at a bad time?"

Becca was not married and probably at home anxiously awaiting my call. She knew I was working on a big project but didn't know all the gory details.

"Now's a good time," she said. "What happened to your face?" she said excitedly.

I'd forgotten the mobile had a built-in camera that transmitted my image to her. She had it off on her end or I could've seen her as well. I made a mental note to switch it off after the conversation.

"It's nothing," I said waving my hand dismissively. "I'll tell you about it tomorrow."

"Is everything okay?" she asked. "How did it go with Mark?"

She met Mark accidentally when she walked into my office unannounced. After I introduced them, Becca asked Mark what brought him to our office. Before I could answer for him, he excitedly said he was part of the new experiment I was conducting. I quickly changed the subject before he said more. Becca seemed curious but let it drop.

"Things went as well as could be expected, I guess. There were some complications. I'll explain everything tomorrow. Can you be at my office first thing in the morning?"

"You emailed me to pick up the test results from Turner Labs and they don't open until nine. I'll come in right after that."

I'd forgotten about the errand I'd given her. Something she didn't necessarily have to do. The lab could email me the results. But I wanted her out of the office, so I gave her some busy work in case I wasn't ready first thing in the morning.

"That'll be fine," I said.

"Are you sure you're okay? Something seems wrong," she said sincerely.

"I'm okay. I'll see you in the morning."

I was okay. Barely. Things hadn't hit me yet, but for the first time in two days, I allowed myself to breathe normally. I set the mobile on remote so it would drive itself.

"What is your destination?" a woman's voice said in a robotic tone.

"Home, please."

"Take me home as fast as possible," I muttered under my breath.

I looked out at the night sky. The rings of Saturn cast a large yellow and gold shadow completely across the horizon. Saturn had sixty-two moons. More than half were visible that night. The reflection of sunlight off of the orbs was causing light to reflect off the rings creating a prism of colors. I'd seen the light show many times. I felt like the light. I felt the chaos.

The light was slamming from one ring to the next, bouncing off, reflecting, speeding to the next ring where it would change shape, direction, and speed. That was what I was feeling inside. Thoughts, adrenaline, guilt, excitement for conducting the experiments were like the various lights bouncing around inside of me.

I found sudden peace in the chaos. Serenity in knowing I had accomplished my task. As hard as it was, the real work could begin. Important work that needed to be done.

I could feel the tension leaving and my heart rate calming. I took several deep breaths and exhaled slowly. I closed my eyes for a moment, but felt better with them open, when I was looking at the sky. The colors were helping me to relax.

"You will be home in two minutes," the woman's voice said.

"I can't wait to get home," I thought to myself. "I'm going to take a shower, get something to eat, and sit on the couch and watch a movie." I already had an excuse ready for the bandage on my face.

The mobile rounded the corner faster than I would have. I was amazed at how well the new ones handled. *I'm really going to like this new ride*, I thought.

The calm and peace suddenly left me. A wave of panic shot through my body as I tried to process what I was seeing. Several mobiles were in front of my house.

Who were they and why were they there?

6

I walked into the back door and was immediately greeted by my wife, Helen, who was fuming mad. I'd forgotten we were hosting a Bible study group from our church which was the reason for all of the mobiles in front of our place. This was the first night, and I was at least an hour late. No doubt I'd already missed the meal. My back was toward Helen, so she wasn't immediately able to see the large bandage on my face. The wound was something I was thankful for at the moment in that it would serve as a reasonable excuse for my tardiness.

"How could you be late tonight of all nights?" Helen said, angrily. The words were spoken barely above a whisper but with intensity. She wouldn't want our guests to hear her. Knowing her, she'd want to maintain her appearance to our guests as the perfect woman with the perfect marriage.

"There was an accident at work, and I was almost killed," I said, turning and facing her so she could see the huge bandage on my face.

That didn't faze her.

"Why didn't you call? I had to do everything myself. I cleaned the house and got everything ready all by myself. Work is always more important to you than anything else!" The words came with such vitriol.

I was amazed. I'd just said I was almost killed, and she had no interest in what happened to me. Her only concern was about how I had inconvenienced her. I paid for a maid who came twice a week, so she didn't have to clean the house. Everyone else brought food for the dinner, so she didn't have to cook. She probably just went by the store and picked up a dessert. Points I would've argued if there weren't people in the other room.

"It couldn't be helped," I retorted.

She was right about one thing. I should've called or at least listened to the several messages I'm sure Helen left me. I didn't bother to check. If I had, I'd have been reminded about the Bible study. Even then, I didn't have a chance to call. That wasn't true, I realized. I'd managed to call Becca. A fact, I'd analyze another time.

"We can talk about it later," I said rudely, walking right past her and into the main living area, leaving Helen with her mouth wide open, ready to say something but no one to say it to. She followed me into the large living room where I counted fourteen people sitting in a circle. Bob and Susan, the leaders of the study were prominently in the middle.

"I'm so sorry I'm late," I said. "I had an accident at work that required medical attention." I pointed to the bandage on my face. Several murmurs went through the group.

"What happened?" Bob asked. "Are you okay?"

"I'm okay," I responded. "I have a bad cut on my face, but it'll heal. Just thankful it wasn't worse." They had no idea how thankful I was. Helen walked past me, slightly bumping her shoulder against me to let me know she was still mad. She sat in one of the two chairs obviously reserved for us. Her cold demeanor in the other room had turned into a warm, but tremendously fake smile. Only I knew what was going on inside her which I would experience later when everyone was gone.

"We were just getting started anyway," Bob said. "Let's go around the room and have everyone introduce themselves and tell us one interesting fact about yourself."

I don't remember any of the names or any of the interesting facts. My mind was on Mark and Clooney and the experiments. My meeting with Becca in the morning to explain everything to her was also prominently on my mind. I wondered how she'd react.

I do remember Helen introducing herself. Everything was all about her. She owned a hair salon and day spa. Had three kids. All grown. Two grandkids. She's been married for thirty-three years. Her interesting fact was she designed her house by herself and picked out all of the expensive furnishings. Of course, she didn't say expensive. I added that word. She also didn't say "we" once. "*We've* been married for thirty-three years, or *we* have three kids and two grandkids." A point I would make in my introduction. I was the last in the group to speak.

"My name is Roger Forrester."

"Dr. Forrester," Helen interjected.

"Roger is a medical doctor and scientist," Bob added.

And a murderer. A slight grin came on my face. Still emotionally torn by the last two day's events. So much so, I wished my house was empty at that moment, including my wife. I wished she was shopping or visiting the grandkids, and I could be alone with my thoughts and a large glass of wine.

"I do medical research," I said, apologetically. Some of the people might have known of my reputation. I didn't care if they did or they didn't. I wasn't nearly as concerned about impressing others as Helen was.

"*We've* been married thirty-three years," I said. "As Helen said, *we* have three kids and two grandkids. A fact you probably don't know is that Helen and I were high school sweethearts. She was the most beautiful girl in school, and I was lucky enough to win her heart."

Helen beamed as I said it. I placed my hand on hers. She dug her fingernails into the side of my hand which was still sore from my earlier confrontation with Clooney. I quickly moved it away.

I immediately felt regret about how bad my marriage had become. I barely remembered my life without Helen. I'd been with her my entire adult life. We'd had a good life. We rarely fought. She was a good mother. We had grown apart over the years and focused on other things rather than each other, mostly the kids while they were growing up. When they moved out, we were left having to rebuild the romantic and loving part of our relationship. We never bothered rebuilding and settled into a comfortable relationship of avoidance.

Bob waited for me to say more, but I was done, not entirely comfortable in that setting. Helen was in her element. She came alive through hosting and parties. That's why she volunteered our house for the Bible study group.

We'd been going to the First Christian Church of Westminster for two years. Anyone and everyone of status went to that church, which is why she insisted we go there as well. I was perfectly satisfied to stay in the background, but Helen was the socialite. Volunteering for committees and helping where she could. Wanting to be seen every time the doors were opened.

That wasn't exactly fair. She did a lot of good work at the church and in the community. I only wished she paid half as much attention to me as she did her philanthropic work. Of course, she wished I paid half as much attention to her as I did my work. We'd settled into a convenient marriage. I provided her with a big, beautiful home, nice mobiles, expensive furnishings, and funded her business enterprise, which lost money but kept her in the social center of the Westminster gossip. In return, she was the beautiful, thin, well-dressed socialite wife any man would be proud to be married to. We both played our roles well.

"Tonight, I want to talk about situational ethics," Bob said, interrupting my thoughts and bringing me back to the reason everyone was at my house. "More specifically, is it ever okay to do something morally wrong if it's for the greater good?"

My mouth flew open. I caught it in time to close it before anyone saw. Of all the topics we could be discussing, Bob was bringing up the one that hit closest to home. I pictured Mark and Clooney lying on the tables back in my lab.

No way I could tell the group what I was doing. Research on monkeys was one thing; keeping two humans barely alive for my research was a whole controversial ethical dilemma.

I was interested in knowing what Bob had to say. But how could I ask questions without giving away what I was doing?

The next thirty minutes should be very interesting.

7

"Can anyone think of an instance when someone might make a difficult choice to do something that's not right for the greater good?" Bob asked a similar question again.

No one answered right away. Everyone seemed a little nervous. Not totally unexpected, considering this was the first question of the first group and no one wanted to take the initiative and answer it. Especially, such a difficult question with many potential right or wrong answers.

Bob was the Associate Pastor of the church and the pastor's right-hand man, experienced and a capable teacher. He wouldn't be fazed by the momentary silence. In looking around the room, it seemed to me the group was made up of the wealthier members, which was probably why Bob was given the assignment to lead the group. I judged that based on the way the women were dressed. I didn't actually know anyone who was there or what they did for a living or their level of income. Of course, I spent most of my time at work and very little of my time in social settings with the rich and famous.

"A lot of men work too much," Helen broke the silence by using me as an example, "and neglect their families, thinking they are doing something good for them when they are really harming them." A hint of resentment directed at me and probably only I caught. Sitting forward in her chair, her legs were crossed and her hands over her knees. She wasn't looking at me or she would've seen a noticeable glare for the obvious dig.

"Thank you, Helen," Bob said. "Would anyone like to respond to that?"

An uncomfortable silence filled the room.

"I don't think that's what Bob meant, Helen," I said, as my own level of resentment rose inside of me.

Helen did look at me when I said it, making sure I saw the noticeable glare on her face.

I looked away from her and continued my thought. "I think Bob's talking about moral dilemmas."

"Do you have an example?" Bob asked. I wasn't sure if Bob noticed the tension between us or not. If he did, it wasn't reflected on his face.

"It's like a man who steals a loaf of bread to feed his family, so they don't starve to death."

Bob nodded in agreement but didn't say anything so I could continue.

"A man who works too much is doing so out of a choice. There might be a reason why he'd rather be at work than at home with his wife." I was tempted to look at Helen when I said it but resisted the urge. "The man who steals the bread may feel like he has no choice. It may be morally wrong to steal the bread, but it's for the greater good of the family."

"That's an excellent example," Bob said. "The exact moral dilemma I wanted to discuss here tonight. Is it okay for the man to steal the bread to feed his family?" Bob asked, thus beginning a robust discussion that lasted for a good thirty minutes.

Until someone raised another moral dilemma. A subject I wanted to avoid at all costs.

"What does everyone think about cloning?" Bob asked.

I began to squirm in my chair.

"I read a report that the Satites had perfected cloning and are creating human beings in laboratories. At some point, people will be able to choose the sex of their child... even the color of their eyes."

"One of the problems with that," Helen said, "is that if a choned baby has genetic deformities, people might decide to kill it in the womb rather than deliver it."

The conversation made me uncomfortable, but at least it wasn't going the direction I thought it might, so I was glad for Helen's observation.

"I hear that the Satites already kill babies just because they don't like the color of their eyes or the sex," one of the men said. His name was David, or Daniel—some D word I couldn't remember.

"That's a good point, Derek," Bob said, clarifying the man's name for me. "The Satites could use the cloning to produce a superior race. Ultimately, they may want to kill the infirmed, the disabled, and those less fortunate. Someone who's not as good looking or as smart could have their life terminated if they don't meet an arbitrary standard."

"They could even create an army of superior warriors," Derek added.

Derek had just crossed the line. The discussion was getting too close to the reality I was dealing with. Clooney was a soldier in battle. The Satites were creating an army of superior men. Men who were bigger, stronger, faster, smarter, and harder to kill, as I had experienced first-hand. I needed to change the subject.

"I'm faced with those types of ethical dilemmas every day in my lab," I interjected. "I'm a medical researcher. We infect animals with diseases in order to test various drugs on them. It's harmful to the animals, but we've found cures for diseases that have saved thousands of lives because of the research. Is that something that's okay to do? Harm animals for the greater good of mankind? I think it is because of all the good we do."

No one answered. They all stared at Bob, waiting for him to answer.

"Let's look at an actual example in the Bible," Bob said, opening a Bible in his hands and flipping through the pages until he finally stopped. He began reading the story of Habar in the Old Testament. When he finished reading the passage, he began paraphrasing the story and pointing out the moral dilemma Habar faced.

"This was written back when the Saturnians were slaves to the Satites," Bob said. We were all descendants of Saturnians. God's chosen people who were constantly at war with the Satites.

"The Saturnians had escaped from slavery and had been given a promise of a new land, a *promised land*, if you will," Bob continued. He was referring to the land we now possessed and were defending against the Satite's aggression.

"The Saturnians sent some spies into the land to stake it out. Habar lived in the Promised Land. She was a woman of ill repute. A prostitute. She hid the spies in her house. The Satites had soldiers going through the city looking for the spies. They knocked on her door. She lied and said that the spies weren't there, when in fact she was hiding them in a back room. The Bible commends her for her faith."

"So, the Bible says she did the right thing?" I said almost like a question.

"Yes," Bob answered. "There are instances when what seems like the wrong thing might be the right thing if it's for the greater good. God commended her for her faith, not necessarily for the lying. She lied because she believed in their God and that they were on God's side. Her ultimate motives were what God commended, not necessarily her immoral action of lying."

A sense of relief came over me. I was suddenly glad we had the Bible study that night. I now had my justification. Many questions still swirled in my head, but I felt more at peace at what I was going to do to Mark and Clooney starting tomorrow.

8

After everyone from the Bible study left, Helen went into the kitchen to finish cleaning up, and I went into my office. Sort of a cold truce. Like two combatants going to their own corners in a boxing match. An exaggerated analogy, but how it felt, nonetheless. I did what I always did and turned to my work for comfort or at least for distraction.

The first thing I did was turn on my *artby*, an artificial brain in a box with a big screen. I could access information all over the world with just the click of a key. I entered my password 06153980. Our anniversary. The screen flickered then roared to life. I was constantly amazed at the power and information available on that one device.

I clicked onto the global space highway and entered a specific road address, and the inside of my lab appeared on the screen. I'd set up a viewer that allowed me to see live images on my artby. I could even access them on my caller if I wanted to. I could move the viewer by remote control and see every area of the lab. This allowed me the ability to check on my patients at any time.

Mark and Clooney were lying in beds next to each other, each hooked up to a machine that kept their heart's beating and their lungs filled with air. The viewer allowed me to zoom in on the machines and read the numbers or I could access the data remotely and pull them up on my screen. Everything seemed normal, so I didn't bother.

I turned my attention to my morning meeting with my assistant, Becca. All she knew was we were involved in a big project but didn't know all of the details. I wasn't sure how she would react. My expectation was she'd be excited. A notable physician in her own right, the experiments we'd be working on would be groundbreaking and could potentially change the entire course of Saturn.

What researcher wouldn't want to be a part of that opportunity once she worked through the ethical issues? Something the Bible study had helped me to do. From conversations, Becca was a stronger Christian than I, and she'd understand the concept of situational ethics. I was convinced she'd be excited about the opportunity. If for no other reason than the large number of rings involved. My lab was to receive fifty million rings in the form of a grant for the research. There'd be a huge bonus in it for her.

Situational ethics. That many rings can buy a lot of things, and a lot of things can justify a lot of compromised behavior. In rethinking it, I didn't think that would matter much to Becca. She wouldn't be as motivated by the rings as much as the research. The same for me. I wasn't motivated by rings or things. I simply loved my job. I'd do it for free. Fortunately, it was financially lucrative, and I got to do what I enjoyed doing as a life calling.

I made some notes as to what I wanted to say to her. I had to describe the Eden Experiments thoroughly. Becca was as intelligent as she was beautiful. Details were her forte. She'd insist on carefully thought-out procedures and meticulous documentation. Checks and balances were vital in research. That's why I wanted her involved in the project. She'd think of things I hadn't or wouldn't think of and experiments that might lead to greater discovery.

In three short months, she'd already established herself as the best assistant I'd ever had. We worked well together. Almost reading each other's thoughts. After nearly a page of notes, I felt comfortable with the presentation. My arguments were compelling and complete. Of course, the project was moving forward with or without her participation. I was too far into it. There was no turning back, for me, anyway. I just hoped she'd want to be involved. I wanted her there with me. I needed her.

She'd get half the credit. I tried to think of every argument, even though Becca wasn't motivated by fame and credit.

Helen walked in just as I had finished writing my notes. She stopped and stood inside the doorway. I turned the screen off so she wouldn't see the images in the lab if she were to walk to my side of the desk. I hoped it hadn't been too obvious I was hiding something.

"You never said you were sorry for being late," she said, matter-of-factly. Obviously, still mad.

"You never asked what happened to my face, so I guess we're even," I retorted.

"You embarrassed me in front of my friends. Left me alone to do everything. You don't even care."

"You don't care that I almost died today."

Helen threw her head back in disgust. "I'm going to bed," she said in a huff as she left the room without giving me a chance to respond.

I started to follow her and continue the argument but thought better of it. I was exhausted. I did nearly die. My head hurt. The cut on my face was throbbing. I didn't know which was stronger, my anger at Clooney or my anger at my wife. Clooney was my enemy. My wife was supposed to be understanding.

How did she not even ask?

I decided to sleep on the couch in my office. I went into the guest room to get a blanket and pillow from the closet. I'd sleep in the guest room, but Helen would be upset that she had to rewash the sheets and pillowcases. I wasn't interested in any more battles, so I went into my office, turned off the light, and laid on the couch, covering myself with the blanket.

I wanted to go upstairs and change clothes, but I didn't want to see her and face a long night of conversation. Helen was the kind who'd stew on it for days until it all came out in a big blow-up. I was the kind who got mad quickly and then got over it just as quickly. I'd forget about it by tomorrow. Or at least I would have adequately suppressed it by then.

The couch was uncomfortable. I suddenly realized I had a sharp pain in my side. I stood and went into the washroom, turned on the light, and unbuttoned my shirt, aghast at what I saw. A large bruise had formed on my left side. An ugly shade of purple, red, and black had formed, running from just above my belt buckle all the way to just under my arm. It was tender to the touch. I didn't remember when I had sustained the injury, but it had to have been in the heat of the battle. Amazed that I was just now noticing it.

That made me even madder at Clooney and even angrier at my wife. "Why do I have to sleep on the couch? This is my house too. We have a big, comfortable bed upstairs, and I'm not going to sleep on a hard leather couch," I said angrily to Helen even though she wasn't in the room.

I stormed out of my office and up the stairs to our bedroom. A light had been left on in the washroom. Helen at least had the consideration to leave it on for me. I stripped off all my clothes and turned on the shower. I stepped inside and let the hot water wash away a lot of the anger.

I felt better. I got out of the shower, put on shorts and a tee-shirt and walked quietly to the bed and got in on my side, trying to be careful not to wake Helen. I wanted to turn my back to hers but that was my bad side. It hurt too much to lay that way, so I stayed facing her. She had her back to me.

A few minutes passed. I settled in to try and sleep. Images of Clooney and our fight kept invading my mind, giving me spurts of adrenaline that kept me from sleeping. I tossed back and forth trying to get comfortable. Helen was motionless. I could only hear soft breathing. I suspected she wasn't asleep, but she gave no obvious signs of being awake.

Until she said in a quiet voice barely above a whisper, "What happened to your face?"

"One of the monkeys attacked me," I said softly, suddenly feeling tremendous guilt. I'd made her feel bad about not asking. Now she did and I lied to her. I felt like a horrible person.

"I really did think I was going to die," I added.

"I'm sorry I didn't ask," she said sweetly.

"I'm sorry I didn't call," I said, leaning over and kissing her on the back of her hair and placing my hand on her shoulder. I expected her to turn over, but she didn't.

I let out a sigh and settled back down to go to sleep.

"How is your new assistant doing?" Helen asked.

"He's great. He's working out really well."

9

Nervous didn't begin to describe how I was feeling. Becca, my assistant would be back to the office at any time for our meeting to discuss her participation in the Eden Experiment. I was already second guessing myself. She should never know about it. As soon as she gets there, I should tell her to walk right out the door and never come back.

It was too late for me. It didn't have to be for her. She knew nothing about the program and had nothing to do with Mark or the Satite's death or anything that had happened to that point. She had plausible deniability. Once I explained to her the program, and she took one action in furthering it, then she was fully culpable. If I went to confinement, she would as well. We all would. We'd lose our medical licenses, be disgraced in the medical research community, and probably lose our freedom.

Too big a risk to ask her to take. On the other hand, if we were successful, we could save thousands of lives and turn the war with the Satites in our favor. Not to mention, make the most important medical discoveries of our generation. She could go down in history as having been a part of it. It's what researchers like Becca lived for.

Selfishly, I needed her. Becca had an undergraduate degree in Biblical Studies from the University of Sigwell. Her graduate degrees were in Biology, Immunology, and Medical Science from Oxnard University. Graduating at the top of her class, she was one of the foremost experts in immunobiological research. The combination of Bible knowledge and medical acumen were exactly what I needed for this project.

Was it too much to ask? Should she risk her whole career for this one experiment?

Becca suddenly appeared in the doorway of my office, interrupting my thoughts. A bright smile on her face was her usual demeanor and the whole mood of the room immediately changed. My negative thoughts dissipated like a thin puff of smoke. I couldn't imagine doing it without her.

She had that unique ability. I was drawn to her. Within one minute of our first interview, I wanted to hire her on the spot. Now I wanted to gloss over the risks and not say anything negative so she wouldn't say no.

Two cups of coffee were in her hand. She had stopped by Joe's *Coffee* on the way back to the office and got my favorite. Just like I liked it, she said.

"Okay, Boss," she said as she sat down right across from me. "What are we doing?"

"Before we go there, you need to know that this project is unlike anything we've ever done before. The mandate is from the highest offices of our government. But it's off the books. No one knows about it except a very select group of people."

"Sounds exciting," Becca said enthusiastically. "When do we start?"

"It's not as simple as that. I've actually already started it. But there are some things you need to know. What we will be doing could be considered illegal by some people."

Becca leaned forward in the chair. Her eyes narrowed in confusion. A half-smile formed on her face.

"Illegal? I can't imagine you doing something illegal."

I handed her a piece of paper.

"What's this?" she asked.

"A confidentiality agreement. This program is top secret. No one can know about it until we have finished our research. We could get in a lot of trouble. Especially if anyone finds out what we're doing."

She pressed her lips together and twisted them in a slight frown, obviously cynical of what I was saying. It wasn't making sense to her. It didn't make sense to me either. The words in my head sounded so unbelievable. So much so, I was afraid to even speak them.

"I don't understand," she said.

My tone turned very serious. I had to give her more information.

"All I can tell you without you signing the agreement is that if the experiment goes wrong, we could lose our careers. Everything we've worked for is at risk. You need to know that. At the same time, it's exciting and groundbreaking research. The President of Saturnians has personally asked me to take on this project. I agreed because I believe in it. That doesn't change the fact that it crosses some ethical lines."

"You mean the end justifies the means?"

"I don't know if it does. We won't know until we get to the end of the project. Will it be worth the risk? There are no guarantees."

"How do I fit in? What do you need from me?"

She brushed her bangs out of her eyes, momentarily distracting me.

I could tell the conversation was making her nervous as well. I was fidgeting in my chair like a kid. I looked down at my notes, trying to figure out which argument to focus on. I wanted her to do it, but I didn't want her to regret it. That didn't seem possible. There was no way I could prepare her for what we were about to do.

"You shouldn't do it," I said emphatically. "I'm telling you that right now. You should walk out the door and never come back."

Becca laughed. "Don't you think you're being a little over dramatic. I just started this job three months ago. I'm not quitting. I love my job. I trust you. If you think this is something we should do, then I'm all in."

"You will make one million rings," I blurted out, immediately regretting saying it.

Anger flashed across her face as her jaw clenched.

"I would never do this for the rings," she said roughly. "I can't believe you would either. If it's about the rings, then count me out. I got into medical research to help people. To help the people of Saturn have a better life. If it's about that, then I'll help you. If it's about rings..."

In my notes, I had scratched through that argument. I knew it wouldn't work with her. It wasn't about the rings for me either. I didn't know why I had even brought it up.

"I'm sorry," I said sincerely. "It's not about the rings. For me either. I just want you to know the whole story. There is great risk to us. There's also the potential for great reward. Yeah, we'll make a lot of rings. There could be a lot of fame associated with it, if we're successful. It's going to be challenging. I'm not going to lie. You're not going to like what I will ask you to do. There may be danger from the Satites. Our lives could even be in danger. Like I said, our reputations could be on the line as well. We could even lose our medical licenses. I'm willing to take that risk, because I believe in the project. I can't ask you to do it without you knowing what's involved."

"Is that what the big bandage on your face is all about? Is that the danger?"

"That's exactly what I'm talking about. It's very dangerous. I could've died."

"Tell me what it is," she said soberly. "Then I can make a more informed decision."

"That's the problem. I can't tell you, until you are in. It's the best I can do. Once you know what's going on, then you assume all the risks. That's just the way it is. But I need a decision. We start right away."

"How does Mark fit into the experiment?" Becca met Mark in my office, and he blurted out that he was involved in the Eden Experiment. She was asking a legitimate question, but one I couldn't answer.

"I can't tell you."

"How does the Garden of Eden fit into it? What does the Bible have to do with it?"

"I'm sorry."

Becca rolled her eyes. She picked up the confidentiality agreement and read through it quickly. She picked up a pen from my desk and started tapping on the document, obviously giving it serious consideration. She laid the pen back down.

"What do you think I should do?" she asked.

"I don't think you should do it."

Becca picked up the pen, signed the document, and handed it to me. "There. It's done," she said with a nervous chuckle.

I rubbed my eyes roughly, trying to decide whether to sign it or not. If I did, she was in, and there'd be no turning back. It wasn't official until I signed it. I picked up the pen and signed it just as impulsively as she had.

"Okay," she said. "That's settled. Tell me about what Mark has to do with the Eden Experiment."

"Mark's dead."

"Dead!" she said, her eyes wide, suddenly forming into a steely stare. "What happened?"

"I killed him."

10

"You killed Mark?" Becca said, her voice raised in intensity. "Why?"

She had bolted from her chair and was standing next to the door with her arms folded. She looked at me with a frozen stare, eyes wide and eyebrows raised.

"I can explain."

"Does it have anything to do with the bandage on your face?" she asked sharply and in an accusatory tone.

"No. That happened when I killed the Satite," I said. "He put up a struggle." I immediately regretted how that sounded. The tension in the office reminded me of an ER room where everything was chaos when an emergency case came in, and we were trying to save someone's life. Becca was responding with expected emotion, and if I didn't calm things down, I didn't know what was going to happen.

"You killed two people! I have to get out of here." She reached for the door. I had locked it from a switch at my desk.

"You can't leave, Becca. You already signed the agreement. You're in this as deep as I am now."

She pulled back and forth on the knob, but the door wouldn't open.

"Let me out of here! Now!" she shouted.

"I can't. You signed the agreement."

"Tear up the agreement. I don't want any part of this."

"I've already told you too much for you to get out now. We can't go back. I told you that some people would consider what we're doing is illegal."

"You said you were doing something illegal. You didn't say anything about murder!" She was yelling now.

Becca pulled on the door again. It wouldn't open. Large steel doors were installed throughout the building as a precaution. I was glad they were working. We believed the Satites would eventually try to infiltrate the building if and when they learned Clooney was there.

The look of disbelief on Becca's face had turned to fear. I wanted to stand and take her in my arms and try to reassure her, but I knew she'd resist. I didn't want a physical confrontation with her. I had to get her to calm down. She didn't have to be afraid of me.

"It's not what it seems," I said in a gentle tone. "You need to give me the opportunity to explain."

"You have two minutes. And then you're going to open this door and let me out of here, and I'm going to call the police."

"The First Minister will have you arrested," I retorted. "You can't go to the police. This project was sanctioned by the highest levels of our government. You don't understand. This is bigger than either of us."

She put her hand over her eyes. Tears were forming.

"I can't believe this. Are you going to kill me too if I don't do what you want?"

"Of course not," I said. "But they'll make you go to confinement until the experiment is over. I told you not to sign it. I told you to leave. I told you to walk out the door and never look back."

"Yeah, well. You didn't tell me about this. I never would've signed it had I known you were going to murder two people. I'm somehow supposed to cover it up like it didn't happen. I can't do that."

I turned my artby screen around, so it was facing her. It showed Mark and Satite in their beds back in the lab.

"Look Becca. They're still alive. After I killed them, I brought them back to life."

She took two steps toward my desk and looked at the screen.

"Why would you do that?"

"It's part of the experiment. We need them to be alive."

"But they are unconscious. This doesn't make any sense."

"That's the protocol for the Eden Experiment. I have to stop their hearts and then bring them back to life. After I inject ancillic acid into their cortexes." This time I was the one who put my hands over my eyes. I couldn't believe the words coming out of my mouth. It sounded so diabolical. Sick.

Becca reacted in the same way as her mouth flew open. Her disbelief had turned to anger. Even rage.

"You did murder him! Mark will never wake up. Ancillic acid into his frontal lobe means he's dead for all practical purposes. The only thing keeping him alive are those machines."
"It had to be done."

"Mark has a wife and family. Kids. How could you do such a thing?"

"He volunteered for it. He made the choice to participate in the experiment. You met him. He was excited to do it."

"Why would he do it?"

"His family got a million rings."

"For rings? That's ridiculous. He basically let you kill him for rings. That's sick."

I realized how that sounded. I wished she'd sit down, and we could discuss it sensibly... without emotion. We were doctors. We dealt with life and death situations all the time. Becca had a logical and practical side and would understand once I explained everything. I was sure she'd feel like the experiment was worth it. I just had to give her time. I had the same reaction when they told me what we would have to do. Once I knew everything, I was okay with it. She would be too. I just had to get her to understand.

"Mark didn't do it for the money. Well... I mean he did. But there was a reason. He was dying anyway. Mark has liver blastoma. He only has six weeks or so to live. In a sense, he's donating his body to science. He's letting us perform these experiments on him so we can do our research. It's for the greater good. He feels like his death can have a higher purpose. And with the rings, his family is taken care of. He felt like this was actually an answer to prayer."

Becca didn't respond right away. I stood and walked around the desk and put my hand on her shoulder. She didn't immediately pull away.

"I'm not a madman. There's more to the story. I told you I believe in what I'm doing. I think you will too, once you have all the facts."

I led Becca back to her chair. She sat down slowly. Deliberately. Her eyes affixed to the screen. Staring at Mark and Clooney. Trying to process all of the information.

"Please hear me out," I implored. "Let me explain everything."

She slumped back in her chair. I turned the artby screen back toward me. The images were probably already seared in her mind. No reason to have her looking at it. I'd take her back to the lab in a few minutes. After she calmed down.

"Who is the other man? Did he volunteer as well?"

"Not exactly."

"If I'm going to be involved in this, you have to tell me everything. Don't lie to me. I deserve to know what I'm getting into."

"I totally agree. I'm trying to explain. It's complicated."

"I'm listening," she said roughly, with her arms folded again. Her lips were pursed with obvious resolve and determination. She had regained her composure. I knew she would.

"The other man is a Satite. We captured him on the battlefield. He's a giant."

"I've studied cloning."

"I know you have. That's one of the reasons I need you for this experiment. The Satite is a superhuman man. He just appeared out of nowhere, just a few weeks ago. He killed hundreds of Christians all by himself in the first few weeks. Our men are no match for him.

Satites have more than two hundred of them already and are creating more. We have to find out a way to stop them."

"So, we're supposed to figure out how they are cloning him?" she asked.

"Exactly. And anything we can do to counteract it."

"What does the Garden of Eden have to do with it?"

I took a long sip of my coffee and a very deep breath.

Where do I begin?

11

The Garden of Eden, before the Fall. Year unknown.

Satan had taken on the form of a serpent and was slithering through the Garden of Eden at mid-morning. God usually came to the garden in the cool of the evening, so Satan always made sure he left the garden before God arrived.

He was looking for Eve.

Another reason he came at that time. She would most likely be alone mid-morning. For the most part, Adam and Eve were inseparable except when Adam was tending to the garden, which he often did around that time, first thing in the morning after breakfast.

Where is she?

He'd been to several places she normally frequented and hadn't found her. The first place he looked was where the four rivers intersected near the tree of the knowledge of good and evil. Eve was nowhere to be found. Being at that spot made him angry. He tried on several occasions to get Adam and Eve to eat from the tree, but they refused. Saturn's Adam and Eve had become more of a challenge than the other planets.

He had another plan. Something different. A trick he never tried before. The new idea came to him a few days ago. He'd come to the garden several times to talk to Eve about his plan but could never corner her without Adam being around.

Will she fall for it?

The garden was a maze of forests, plants, flowers, streams, rock formations, and she could be in any of a thousand places. He searched for what seemed like an hour. He came around a corner that opened into a large and lush field with dark green grass and beautiful flowers surrounding the edge of the field.

He suddenly heard a noise. A woman laughing.

Eve.

There in the center of the field was Eve, playing with a Termaxasaurus. The largest of all the animals God created. The humans had nicknamed him T-Max. A mammoth creature, he was at least forty feet long, twenty feet tall, and weighed approximately seven to eight tons. Eve and T-Max were tossing a fairly large stone back and forth. Eve would throw it, and T-Max would fetch it and bring it back to her, and they would repeat the activity. The gravitational pull on Saturn was not as strong as on some of the other planets, and stones felt lighter and easier to throw. That's why Eve was able to toss it with ease, even though it probably weighed fifty pounds on other planets.

T-Max growled slightly and showed his teeth upon seeing Satan.

Eve barely noticed and didn't acknowledge Satan, making him even angrier at her.

He couldn't let her see his frustration. She was made in the image of God, and he hated everything God created. He wanted to be God and thought he should be. It was his right.

He crossed the field with purpose in no time, his body moving like a wave in an ocean. Within seconds, he was next to her.

"Hello, Eve," Satan said. "You're just the person I want to see."

She gave him a slight wave of the hand but continued playing. Eve had no knowledge of good and evil, so she had no fear of anything. Really didn't even know how evil Satan was. That made it easier for him to approach her.

"Can you quit throwing the stone so we can talk?" Satan said roughly. He could speak that way to her. With no knowledge of good and evil, she couldn't be offended. She just kept smiling and was always in a good mood. Getting her attention was the hardest part.

Eve was laughing and running around like she didn't have a care in the world, which Satan knew she didn't. Hopefully, that wouldn't last much longer. If his plan worked. He glanced furtively in every direction. Not seeing Adam, he bolted toward the stone when Eve threw it and got to it before T-Max could get there. He snatched it from the ground with his two stubby arms and held on to it.

"Go play somewhere else," Satan said strongly to T-Max. "I want to talk to Eve."

Eve sat down on the grass and brushed her hair aside which had become mussed from playing. T-Max came and laid beside her like a dog lays next to his owner. Eve stroked his head, and he grinned widely. She let out a huge sigh, not so much out of breath, but it sounded more like a sigh of satisfaction.

Satan couldn't help but notice how beautiful Eve was. Golden brown hair, green eyes, with perfect features. She was wearing a crown of glory given to her by God which covered her body with a glow, an aura, so to speak, that radiated and intensified her beauty. As she'd been since creation, she was totally unashamed and without guile though she wasn't wearing clothes.

The sight of her beauty caused anger to rise further inside him. At one time, he'd been even more beautiful than she was, back when he was the worship leader in heaven. Before he lost his glory. He'd once been perfect in every way. Every precious stone was his covering. Sardius, topaz, diamonds, the beryl, the onyx, and the jasper, the sapphire, the emerald, and the carbuncle, and gold. Lots of gold. The craftsmanship of his taborets and pipes were astonishing. With cherubs at his feet, he stood daily on the mountain of God in the midst of the stones of fire, leading the people in worship. For eons he was the angel most favored by God.

Until God found iniquity in him, and he was cast out of heaven along with a third of the angels. He'd tried to lead them in a coup, unseat God, and take over his throne. If only he'd been able to get more angels on his side. If there had been more than half, maybe things would've been different.

So many regrets of what might've been.

Instead, he was at the mercy of this inferior creature. A beautiful woman, but nothing compared to him. He had no authority on Saturn unless she gave it to him by eating from the tree. But he had another plan. A diabolical way to get it. He would leave his domain and take on strange flesh and become human. He just needed Eve to agree. To do so, he had to win her trust. Trick her if necessary. Lie. Seduce her. Anything to get her to fall.

"Of all the Eves who have ever lived," Satan said, in a lustful tone, "You are the most beautiful of them all."

Eve's eyebrows were raised, and her lips pursed into a frown.

"I don't understand. What do you mean? I'm not the only Eve?"

"No. You see all the moons in the sky. There's an Eve on each one of them. And an Adam."

"Wow!"

Eve tilted her head up and scanned the sky as a more confused look came upon her face. She was obviously thinking, contemplating that new information.

Satan lied. Saturn had sixty-two moons, about half of which could be seen in the sky at any one time. God created many different planets through the millions of years. On each planet, God had created an Adam and an Eve, a Garden of Eden, and a tree of the knowledge of good and evil. God forbade each Adam and Eve to eat of the tree. Satan persuaded all of them to eat the fruit even though it was forbidden.

While there'd been life on other planets, there were none on the moons. Eve would never know he wasn't telling the truth.

"I didn't know that," Eve said slowly. "What are they like?"

"They are like you, just not nearly as beautiful. God was showing off when he created you."

"Oh... That's a sweet thing to say."

"Have you thought about the fruit on the tree?" Satan asked.

"I've thought about it."

"Did God really say, 'You must not eat from any tree in the garden?'"

"We can eat of the trees," she responded. "But God did say we couldn't eat from the tree in the middle of the garden. He said if we were to touch it, we would die."

"You won't die," Satan said, laughing diabolically. "All the Eve's on the other moons have touched the fruit, and they didn't die. They all ate it, and their eyes were opened, and they became like God. Wouldn't you like to become like God?"

"How would I become like God?"

"You will know good and evil. The fruit is good for gaining wisdom. Don't you want wisdom?"

"I guess."

Satan took her hand and began stroking it.

"You need to trust me. I know what's best for you."

Eve pulled her hand away.

"I don't think so. God has been so good to us. He told us not to touch that tree or we would die. I don't want to die."

"It doesn't matter," Satan said dismissively. "I don't care if you eat of the tree or not. That's your loss. God knows if you eat it, you'll live eternally and be like God. I was just thinking of you."

Eve stood to her feet. He had to get to the point. She would leave soon. This was his opportunity.

"I should go," Eve said abruptly. "Adam will be back soon from tending to the garden. We're going to eat lunch together."

"Before you go, I have something I want to ask you," Satan said.

He moved closer to her. His face was only a few inches away.

"I have an idea. Something you and I can do together. Better than eating the fruit. It's another way you can become like God. No one can ever know about it. It'll be our secret."

"What's that?" Eve asked, moving back a couple of steps so his face wasn't right in hers.

"I want you to have my child."

12

"I want you to have my child," Satan had said.

Eve was confused. She wanted to talk to God and Adam about what Satan was asking her to do. She loved her life with Adam, but what if there was more? What if she really could become like God? God seemed all powerful. He could come and go seemingly anywhere in the universe whenever he wanted. God also had so much wisdom. She could do so much more if she was like him.

Think of the possibilities, she heard a voice in her head say.

Kafi watched the conversation in the garden between Satan and Eve. He was a guardian angel assigned to Eve by God to protect her. What he heard was deeply concerning. Satan had never used this tactic before. While a fallen angel having relations with a human was physically possible, Kafi was certain God wouldn't allow it or at least wouldn't condone it. He wanted to go and tell God about the conversation but didn't want to leave Eve alone. A number of fallen angels had gathered, and he was now considerably outnumbered.

One demon named Raz was showing particular interest in the situation and looked as though he was trying to persuade Eve's thoughts. He had just told her to think of the possibilities. Kafi wasn't going to let him get away with it, if at all possible. The problem was that God had made Eve a free moral agent, capable of making her own choices, and Kafi's power to protect her was limited.

He couldn't protect her from herself.

"If you have my child, he will be like God," Satan said to Eve in a commanding voice.

"God said Adam and I are to have children," Eve responded. "He told us to be fruitful and multiply Saturn with our sons and daughters."

"Good answer," Kafi whispered to Eve in a still small voice in her mind. He had the ability to speak to her audibly but didn't have permission from God to do so at that moment. He could also appear to her physically but only when directed by God, and his experience had been that God rarely granted that permission.

"You already have everything you need," Kafi said. "You'll lose what you have if you believe Satan."

"Your children will be limited to Saturn," Satan retorted. "I can fly anywhere, anytime I want in the heavenlies. Like God does. Our child could do the same."

A lie, Kafi knew. The child would have the same limitations as humans. The spirit being would be trapped in the body of the child. Able to control his will and emotions and physical attributes, but with human limitations. He imagined the child would have superior size, weight, and strength. He shuddered at the thought of Satan's plan actually working. The being would be evil in every way. Every intention of his heart would be against God and the ways of God. It would allow Satan to wage war in the earthly realm as well as in the heavenly realm where it was now confined.

"Flee from him," Kafi implored Eve. "He's evil."

Eve had no concept of evil since she had not yet eaten of the fruit. He wondered how he could make her understand not to fall for the lies.

Raz suddenly appeared to Eve, startling Kafi at the quick transformation. Eve had taken a step back as well, clearly not sure what to make of the strange being suddenly appearing out of nowhere. Raz had taken on the form of a human by distorting the light. At least it looked that way to Eve. If she had looked closely, she could discern he wasn't real. A very clever disguise. This was a new battle they were fighting. Kafi made a mental note to ask the archangel Michael how to effectively fight that strategy.

Raz flew around like a blur and landed next to Eve with a wide grin on his face.

"Look at me," he said gleefully. "That's what your son can be like. He can fly and go into the heavenlies like me."

Just as quickly as he appeared, Raz disappeared. Like a puff of smoke. But not before whispering in her ear, "Don't you want to be able to do that?"

"I want to do that," Eve repeated the thoughts that had entered her mind saying them out loud. "Will my son really be able to do that?" she asked.

"He can do that and more," Satan bellowed. "Our son will be like God. If you eat of the fruit, you will be like God, and you'll be able to do it too."

"That's not true. Don't believe him. It's a lie." Kafi whispered to Eve even though she didn't know what the word *lie* meant.

* * *

Eve could hear the conflicting voices in her head. One was telling her Satan was lying, whatever that meant. She thought she knew but wasn't sure. Satan was saying God wasn't telling the truth. The voice in her head was saying Satan wasn't telling the truth.

I don't know who to believe.

I should believe God. He's always been good to me.

A reaffirming thought came to her, giving her a sudden peace.

Eve suddenly felt certain she wouldn't do it.

* * *

"Don't you want to be like the other Eves?" Satan said, repeating his previous argument and disrupting her good thoughts sent by Kafi.

"You can be the greatest of all of them!" Raz shouted in her head. The other fallen angels chimed in with various comments, drowning out everything Kafi was saying to her.

"There are no other Eves on the moons," Kafi said, but Eve didn't even seem to hear him speaking to her over the din.

He needed help. They were playing on Eve's emotions and exploiting her vulnerabilities. Throughout all the years and all the planets, Satan always tried to get humans to doubt God. This Adam and Eve had lasted longer than most. Generally, the humans ate from the tree the first time Satan tempted them. God never told humans about life on other planets. He had his reasons. Satan was violating protocol and going against previous precedent with other planets. He was obviously growing more desperate as each planet ended in the defeat of his plans.

Kafi decided he needed to go get Adam. Eve was not as strong as she had been previously because she was losing the fight in her head as the evil forces were overwhelming her thoughts. If he didn't hurry, Eve might do something foolish.

He raced to find Adam. Adam was on the other side of the garden tending to it. His angel, Asa was with him. Kafi quickly told Asa what was happening. Asa spoke the thought to Adam that he needed to go to Eve. He put a sense of uneasiness with the thought. It wouldn't do any good to try and make him feel fear or panic. Adam had no knowledge of good and evil. As far as Adam knew, there was never anything to fear.

Araq, the fallen angel assigned to Adam, was also there and implored him to finish his work before he went.

Adam listened to Asa and dropped what he was doing and set out to find Eve.

Satisfied, Kafi flew back to the field where Eve was now surrounded by a large crowd of angels and fallen angels. He had to push his way to the front of the line so he could see what was going on.

Several of the fallen angels tried to stop him, but he was determined and pushed them aside roughly.

"Get out of my way!" he shouted. "I'm her angel. I'm supposed to be here."

When he finally made his way to the front, he saw Satan take Eve by the hand. He strained to hear what she was saying. He could see that Adam was still far away on the other side of the garden.

"Okay," Eve said. "I'll do it. I'll eat the fruit. I'll have your child."

Those were the last words he heard as they walked off in the direction of the tree of the knowledge of good and evil.

13

Present Day, Sat-4013

By the look on her face, Becca was still not convinced. Her arms were still wrapped tightly within each other, folded, pressed into her chest. A stern but emboldened look had come on her face as she appeared to be gaining confidence over her fear. I had just started explaining the Eden Experiment and what we were trying to accomplish. She still seemed skeptical although the vitriol had subsided some.

Her lips were still tightened in skepticism. I couldn't help but notice how attractive she looked when she was mad, even given the gravity of the situation and the conversation. It took all my effort not to smile at her. I didn't want to make things worse by making her feel patronized.

Focus.

I tried to keep my mind on the task at hand—convincing her to help me with the Eden Experiment. The success or failure might very well be determined in the next few minutes of our conversation.

I had on my desk, the first step in the experiment—the DNA tests and blood work. Becca had picked those up for me at Turner Labs first thing in the morning, and I was curious as to what they revealed. I wanted to look at them, but Becca was not yet on board. We'd look at them together if and when she was. A good argument was crystalizing in my head.

"Becca, we are in the middle of a war with the Satites," I argued. "They are cloning a superior race of warriors. If we don't stop them, they'll take over the world. You know what they'll do to anyone who's a Christian."

"I get that," she responded. "I can see why you need to examine the Satite. I suppose all's fair in love and war as they say. But I don't understand why Mark had to die. We don't need him to do research on the Satite."

A bolt of excitement rushed through me. This aspect of the experiment was what drew me to it.

"We can compare Mark to Clooney," I said.

"Who is Clooney?" she interrupted.

"Sorry. That's the nickname I gave to the Satite. It's a play on the word, chone."

A faint smile came on her face.

I was making progress. "The Satite is void of any knowledge of good and evil. In a sense, so were Adam and Eve in the garden. But Clooney is different from them. He's evil. They weren't. Clooney isn't capable of anything good. I don't think he's even capable of being saved. He doesn't have a spirit, or at least I don't think he does. He just has a body. A genetically modified body structured to be a powerful warrior. You should've seen him when he came in the lab. Pure evil. All he wanted to do was kill me and everyone else in his path. The look on his face was like looking at Satan himself."

"I can hardly blame him. You were about to kill him. I'd be pretty mad too."

"It wasn't just that. Yeah, he was angry. But he's different in some way. His body is obviously different. But something is different in his soul and spirit. Deep down."

"How so?"

"It's like he's not human. He has all the human attributes, but he is devoid of a spirit and a soul. Becca, this might be our chance to discover where the spirit is in the body."

The pace of my words had quickened, and my voice had a sense of urgency as genuine excitement filled the room. Becca responded to the energy and unfolded her arms.

"I get it! We can compare Mark's body to the Satite's." Becca said with the same level of excitement. "Think about this. Mark is a Christian. The Satite is not. So, the spirit of God lives inside of Mark. By comparing the two, we can discover the difference, if there is one. There has to be."

"Yes!" I said. "We can do brain scans. Full body imaging. Explore organs and cells. Observe the difference in Mark's body contrasted with Clooney's."

"They have to be different," Becca said with excitement. "Clooney was formed in a lab. I've never thought about that before. Was he born with a spirit, like normal humans made in the image of God? That's a very interesting question."

"That's why we need both of them. I didn't want to do this to Mark, but he was going to die anyway. This way, his life can have meaning beyond his death."

"There are so many ethical issues to consider." Becca kept nervously changing positions in her chair. Crossing and uncrossing her legs. Brushing her hair away with her hand.

"Trust me, I've thought about them all," I replied. "I've had trouble sleeping at night, wrestling with all of the consequences. And I don't think the end justifies the means. You have to know that about me. I live my life by a moral code. I don't take it lightly when I deviate from it."

I paused to let that sink in.

"That's the very reason the Satites choned Clooney," I continued. "Their end is to annihilate Christians. They hate us. They'll do anything to get to those ends by whatever means necessary. We can't be naïve enough to not do everything we can to stop them. Within reason. Obviously."

"What happens if we do discover the location of the spirit in the human body? What then?" Becca asked.

"I haven't thought that far ahead," I said. "But the medical possibilities are endless. And the religious ones are as well. Scholars and theologians have debated this question for centuries. The location of the spirit in the human body has evaded scientists for centuries. I've read as many theories as I could find. None of them make sense."

"I think we're going to find the answer," Becca said, looking me straight in the eye.

My heart leapt and I could feel the tension leaving the room. She was going to help me with the experiment.

"We?" I asked. "Does that mean you'll help me?"

"Sounds like I don't have a choice."

"So, you don't think I'm a monster?"

Becca rolled her eyes as she let a grin come over her face.

"Seriously. I couldn't stand it if you hated me," I said sincerely.

I stood and walked around the desk and stood next to her and leaned back against the desk. Becca was still sitting in the chair. I was towering over her which was not my intention, but I wanted to be next to her. Reassuring her that we were in this together.

"I don't hate you," she said as she looked away while waving her hand dismissively. "I understand better why you would do it. A lot of good could come out of this. If nothing else, I'm really curious. You're right. This is a great opportunity. Whose idea was it to add Mark to the experiment?"

"Mine," I said hesitantly. "I didn't think we'd learn much just experimenting on Clooney. I mean... we'd learn some things. But by comparing Clooney's body to Mark's, we can learn so much more. Maybe we can even solve one of the mysteries of the universe. I'm a researcher. It's what I do. It's in my DNA."

I abruptly stood straight up sending a jolt through the room.

"What is it?" Becca said with concern in her voice, the smile suddenly leaving as quickly as it had come on her.

"DNA. That reminds me."

"What about it?"

"The package you brought back from Turner Labs has the results of Mark and Clooney's DNA tests. With our conversation, I haven't even had a chance to look at it."

I picked the package up off the table and waved it around nervously, almost like I didn't want to open it.

"This is the first step in the experiment," I explained. "I took their blood and extracted DNA from several places in their bodies. I swabbed their mouths and extracted DNA from their bones. I also took a hair sample from each and got a urine sample."

"You certainly covered all the angles," Becca said. "I would think each of the tests would show the same thing."

"I would think so too, but I wanted to be sure."

"Open it up," Becca said excitedly. "Let's see what it says."

She stood to her feet, sidled up next to me, and watched as I opened the envelope. My hands were shaking. Perhaps from the anticipation of the test or the intensity of our conversation. Probably both.

I tore the secured tab off the top and opened the envelope. Inside were several sets of papers. The one on top was from Specimen A. Mark's results. I went right to the section with the results. A quick glance and they seemed unremarkable.

"Specimen A is Mark."

"His results are normal," Becca said as I nodded in agreement.

Specimen B was Clooney's DNA test results.

"Oh my!" I said as my mouth flew open at what I was reading. I handed the page to Becca.

She started scanning it. She looked up at me in disbelief, obviously feeling the same shock. Unable to move, her look penetrated me to my very core.

A wave of fear flooded through my body.

"I can't believe this," I said.

"This is amazing. I think I know what it might mean," Becca said, solemnly.

I wasn't sure I wanted to hear it.

14

Still Present Day

"This is a disaster," the demon Raz said aloud to himself. "I'm going to get blamed for this."

He was observing Roger and Becca from the heavenlies. They were on the verge of discovering the true identity of the Satite, which Satan had so cleverly tried to conceal and had sent him to monitor. Raz had risen to the level of ruler after successfully manipulating Eve into eating the apple in the garden of Eden and having the evil one's child centuries ago.

Now, he had been sent for damage control after the demon in charge of the Satite had failed to protect him. After he arrived, he found that the Satite had been captured and then killed by the doctor and now lay in the laboratory basically dead for all practical purposes.

He listened intently to what was being said. He could see Roger, the doctor, and Becca, his assistant, sitting at the conference table in his office with the DNA results for Mark and for the Satite spread out on the table.

"What is the meaning of the DNA markers?" I asked Becca.

"That's what I'm trying to figure out," Becca replied. "I've never seen anything like this before."

"Look at Mark's number," I said. "They're perfectly normal."

"His G-WACS are consistent with an adult male," Becca responded. "The sequences and patterns are exactly what you'd expect to see."

"Mark's mutation sequences are also of little to no consequence," Becca continued. We both stared at the numbers. I had some knowledge of DNA results and knew my way around them, but she was more of an expert.

Humatile 5817

Motile 413

Unknown 18,578

Humatile represented the number of entries with good DNA. Motile was bad DNA. Unknown was DNA that was unmatched. Good and bad were self-explanatory. The unknown was where things were open to interpretation. We still didn't know a lot of things about DNA, and no test gave us all the answers. Most people on Saturn had similar numbers.

"Look at Clooney's same numbers," I said, pointing to a different page.

Becca was sitting in the chair with her legs underneath her, leaning over the table.

Our heads were nearly touching as we reviewed the numbers. I could smell the shampoo she used on her hair that day. A flowery scent. I consciously made myself turn my attention back to the results.

Humatile 0

Motile 10,666

Unknown 41,616

"Humatile is zero," I said. "How is that even possible?"

"Clooney doesn't have one good DNA marker," Becca said. "That's impossible. I wonder if there was an error in the test?"

"I followed standard procedures in extracting the samples. If you look at all three tests, the numbers are the same with very little variance. The mouth swab, urine analysis, and blood work all come up with the same levels of DNA."

"Motile is through the roof," Becca responded. "10,666. The bad DNA." She said the last words almost to herself.

"Unknown mutations are 41,616," I added.

"Look at how many times the number six is in his DNA markers," Becca said as her voice raised in urgency. "It's what we call prevalence. It's very high."

I couldn't help but notice the deep level of concern in her voice and on her face as she said it. Her head tilted to the side almost as if in disbelief.

"Clooney has a high prevalence with the number six," Becca continued. "Aleas is six. Proteas is sixty-six. Cocrease is six hundred and sixty-six. I could go on and on. There are at least a dozen numbers with six in it."

A shudder went through my body. A wave of fear. I knew that the number 666 had significance in the Bible and the end times, but I didn't remember what it was.

"Six is the number of man in the Bible," Becca explained as if reading my mind.

"Three sixes is the number of the beast or anti-Christ in the book of Revelation," she continued, her voice elevating in pitch and tone.

This was where I knew her knowledge of biblical studies would be invaluable. This sounded bad.

I was looking on the first page of the report when I noticed something highly irregular if not unexplainable. "Look at this," I said excitedly. "We should've looked at this first. What does this mean?"

"What?" she said, matching my excitement.

"Clooney's sex. We never thought to look at it."

I handed her the first page of his report.

"SXY-STN," Becca read out loud the letters in the box that identified the sex of the subject.

"STN. What is that?"

I knew from my training that female was SX and male was SXY. I'd never seen anything but one of those results in that box.

She didn't answer right away.

"Becca," I said strongly. "What does this mean?"

She stared at the page with her mouth wide open.

"It means Clooney is only half-man."

"So, he's half man and half woman?"

"No. He's half man and half something unknown."

"Any guess as to the unknown?"

"I hope I'm wrong."

"You're scaring me," I said.

"I think Clooney is half man and half demon."

* * *

Raz had heard enough. Time to execute his plan. He'd met with the evil one for this exact contingency. The humans now knew the truth about the Satite. Or at least enough of the truth that they'd eventually figure it out. He'd been given specific instructions of what to do if this happened.

In his position of ruler, he had authority over a multitude of spirits and demonic beings. Several were gathered around him, awaiting his instructions.

"Spirits of lust and adultery, you are now assigned to the doctor," Raz barked with anger and authority. "Don't hold anything back. You are free to tempt him in any way possible. If he opens the door, even a little, you are free to devour him. You do not have permission to kill him, though."

The two demons obediently flew away without a word of questioning.

Raz addressed the others.

"We are going to attack his family. Especially his wife. Spirits of fear, anxiety, and jealousy, you are not to leave her side. I am going to put a disease on her. She's already opened the door. I've heard her say several times how fearful she is of getting sick and dying young. You do have permission to kill her, just not right away. Draw it out so she will suffer. Make it six months. I must warn you, though, she has a lot of people around her who will be praying for her."

Raz raised to his full height. He spread his arms which were more wing-like. His voice was raised and echoed through the heavenlies. He needed to rally the troops.

"We are in a battle. You must fight to win. We have lost too many of them on other planets. You must not let us down."

"What are we to do, if she speaks the name of you know who?" one of the demons said, not able to actually speak the name of Jesus.

"You will have to flee and leave her alone," Raz said. "But I don't think she will. She is not that strong in her faith. Others around her are, though. They will be praying for her and asking God to heal her. Don't let those prayers get through. Do everything you can do to hinder them. Bring doubt, anger, and a root of bitterness to her. Get her to be angry at God."

"We won't let you down," one of them said confidently.

"You will regret it if you do," Raz retorted. "The punishment will be severe."

The demons flew off in a rush, like a swarm of bees leaving a hive suddenly released into the air.

I hope this works. If it does, I might get my own principality. If it doesn't... my punishment will be even more severe than theirs.

15

"You only have six months to live," the doctor said to Roger's wife, Helen.

She sat in his office having just finished her annual exam. The words hit her in the gut like a punch. The last words she ever expected to hear had left her stunned. A sudden tightness came on her chest, squeezing like a vise or a large boa constrictor.

"I don't understand," she said. "I feel great. What's wrong with me?"

"You have pancreatic blastoma," the doctor said. "It's incurable at this time. I'm sorry. Your body is attacking itself with blastoma cells."

Helen's life flashed before her eyes. Not her past, but her future. A future she wouldn't have. She wouldn't see her kids grow older, or her grandkids get married and have their own kids. Her parents were already older. They would need her in their old age. What would they do without her?

I'm going to miss all of them. Kids aren't supposed to die before their parents.

Helen's guardian angel, Mica, was watching and listening intently.

* * *

Helen suddenly felt strength. An inner peace. The tightness went away momentarily. She took a deep breath.

I will be strong. God will work this together for my good.

A number of Bible verses flooded into her mind.

"You're doing good," Mica whispered to Helen. "Let God give you his peace."

Suddenly, she felt overwhelming sadness. *How will I tell everyone?*

Chaz, a demonic spirit, was hovering over the doctor's office. He flooded her mind with a barrage of negative thoughts.

Mica was trying to counteract them.

All kinds of thoughts were running through Helen's mind.

Is it strange that I didn't think of my husband first?

He won't even care.

Where did that thought come from? Of course, he cares.

I don't want to die. I'm not going to die.

I'll fight this. The doctor said it's incurable.

"There is a medication you can take," the doctor said, interrupting her thoughts. "I have to be honest, though. The side effects are very difficult to live with. And it doesn't do anything to cure the disease. It might extend your life by a month, maybe two. But you have to think of the quality of your life."

"I don't think I want to do that," she said. "But I'll talk to Roger."

I can't believe this is happening.

Why would God let this happen?

By his stripes I am healed.

What if he doesn't heal me?

A sudden fear came over her. The doctor was talking about the end of her life and what it would be like. What suffering she should expect over the next few months and how her body would slowly break down. She barely heard what he was saying. Six months wasn't a long time. She suddenly felt anxious. *I have so many things to do. Where do I begin?*

"Don't be afraid," Mica said in a still, small voice. "Be anxious for nothing. Jesus will never leave you nor forsake you."

"He already has forsaken you," Chaz retorted in the deep recesses of Helen's mind. "If God loved you, he wouldn't have let this happen. It's you. You've sinned against God. He's punishing you."

"God is love," Mica countered. "Perfect love casts out all fear. There is no condemnation to those in Christ Jesus."

The competing thoughts were like a seesaw inside her. Mostly, she was ignoring them. More out of shock than anything else.

"Is there anything else I need to know?" Helen asked the doctor.

"I'm writing you a prescription for anxiety. Take it as needed."

"I don't feel any anxiety. I don't feel anything. I feel normal. That's what makes it so hard to believe."

"Good," Mica said to her affirmingly. "Keep speaking positive words. Everything is going to be okay."

"You are dying," Chaz said to her. "Just accept it."

Mica watched as Helen felt a sudden pain in her side and doubled over.

Fake. A lying symptom put on her by Chaz.

As quickly as it came upon her, the pain left. Mica had picked Chaz up and threw him aside. He pounced on him and struck him relentlessly. A flurry of demons surrounded Mica, trying to pull him off of Chaz. Fiery darts were thrown at Mica, but he easily deflected them.

At least they are throwing them at me and not at Helen. He had accomplished the desired effect. The demons were distracted long enough to stop the attacks on her.

While they were waging battle, none of them noticed that Helen had left the office and was in her airmobile.

* * *

Helen decided to go to her husband's office. *I need to tell him.* He wasn't her first thought, but now she needed to be with him. He's the first one she wanted to tell. He'd always been her strength. Her rock. They had lost two children together early on in their marriage when she miscarried. He'd been so strong. She needed that strength. He'd put his arms around her and tell her everything was going to be okay.

Helen allowed herself to cry for the first time since getting the news.

Mica was back with her. For the moment, he had thwarted Raz. He knew it would only be for a short period of time.

"It's okay to cry," Mica said. "But joy will come in the morning."

Helen held back the tears. There'd be time for that later. She needed to be able to get the words out. Telling Roger would be hard. They'd grown apart, which she now regretted. Often, it took times like these to realize what one has. She loved him, and now she needed him. Roger was also a doctor. He would know what to do. Maybe they'd get a second opinion. Roger would have an opinion and maybe even know of a cure.

"Doctors are not always right," she could hear him say.

She pulled into the parking lot already feeling better. While tears were still running down her face, she could feel an inner strength. Her hands were wet from wiping them away, so she wiped them on her skirt. She looked at herself in the rearview mirror and laughed lightly. Her makeup was smeared. Everything wasn't perfect. She always looked perfect in public.

Oh well. I think Roger will understand.

"We are facing a battle," she'd say to him. "A battle we're going to win."

The urge to tell everyone in the Bible study group suddenly came upon her. They can start a prayer chain and get the entire church praying. They'd all fight this together.

Seeing Roger's airmobile already bolstered her strength. She imagined how much better she'd feel when she was actually with him.

There were two airmobiles in the lot, Roger's and one other. She had pulled in next to the other.

Helen took a deep breath and let it out slowly. *What do I say?* She decided to say what was on her heart. *I'm going to cry.* Be strong, without crying. Was that even possible?

The thought suddenly entered her mind that maybe she should wait until tonight. Later, after work. *I'll cook him a nice dinner.* They'll have a glass of wine. That would help her relax a little. He was probably busy right now anyway and would be distracted. She started her airmobile, having decided to leave and give herself more time to prepare what she'd say.

At that moment, the door to his office opened. A woman walked out. A pretty woman. Young. Thin. Someone she didn't know. Must be a visitor or a customer; although, she was in a lab coat. Maybe she was making a delivery.

The woman saw Helen and walked toward her airmobile. Helen hit a button that rolled down the driver side window.

"Is there something I can help you with," the woman asked.

"No. I'm just here to see Dr. Forrester," Helen said.

"Okay. He's in there. The door's locked. You'll have to use the intercom and let him know you're here."

"I will," she said as she rolled the window back up.

Helen opened the door and stepped out of the airmobile. The woman was now at her vehicle opening the door.

"And who are you?" Helen asked.

"I'm Becca, Roger's assistant." She smiled warmly. "See you later," she said with a wave.

"Go! Now," Raz ordered several of the demons. "Fear, anxiety, jealousy, anger—every spirit—hit her at once."

Helen collapsed back into the airmobile and shut the door. Tears were pouring down her cheeks.

"He lied to you," Raz said.

He's such a liar. He said his assistant was a man.

The demons were overwhelming Helen with thoughts.

Why would he lie?

"She's pretty," Raz said to her.

And younger! He's twice her age.

"He's having an affair." Raz needed to keep the pressure on her.

I can't believe he's cheating on me!

"They've already had sex. He's probably planning on leaving you." Raz would say anything to make her feel pain.

Of all the nerve!

"You don't deserve this."

I can't deal with this right now. It's too much.

"You're going to die!"

I'm so afraid.

What am I going to do?

Helen couldn't start the airmobile and get out of there fast enough. So fast she almost hit the sign as she was leaving. The pain in her heart was so intense she could barely breathe. Her eyes were filled with so many tears, she couldn't see the road clearly. After nearly hitting another airmobile, she pulled to the side of the road.

Sobbing. Doubled over. Slumped over the wheel. She kept saying over and over again, "I don't know what to do."

"Faster! Harder!" Raz shouted to his demons. "Don't let up." He ordered more fiery darts. More thoughts. More demonic attacks.

Anger flooded Helen like a tidal wave.

I hate him. I'm dying, and he doesn't even care. I'm so embarrassed. I've been such a fool. I've given him thirty-three years of my life. I can't believe he did this to me. I hate her.

"Get her to say those things out loud," Raz shouted at his minions. "It's not enough to have the thoughts. She must speak the words."

"I'm going to die and get a divorce all at the same time! My life is over!" Helen said angrily.

"Perfect." Raz said. "She opened the door. Now we can sift her like wheat. We'll kill, steal, and destroy her and her husband. Get ready! Our work has just started!"

16

Valley of Noh, Eighty-three years after the fall

Cassie hesitated. How could she tell her husband, Abiel, not to go?

"You stay here," Abiel said to his wife.

"I want to go with you."

"Stay with the kids. It'll be alright." Abiel was referring to their seventeen-year old son, Noha, who was the youngest of several boys, Noha's wife, Chloe, and a thirteen-year-old daughter, Mira, the youngest of numerous daughters, who all had husbands and kids. Noha, Chloe, and Mira were the only ones who still lived with them.

"You haven't seen your brother in twenty plus years," Cassie said. "He almost killed you the last time you saw him."

Bale was one year older than Abiel and was the first-born child of Adam and Eve. Abiel was the second born, two years younger.

"I know," Abiel said. "I'll be careful. God told me to go. I have to. We're both supposed to bring an offering."

"I understand. I just don't trust Bale. He's pure evil. I still think he's the one who killed your mom and dad."

Adam and Eve were found dead in their tents twenty years ago. Run through with a sword, apparently killed in their sleep. Abiel suspected his older brother Bale but couldn't prove it. He confronted him and was attacked and nearly killed, escaping just at the last second. He fled to an area of Saturn miles away from Bale in the valley of Noh.

Bale and his descendants were giants. Significantly bigger, faster, and stronger than Abiel and his descendants. From everything Abiel had heard, his brother did evil in the sight of the Lord. Every intent of Bale's heart was to do evil, continually. Fortunately, Bale and his people had stayed on the other side of Saturn and had left them alone. They called themselves Balemites.

That morning, God commanded both Abiel and Bale to bring an offering to the Lord. Cassie, his wife wanted to go with him, but he doubted his brother would even show up.

At least that's what he hoped. If he did, it would be too danger-ous for Cassie.

Abiel prepared his sacrifice—the fat portions of the firstborn of his flocks. A herder by trade, he frequently sacrificed the firstborn of his flocks to the Lord as an offering. From what he heard, Bale tilled the soil, and would likely bring crops. Others in their camp grew crops as well, but Abiel focused on raising the animals. He loaded the sacrifice onto donkeys, kissed his wife goodbye, and set out for the location not that far away. Several of his older sons went with him.

They came over the hill, and Abiel's breath suddenly left him. Not only was Bale there but a whole army camped behind him on a hill. At least several hundred. All giants. All appeared to be armed with swords. Bale stood alone in the valley near a make-shift altar, with a fierce scowl on his face.

Bale's height had to be at least eight feet tall. He wore a bronze helmet on his head and a coat of armor of bronze. Abiel couldn't help thinking the armor alone must weigh more than a hundred pounds. On his legs were bronze greaves, and a javelin was slung on his back. His spear shaft in his right hand was as long as Abiel was tall. Bale had a shield in his left hand that appeared to be four feet in diameter. Probably made of iron.

Abiel's legs were wobbly as he came down the hill and into the valley and neared Bale. He and his sons were unarmed. He motioned for everyone to stop several yards away as he continued walking to-ward Bale.

"Brother, why do you come lined up for battle?" Abiel shouted, his voice shaking as he spoke. "We are here today to worship the Lord with an offering, not to fight with each other."

"This day, I defy the God of Abiel," Bale shouted in a booming voice, raising his arms, creating a span of several feet. "Nevertheless, I brought an offering today. If God accepts it, then I will let you live. If he doesn't, then all your men shall die, and your daughters will become our slaves."

"Why should my life and the life of my descendants be based on your offering?" Abiel cried out. "Bring your sacrifice. If you do what is right, will you not be accepted? If you don't, then God's favor is his own to give. It has nothing to do with me."

"Bring your offering," Bale said sarcastically. "Maybe my master won't accept your offering."

Abiel took his offering off of the donkeys and laid it on the ground. He made his own altar to the Lord out of his sacrifice. The Lord looked with favor upon Abiel and his offering as it was suddenly consumed with fire to the extent that nothing was left, not even ashes. Abiel backed away from the offering cautiously, facing Bale, not willing to turn his back on him.

Bale ordered his men to unload his offering from a makeshift wagon. Abiel had never seen anything like this wagon. It had four round stones attached to long pieces of wood. The wheels rolled along the ground carrying the sacrifice. The men set the crops from the field in a large pile in the same spot where Abiel's sacrifice had been.

All of Bale's men towered over Abiel and his sons.

One of Abiel's sons remarked, "We are like grasshoppers before them." They'd heard of the men but had to see them in person to really appreciate how big they were.

They all stood and watched the sacrifice in anticipation. Nothing happened.

God did not look with favor on Bale and his offering. The crops were still where they lay, mostly rotten from the journey. Bale had obviously not brought the best crops of his field. He brought those that were rotten and couldn't be eaten anyway.

Abiel could see anger raging in Bale as his whole demeanor became more menacing. He spread his arms and looked up at heaven, cursing God. Abiel and his sons trembled in fear. Abiel turned to run.

Bale raised his spear and flung it at Abiel, hitting him in the back. The force of the spear penetrated through him, so the tip was sticking out the front of his body as he fell to the ground, dead.

"Kill them all!" Bale shouted to his men. "I want every male descendant of Abiel, hunted down and killed. Bring all the women and girls to me. Do not touch his wife. She's mine."

A large shout went up from the throng of soldiers.

Abiel's sons tried to run away, but Bale's men were faster and easily overtook them. Not one man was left standing. They were all killed that day. The men continued running to the camps of Abiel, determined to carry out the commands of Bale.

* * *

Cassie could hear the commotion and the shouts of the men, along with the cries for help. Her worst fears were realized when she saw Bale come over the hill toward her tent. No sign of Abiel. Bale was walking in large strides, his eyes like coals of fire, raging and burning fire of hate.

She let out a scream.

"Noha!" she shouted to her son as she ran into their tent. "Hurry. We have to get out of here." Chloe was in there as well. Mira was not.

"Quick," Noha said. "Out the back. Head for the fields." They crawled underneath the back flap and took off running. Cassie looked back just long enough to see Bale destroy the tent and send it flying through the air with just one swipe of his sword.

"Where's Mira?" Cassie asked as Noha and Chloe ran ahead.

"She's down at the river," Noha shouted back over his shoulder.

"Head that way!" Cassie shouted. "I'll try to get him to follow me. Go to the river. Get on the raft and go down the river as far as you can. I'll try and meet you there. Don't wait for me. Hurry!"

Cassie veered to the left. Noha and Chloe disappeared into the fields in the other direction. They'd be hard to find in the maze and rows of crops. Cassie rushed into another adjacent field, knowing she'd be hard to find as well. Bale was closer to her and came her direction. So close, she could hear him panting and taking large, deep breaths.

Her breath quickened and her pulse raced. She looked back and saw him enter the field and take a swipe at her. Cassie let out a weak scream and circled back behind him, trying to use her agility as an advantage. He was bigger. She was quicker. She needed to put distance between them. Going to the river was no longer an option. She'd lead Bale right to them. She had to stay in the cover of the fields. If she went out into the open, he'd catch her in no time.

Think.

She tried to focus on her escape. Hopefully the kids would make it to the river and get away. Cassie was certain her husband was dead. For a moment, she wanted to stand and fight, and avenge her husband's death, but she had no weapon. It wouldn't matter anyway. He was too big and too strong. She picked up a rock off the ground and gripped it in her hand. It was only a small stone. A pebble really.

The thick area of the field was providing some cover, but her breathing was so heavy she was sure he could hear her.

Bale swung his sword wildly left and right, making huge swaths through the field. Incredible how much ground he was gaining on her. He got closer.

Then he saw her, and set out in her direction. In two steps he was on her, attempting to wrap his huge arms around her. She wiggled away by slipping under his arms and darting out of the field into a clearing. At that point, she had no option but to stand her ground. The pebble was all she had.

"God deliver me," she prayed.

Bale emerged from the field and stopped, laughing diabolically. A memory from Eve, came over her. She remembered her mother-in-law's warnings. Bale was evil, she had said. "He's not a real man." Eve's words flooded back in her mind.

Cassie didn't understand what Eve was trying to tell her at the time, but it suddenly came to her.

Bale was evil. There was no way he could be Adam's son. Adam was the kindest man she'd ever met. Gentle and loving. Bale looked nothing like Adam. Abiel was Adam's spitting image. They were almost identical in build, features, look, and in their love for God. Bale looked like how Eve described Satan in the garden. Almost serpent like.

"Don't come any closer," Cassie warned Bale sternly. "On this day, the Lord is going to give you into my hands!"

She showed him the pebble in her hand.

He roared with laughter.

"Am I a dog that you come to me with a stone? Your husband is dead. Today I will take you as my wife. You will have Satan's seed."

Satan!

Is that possible? Could Bale be Satan's son? He had to be. It's the only thing that made sense.

"You come against me with a sword and a spear," Cassie said in a loud voice. "I come against you in the name of the Lord Almighty who you, on this day, have defied. Prepare to die."

Cassie gripped the stone, then reared back and let it fly. The stone spanned the distance in no time. Before Bale could react or turn away, it struck him on the forehead and buried deep into his skull. Bale fell, face-first to the ground. He didn't move.

Is he dead?

Cassie let out a shout of victory. She turned around to flee. Instead, she stopped in her tracks. More than a dozen of Bale's men were standing there, facing her. She backed away but several had circled behind her.

She was trapped. Surrounded.

Cassie could hear the screams throughout the camp and the shouts of Bale's men from a distance. Their worst fears had come to pass.

I just hope Noha, Chloe, and Mira made it to the river.

God, please save them.

It was too late for her.

17

The archangel Ovel had never seen it this bad, not on Saturn and not on any other planet. While a war was waging on Saturn, an even greater war was waging in the heavenlies. For the most part, he had avoided the hostilities. He'd been given another assignment by God—to make sure at least one man and one woman of Abiel's descendants survived the battle and remained untainted by Bale's descendants.

His mission complete, Noha, Chloe, and Mira were safe on an island many miles away from the Land of Noh. They had made it to the raft and onto the river Elin. The raft had carried them safely down south to an unexplored territory unknown to the evil men.

Back in Noh, Ovel was assessing the damage. All of the men and boys who were descendants of Abiel were slain. Their bodies were strewn everywhere, and the birds of the air were consuming what was left of them. The women and girls were taken as slaves. They had been corrupted by Bale's men.

As bad as Ovel felt for them, they had brought this on themselves. Eve started it by eating the apple and giving in to Satan's seductions and having his child, Bale. Adam continued it by allowing Eve to persuade him to eat the apple. Even though Adam and Eve eventually regretted it, sin and death had been brought into the world, and at least half of the people on Saturn, the descendants of Bale, were only half human.

God had commanded that none of Abiel's descendants take foreign wives, but they had. Several of the men had married Balemite women and were bringing the corruption into Abiel's line of descendants. That was the main reason why God had allowed Bale and his armies to destroy them. God had protected them for years from the Balemites. Once they opened the door, disobeyed, and took foreign wives, things had gotten so bad, God removed his hedge of protection.

Even though Bale was dead, over time, things had gotten even worse.

The Balemites had a new leader whose name was Cane. He was every bit as evil as Bale, and his wickedness was as great. Under the instructions of the evil one, he allowed his men to take the captured women and girls of Noh as their wives, but the virgins were to be set aside for a greater purpose. More than two hundred fallen angels descended onto the earth, took the form of humans, and made the virgins their wives, each choosing whom they wanted.

Their descendants became known as Nohelims. They were giants and of evil seed and did evil continuously before the Lord.

* * *

One hundred years later.

Ovel was called back to the presence of the Lord along with a number of other angels where they were awaiting further instructions. No doubt, related to the new developments on Saturn.

Suddenly, the Lord appeared and began speaking in a commanding voice.

"The wickedness on Saturn is great," God said. "The mighty men, the Nohelims of renown, are great on Saturn. The intents of their heart are evil continually. There is none righteous, no not one. I'm sorry I even made man on Saturn."

Ovel could tell the Lord was grieved in his heart. The words came out with obvious pain behind them. He knew how much God loved all of his creation, now compromised by the fallen angels. Not only did angels rebel against God and lose their positions in heaven, they had now corrupted man, leaving their domains and taking on strange flesh, contrary to everything God had commanded and designed for the angels and for man.

"I will destroy man who I have created off of the face of Saturn, both man and beast, creeping things and birds of the air; for I am sorry that I have made them," God said.

The words hit Ovel like a lightning bolt.

"No!" he wanted to shout. "What about Noha, Chloe, and Mira and their descendants?"

Ovel knew they were not corrupt. That's why he'd been instructed to save them. They were living just and perfect lives on the island. Noha had even refused to have relations with Mira, his sister. He believed God had called him to be married to only one woman. They had a son, and that son took Mira as his wife and they had sons and daughters. God had blessed them. They began to multiply on the island, continually bringing sacrifices to the Lord.

How could God destroy them? If he did, then all his efforts to save them would have been in vain. He'd wait to say anything until God quit speaking. Then he'd plead for their survival.

He didn't have to.

"Noha has found favor in my eyes," God said, much to Ovel's relief.

Pure joy flooded him at the mention of Noha's name and that he'd found favor with the Lord.

"Ovel," the Lord said.

"Yes, Lord," Ovel replied upon hearing his name, stepping forward to the front so God could see him.

"Come with me," God instructed.

In the blink of an eye, Ovel and the Lord were looking down upon Noha.

* * *

Noha was in the fields, preparing the crops for harvest as he had been taught by his father Abiel. Suddenly, an angel of the Lord appeared before him, and he heard God's audible voice call out his name.

"Noha," God said.

"Yes, Lord," Noha replied, dropping his tools of harvest.

"All flesh on Saturn has been corrupted," God said, "except for you and your family. That is why I instructed my angel to save you... so an incorruptible race could continue on Saturn."

"The end of all flesh has come before me," God continued, "for Saturn is filled with violence, and I will destroy every living thing on Saturn."

A sadness came upon Noha. He often wondered what had happened back in the Land of Noh. Did his mother Cassie survive? Were they taken as slaves? They were down current from Noh and there was no way for them to make their way back there. They were stuck on the island. While they had made a good life for themselves and their families, Noha still thought about Noh often and regretted not knowing what had happened to his family. He'd give anything to go back there, even with the danger.

Now he was learning that some had survived. God wasn't being specific, but whatever happened must have been horrible if all of Saturn was now filled with violence. So much so that God was going to destroy them all. A jolt of fear came upon him as he wondered if that meant him and his family as well.

"I want you to build an ark," God said. "Made from wood. Make rooms in the ark and cover it inside and outside with pitch. This is how you will make it."

For the next few hours, God gave Noha specific instructions on how to construct the ark. Many times in the past, Noha thought about how to construct some kind of craft to get back on the river and propel himself back to Noh. He never could figure out how to do it. He was fascinated by the creative design of the ark God was instructing him to build. Nothing less than ingenious. He could've thought about a design for the rest of his life and never come up with something so practically perfect for floating on water.

"You shall make a window for the ark, and you shall set a door on its side."

Noha took careful notes, writing the design on the ground in the sand with a stick.

"I am bringing floodwaters on Saturn," God said soberly. "They will destroy all the flesh in which is the breath of life," God paused, maybe thinking about his next words, maybe letting those words sink in.

"But I will establish a covenant with you, and you shall go into the ark—you and your wife, your sons and daughters, and their husbands and wives and children. They shall go on with you."

Joy came over Noha.

We will be saved.

What God said next was incredible to him.

"You are also to take two of every bird, two animals of every kind —two of everything—and you are to keep them alive."

What?

How was that possible? Some were wild animals. Wild animals on the ark who would prey on the other weaker animals. How would he keep them separated? He'd have to round up two of everything. Lions, tigers, elephants. How will two elephants fit on the ark?

The smell.

His thoughts were interrupted as God continued. "And you shall take for yourself all the food you will need and enough for the animals."

How will we store the food? Cook it? Keep it fresh?

Just as quickly as he appeared, God was gone.

Ovel was still there, instructed to stay with Noha and protect him through the task and keep him from getting discouraged. Ovel already noticed Noha had many doubts.

"How long will we be in the ark?" Noha asked himself out loud. God didn't say. The task suddenly seemed daunting to him. He calculated it would take him at least a hundred and twenty years to build the ark. How would he convince his family that he wasn't a madman? They were going to think he's crazy for building a huge boat for rain when there wasn't a cloud in the sky.

Ovel sent Noha words of encouragement.

Even with all his doubts, Noha did everything according to all God commanded him.

The flood lasted for forty days and forty nights.

The evil men and the corrupt flesh were all destroyed.

Saturn was given a second chance.

PART TWO

"This is not some silly game… This is life and death.
Angels and demons."

— Melissa de la Cruz

18

Satite Cloning Lab, Present Day

Eval stood by a large window overlooking what was now forty years of his life's work. More than four thousand incubators held four thousand chones. Chones were inhuman beings choned from the DNA of the Balemites. Twenty years before, a bone had been found in a cave, perfectly intact. Predating the Great Flood. Eval presumed when the rains started, somehow a Balemite man had managed to find a cave and roll a stone at the entrance. Satite archeologists found the remains after rolling the stone away and exploring the cave. While the shelter didn't protect him from dying, his skeletal body was still intact. As was his DNA.

Eval was able to extract DNA from the Balemite's arms and legs. One arm was more than five feet long, so he had a lot of raw material to work with. What he discovered in analyzing the Balemite's DNA was astonishing. The man was half human and half demon. Proof positive that a superior race of people spoken about in ancient writings most had dismissed as a myth or a fable did actually exist.

Now he'd brought them back to life.

An expert in cloning and DNA, Eval was able to unlock the genome code and duplicate the DNA markers of the man creating his own superhuman being. The process hadn't been without challenges. For years, he experimented with the code, perfecting it. Once he was certain he had the correct genetic formula, his problems really began. The incubation created almost insurmountable issues.

Women couldn't carry the beasts for longer than a couple months. His early surrogates, Satite women who were forced to carry the children, died when the beings grew beyond the capabilities of the women's wombs and their insides literally exploded from the womb rupturing, killing the women instantly along with the child. More than a thousand women died in the experiments.

Now the women carried the creatures from inception to the first month until the first heartbeat, and then the creatures were surgically removed from the wombs and placed in the incubators with artificial umbilical cords providing enough nourishment to bring them to adulthood within three months.

Once full grown, the being reached a height of eight-to-nine-feet tall and weighed more than five hundred pounds. The first chones only grew to a height of between six and seven feet. The process was more refined now and the next group of warriors would be so large and lethal they would be unstoppable. After a month of training and download, Eval was able to transform the man into a fighting warrior, capable of killing thousands of people with the skill to avoid being killed himself. The biggest challenge now was training the beasts without his own men dying. He had to channel their evil toward the Christians. The chones had no knowledge of good and evil. They had to be trained to know nothing but evil while knowing enough to focus their hatred and murderous appetites on the enemy.

The first group of chones—two hundred of them—had survived the process and were in the field. MC-43 was the most successful, having killed as many as eight hundred Christians at one time, according to the latest reports.

The ring of his caller suddenly interrupted him as he admired his handiwork.

Damian is calling.

Damian was the Vice Chancer of the Satites. As Supreme Commander, he was the one funding all of his efforts and in charge of their part of the world. A ruthless dictator, Damian was obsessed with killing Christians and taking over the world, making sure that nothing good was left on Saturn. Eval presumed Damian had made a pact with the evil one and was mostly following his directions.

"Damian. To what do I owe the honor of your call," Eval said. The Vice Chancer only had the one name which everyone was required to call him. Modeled after Satan, who was sometimes called Lucifer, but generally was referred to by the one name.

"I am calling on the status of things," Damian said in a growling, raspy voice. Not in a way that alarmed Eval but in his normal manner and tone.

"When will the next generation of warriors be ready?" he continued.

"Two hundred more are in training now. Four thousand will come out of the incubators within days."

"How many of those will survive?"

"I expect more than half of them. About eighty percent will come out of the incubators, alive or at least functioning. The others will have some genetic mutation that can't be fixed and must be euthanized. Another group will not be able to download the training and process it. They must be separated from the others. They too have to be killed. We salvage their DNA so it can be used in the future."

"How many will be ready for battle?" he said roughly.

"At least three thousand. You asked for two thousand. I'm giving you a thousand more than you requested."

"Excellent. With an army that size we will annihilate the Christians and will rule the world and make them our slaves within no time."

"How are the two hundred already in the field doing?" Eval asked.

"We lost one," Damian replied.

"What do you mean you lost one?" Eval asked with alarm in his voice.

"He's missing."

"Why wasn't I informed?"

"It just happened in the last few days. Somehow, he just disappeared."

"Which one?"

"MC-043," Damian answered.

"The chones have a chip in them, with a locator," Eval replied. "It's a beacon device. I can find him by just tracking the chip. Let me call you back."

The line went dead without a word from the Vice Chancer.

Eval strode back to his desk and powered up his artby. All of the information for every chone was in the box at his fingertips.

"MC-043," he said to himself as he typed in the information. The best of all the chones to date. He'd immediately become obsolete as soon as the new ones came out of the incubator, but he'd been the first to really excel in the training. They perfected the process through him. Eval had a deep affection for forty-three. He had named him Herculeum.

The locator was still on. Herculeum was in enemy territory. He zoomed into the location.

Forrester.

He knew the location immediately. The blue dot was flashing at the SR & MDA research facility. Dr. Roger Forrester was the foremost medical researcher on Saturn. Second in skill, only to himself. The doctor had somehow gotten his hands on the chone and was no doubt conducting experiments on him.

I should've known.

He dialed the number of the Vice Chancer who answered on the first ring.

"I found the chone. The Christians have him. He's in their medical lab."

Damian cursed on the other end of the caller. "There's no way we can go in and get him until the new warriors are ready," Damian said. "How long will that be?"

"About two to four months. I'll find another way to get him back. Let me call you later."

The caller disconnected again.

He scrolled through Forrester's website, searching for information. *Hmm. Forester has a new assistant.* A woman named Becca Holmes. Eval did some research on her. He didn't find much, but what he did find was enough to form a plan.

This will work.

19

"Mom! How could you do that?" Becca asked, exasperated with her mother. "I told you I wasn't interested."

She stared at the box message on her artby telling her she'd been enrolled into matchworks.sat. An online dating site that matched men and women based on their DNA.

"Honey, you're thirty-seven years old," her mom retorted. "Never been married. You haven't brought a boy home to meet us in ten years. You're not getting any younger, you know."

"I don't have time to date anyone," Becca said strongly. "I'm in the middle of a big project right now. There's no way I would even have time to think about dating."

She couldn't possibly tell her mom how big the project was. The entire future of Saturn might depend on it. While she'd been skeptical at first, appalled really, now that she was in the throes of it, she'd excitedly thrown all her energy into it. She now had pages of notes and ideas on how to conduct the research on Mark and Clooney. Dating was the last thing on her mind.

"That's what I'm talking about," her mom replied. "You never have time for us. It's been months since we've seen you."

"I was there two months ago, remember? We had dinner."

"Two months is a long time. Your father and I are not getting any younger."

Becca decided to ignore that comment. They were in such good health they might outlive all of them.

"Just go on the website and see who they match you with. Aren't you curious?"

"Not at all," Becca said roughly. Immediately regretting the tone. She was mad at her mother but didn't want to be mean.

"I already put your profile on the site."

"What? Mom!"

Becca scrambled to get on the site to see what her profile looked like. Now she was really getting angry. It was one thing to sign her up but quite another to set up an entire profile without her permission.

"I even downloaded your DNA," her mom said. "Look! You already have a match."

She never stayed mad at her mom about anything for long, but at the moment, she was fuming. A picture of her stared back from her artby screen. Complete with a full profile of her height, weight, hair color, and DNA coding.

Oh My Gosh!

The site was actually an ingenious idea. With her background in DNA research and cloning, she found the concept fascinating. Matchworks processed the uploaded DNA through their algorithms, searching for who they believed would be most compatible based on DNA results. Tens of thousands of people had used the services and swore by them. Commercials claimed more than a million successful matches.

"Why did you use that picture, Mom?" Becca asked.

"I like that picture."

"It's ten years old. I don't look that young anymore."

She actually did still look like that picture. Except for a few more wrinkles. It's not the picture she would've chosen but not the worst choice either. As far as a profile goes, it could've been worse.

"My profile says Dr. Becca Holmes. That sounds too stodgy and uppity. Like I'm trying to show off."

"You're a doctor. You should show off."

"That would scare a lot of men away. Some men are intimidated by a successful woman."

"Of all my children, you're the smartest. Don't be embarrassed by it. Respond to the notification. You have a match. If you don't, then I'll respond for you."

"Don't you dare. I'm changing the password right now."

Becca furiously typed, trying to get into her profile. She couldn't. Her mom had set up the account so only she knew the password. She'd have to play nice to get it from her. Knowing her mom, she wouldn't give it to her until she agreed to at least look at the match.

"Becca, honey, Mother knows what's best for you. You need to get out more. Give it a chance. Besides, I need grandkids."

"You already have fourteen grandkids and two on the way!"

"I don't have any from you. You're my baby."

Becca was the youngest of six kids and the only one not married. Something obviously of great concern to her mom.

Sometimes it's so hard to honor your father and mother.

"You have to give me kids before I die," her mother said before she could respond.

Becca laughed out loud.

"Don't be ridiculous. You're as healthy as a cat with nine lives. You'll live forty or fifty more years."

"At this rate, it might take you that long to get married."

"I'm hanging up now."

"I looked at the match. He's cute."

"Hanging up! This is me saying goodbye. Love you."

Becca disconnected her caller and ignored the flashing light on the artby, signifying a match on her profile page. She went to the washroom and stared at herself in the mirror, talking to herself, not sure what to do.

"I don't need this right now," she said out loud, picking up a brush and angrily running it through her hair.

"She had no right to sign me up. Even put my DNA on there!"

Her mom would have all of her vital information in a file, knowing how organized she was. Not that it was hard to get. Anyone could access the information for a fee. Privacy was non-existent on Saturn. Several companies gathered and sold the information to whoever paid for it. Her age, address, medical records, ID number, retina scan, fingerprints, financial credit history, school grades, and DNA test results were all available for twenty rings to anyone willing to pay for it.

The government thought it necessary to have one large database of information. Transparency led to security they had promised. She wasn't sure. She thought DNA results should be private. Being an expert in the field, she knew a lot of information could be extracted about someone and used against them if in the wrong hands.

She was curious. Matchworks flooded the VT vision screens with commercial ads promoting their success. As a doctor in the field, it would be interesting to see who they matched her up with. Would it be accurate? Was it all a scam?

Go and look.

No.

A debate was raging inside her. *I don't want to know.*

Her caller rang, startling her.

"Mom!"

"Not Mom. It's me. Have you looked at his profile yet?" Cherry, her oldest sister said excitedly.

"I can't believe Mom did that. Signing me up without my permission."

"Yes. You can believe it. You know Mom."

"I suppose. But I'm happy with my life," Becca said sharply. "I don't need a man to complicate it. No offense. You found a good one. If I could find one like Bill, maybe I'd get married too. But you got the last good one."

Cherry laughed. "I tried to set you up on a date with his brother," she said.

"That's too weird," Becca retorted. "That's like incest or something."

"No, it's not. It's perfectly normal. Incest is if you marry someone in your own family. Too late now anyway. He's happily married. You missed your chance. You could wait until their son is grown."

"That's not funny."

Maybe she was missing out on something. She loved her independence. Every once in a while, she felt lonely. But not often. When she did, she ate some ice cream, watched a movie, and felt better. At the end of the day, she was thankful she didn't have to take care of another person.

"That's Mom calling me," Cherry said. "I'll put her on our call."

"No..." Before Becca could object, her mom was now in the conversation.

"Have you looked at the match?" her mom said.

"I have not, and I'm not going to."

"His name is Ed. He's cute."

"He's cute," Cherry added.

"You've looked at it too? I guess I don't have any privacy in this world. Everyone's seen his picture but me."

"Dad approves too."

"Mom!"

"The Bible says it's not good to be alone," Cherry said.

"It also says if you're single, you've chosen the better way and you should remain that way," Becca retorted.

"Only if you can control your sexual urges," her mom said.

"I can't believe we're having this conversation."

"Promise me you'll look at his picture."

"I'm not going to promise."

"Promise me."

"Okay mom. I promise. But I'm not going to accept the match. I'm not going on a date with a total stranger. He could be a murderer for all we know. I'm hanging up now. Love you both."

20

Eval's artby screen came alive. A ding signified a notification. It could be anything. He hoped it was what he had been waiting patiently for.

He opened the webpage with anticipation. "Perfect," he said as he dialed a number on his caller. Damien answered again on the first ring.

"I have good news," Eval said. "My plan is in motion. We will have the chone back in no time."

"I'm counting on you. If the Christians find out what we're doing, they might be able to stop it. I don't have to tell you how important it is to get the chone back. Or at least destroy him so they can't research him."

"I'm aware of the gravity of the situation," he said with some irritation. "You can count on me."

He hung up his caller and turned his focus back to his artby. Roger Forrester had an assistant named Becca Holmes. Not much was known about her on the web, except that she was a renowned doctor of immunology and an expert on cloning.

A disaster.

She had the skills to unlock his genome code and create a mutation to stop it. She was, no doubt, assisting the scoundrel Forrester in the examination of MC-043. Fury raged at the thought of the Christians touching his creation. Probing it. Cutting him open. It wouldn't take them long to discover his origins. Eval had to unball his fists to even type in the information.

They will pay with their lives.

Fortunately, Becca Holmes had a profile on a dating website. When he discovered it, a plan had formed in his mind. He set up an online profile under the name Ed Tansa. The last name, an acronym of the evil one. He analyzed Holmes's DNA profile and calculated a DNA match based on what he knew about the website's algorithms. Just as he suspected, the site matched Tansa's profile with Dr. Becca Holmes.

And she had fallen for it.

A flashing light on the site said she had accepted the match. They could now communicate. He started to type her a message but paused to think about it.

I have to say just the right thing.

Hello, Becca... He hit backspace several times. *Hello, Dr. Holmes. May I call you Becca? You can call me Ed.*

He stared at the screen in anticipation, anxiously awaiting a response. If she was a typical Christian female, she'd be skeptical and hesitant. Dr. Holmes was a brilliant scholar. He'd have to be careful or she'd see right through his ruse.

You can call me Becca. It's nice to meet you.

I have to be honest, Eval typed, *I don't think I'm qualified to be matched to someone of your esteem.*

Eval laughed out loud at his cleverness, but more from him saying he had to be honest. There wasn't an honest bone in his body. And that's exactly how he liked it. He would sift this woman like wheat. He'd become her worst nightmare.

Don't sell yourself short, Becca responded. *I've read your profile. You are accomplished in your own right.*

I've never done anything like this before, he responded. A conversation formed in his mind.

Me either. To be honest, I'm kind of nervous.

Me, too! My sister talked me into this, Eval typed, laughing diabolically.

He noticed on Becca's profile that she had three sisters and a mother who was still living. Pictures of them were all over her profile. No way Becca signed up for this without her sisters and mother knowing about it."

That's funny. My mother signed me up.

Eval smiled again. He was enjoying this. Creating an online image and seducing this girl was sending jolts of excitement through him. This woman was already falling for his online wit and charm. And his lies.

Do you think we should meet? He typed in the words but hadn't yet sent it. Was it too soon? He hit backspace deciding it was too soon.

How is a man like you still single? she asked.

He breathed a sigh of relief, feeling glad she was keeping the conversation moving. He thought of a good lie in response.

I was married, but my wife died a few years ago. Blastoma.

She was a doctor so she would know that Blastoma was a disease of mutated cells. He would play on her heartstrings. Make her feel sorry for him. For Ed.

I'm sorry, she said with a sad mojo face next to the words.

Thanks. I've had a hard time getting back into dating. My mother tells me all the time I should. I don't know. It's hard. You never really get over your first love... I guess.

Eval immediately regretted sending that last post. No woman wanted to be with a man still pining over his ex-wife.

Dead wife.

Whatever.

I understand. I can imagine how hard it is.

Change the subject, he decided.

Do you think we should meet?

He needed to move the conversation along. Before he made another mistake. Seconds passed. Then they turned to several minutes. She was obviously considering the question. If she answered no, his efforts were in vain. He'd have to come up with another plan. If she said yes, he'd have to get one of the chones trained to meet her.

He already had one selected A reject from the first two hundred. Not big enough. He was only six foot tall. Brilliant though. The cloning had produced a highly intelligent being. The only problem was that he was pure evil. He'd have to somehow program the appearance of a kind and gentle, loving, caring person.

Eval shuddered at the thought. He knew how to program evil into the chones. Programming something good into them was counterintuitive. Knowing it was for evil gains was the only reason he'd do it. If he could do it. No way he could perfectly balance the good and the evil in the chone.

The chone was intelligent enough and handsome enough to pull it off. But there would be telltale signs. He had to make sure Becca fell for him hard and fast so she'd overlook his obvious flaws. Christian women were weak in that way. If they thought they were in love, they'd ignore the warning signs. Becca would be blinded by the feelings. If the chone could get her to fall for him fast enough... it might work.

Especially if she would have relations with him. Then she would be contaminated. Her DNA would mix with the Balemites. She'd become as evil as he was. He'd have to program romance and lust into the chone. Lust was already there. But it would have to appear to be the good kind.

His thoughts weren't making sense. There was no good kind of lust. Just that the Christians had come to accept certain lusts and behaviors over the years as commonplace and good. They tolerated a certain amount of evil thoughts, impurities, and lusts. He had to strike the right balance in the chone. Make him appear to be a normal male with normal desires.

First, she had to accept his invitation. The minutes dragged on. No response. Eval thought back over the conversation. Did he say something wrong? Was he moving too fast? She might have become suspicious. This woman was smart. She wouldn't be easily fooled.

A ding. A notification. He was almost afraid to look at it.

Elation. She was easily fooled. He read the message aloud. "We should meet. How about this Friday night? For dinner."

Another rush of panic.

I only have one week to get the chone ready.

It can be done.

Friday night's great, Eval responded with excitement building.

Where should we meet? Becca wrote.

You choose.

Perfect response. Let her feel like she's in control right up to the point when she wasn't.

21

Helen acted cold toward me. Belligerent really. More so than usual which was why I even noticed. I'd grown accustomed to a certain level of iciness in our relationship. This was the first time we'd really seen each other in the past week, and I successfully avoided having to interact with her. I'd been working from early in the morning to late at night at the office, conducting experiments on Mark and Clooney. She was asleep when I left in the morning and asleep when I got home at night. Or at least pretending to be.

That's probably why she was mad at me. I was working too much. I knew that and would try and change it once I was through with the experiments. At least tonight, I was home in time to help her prepare for the Bible study. I wondered if she even appreciated it. The guests would be arriving soon and, for a few hours anyway, she would be civil toward me and put on a show for her church friends. I wanted to get it over with so I could go back to thinking about my work.

We'd made no real progress in the experiments other than discovering Clooney was half man and half something else. Something else was a mystery we were still trying to unlock. Becca thought he was half demon. How do you prove that? The Bible had some vague reference to fallen angels leaving their domain and uniting with strange flesh, creating giants.

They were called Nohelims in that they came out of the land of Noh, which at one time was where the first descendants of Adam and Eve lived. After they came on the planet, God destroyed Saturn with a flood because of their evilness. Becca thought it was because every human was infected with the DNA of the fallen angels, except for Noha and his family, which was why they were saved from the flood. Somehow Clooney was a descendant of them in some way, according to Becca's reasoning.

Seemed like a plausible theory. Clooney certainly fit the narrative. Proving it was another challenge in and of itself. We needed some new ideas and direction. We'd done more blood work, body scans, brainwave measurements, x-rays, cellular imaging, and every other test imaginable on both subjects. Nothing of significance was found. The answer had to be there. Clooney and Mark were as different as black and white. The difference in DNA and origin of birth had to result in changes to the body in some way.

Becca had poured into the Bible to look for an answer. I didn't know the Bible very well, so I wasn't much help. She focused on what it said about a person's spirit. A person without Christ was dead inside. Or really, his spirit was dead. The spirit came alive when a person was saved. This transformation had to be seen somehow in the human body. Mark's spirit was alive, and Clooney's spirit was dead. There had to be a way to find that difference in their bodies.

According to Becca, the Bible even tells the Christian to walk by the spirit and not by their flesh. How is that possible unless there is a physical change to your flesh? What did that physical change look like? We were determined to find it.

The eating utensils came together roughly with a loud clang, bringing my thoughts back to the present moment. Helen had obviously thrown them together on purpose to get my attention. To let me know she was mad. I could tell she was about to say something but was interrupted by the sound of knocking at the door.

"I'll get it," I said, thankful for the opportunity to avoid whatever harsh words and tone she was about to send my way.

* * *

The demons were out in force that night. They had been ever since the capture of the Satellite and Roger's involvement with him. Satan was deeply concerned that the doctor had found out the Satellite was from his seed. After the flood, God had forbidden the fallen angels from having relations with human women. God killed all the Nohelim's in the flood, and Satan's grand experiment of mixing the seed of fallen angels with man had come to an end.

Until Satan had the idea to bring them back through cloning. God hadn't forbidden that. Now, Roger and Becca were on the verge of thwarting that plan as well. Something the principalities and powers on Saturn were doing everything they could to prevent.

Chaz and Roki were the evil spirits assigned to wreak havoc in Roger and Helen's lives. Chaz was assigned to Helen. Roki was a new spirit assigned to Roger by Raz. They were watching the evening's events with great caution. The most dangerous times were when Christians gathered together in prayer. Two or more could stop any of their plans if they were in unity and implemented their power properly. A lot of progress had been made over the last week and could be all for naught in a moment's notice. God, through the Holy Spirit, had that kind of power to blindside them at any time.

They had Roger and Helen right where they wanted them. Helen believed Roger was having an affair, even though he wasn't. At least, not yet. She opened the door to anger, resentment, fear, and a root of bitterness had taken hold and was firmly entrenched in her mind and body. The thoughts tormented her day and night. A movie of her husband with his assistant played over and over again in her head. She imagined what their interaction was like. The hurt diving deeper into her soul with each painful thought.

So far, Chaz had managed to keep her silent and not confront her husband. If she said something to him, she would probably discover the truth—a demon's worst enemy. She must continue to believe the lies as long as possible.

Originally, the plan was to get Becca to have an actual affair with Roger. That plan had no chance. Roki knew Becca would never fall for the scheme. She was too strong in her faith to give in to that temptation. That's why Satan had come up with the idea of the dating site. Becca might very well fall for the evil wiles of the chone. That remained to be seen. They'd have their date later in the week.

Another plan had formed.

Helen's animosity and the spirit of lust Roki had put upon Roger, made him more vulnerable to an affair. All he needed was opportunity. They needed time to make it happen. But time wasn't something they had much of. Helen could reveal her sickness at any time. Once she does, there was no way Roger would have an affair. He'd feel too guilty. He might even turn his heart back toward his wife.

They needed to put a potential liaison in front of him right away. The Bible study wasn't the ideal setting to implement the plan, but they didn't have a choice. Roger was always either at work or at home. His only real interaction with women of the opposite sex was in the Bible study. The group of women there the first time the study met weren't good candidates. They needed to introduce a new subject.

She was walking up to the door right now.

Roki sent several thoughts into Roger's head in preparation for their first meeting.

I can't live like this. I don't want to live without physical intimacy.

Those thoughts raised all kinds of negative emotions in Roger. Frustration. Anger. His own unforgiveness toward her. Roger and Helen had not had sexual relations in several months. For a while Roger didn't care. Now, with the spirit of lust working, the desire for sex had returned and so had the frustration. Exactly the inner turmoil Roki needed to work his plan.

Roki had one final thought to put in Roger's mind before he opened the door.

I should think about getting a divorce.

Where did that thought come from? Roger wondered to himself as he walked to the door. Has it come to that? He'd never considered a divorce before. He always thought they would be together forever. Their vows were until death do us part. Now he wasn't so sure.

No time to think about it.

He opened the door, and a couple were standing there with broad smiles. She had a dish in her hands.

Wow! She's a knockout.

Was she here last week? I don't think so. I would've noticed her.

The woman was tall and thin. The blouse was red and had a plunging neckline borderline inappropriate for a Bible study. She'd clearly had an augmentation to her breasts and was more than willing to show off the doctor's handiwork.

Money well spent.

Roger tried to keep from looking at them, but his eyes kept being drawn to her. She was probably fifty-three, blonde hair perfectly in place, with heavy makeup, long, fake eyelashes, painted nails, all accented by expensive clothes and jewelry. When she touched Roger's arm and said her name was Misty, chills skittered up and down his spine.

The spirit of lust intensified the feeling in Roger so it would have a greater effect.

Roki was pleased. Misty would keep Roger's attention through the entire evening. The lust would burn inside of him. Misty was perfect for those goals. Twice divorced, she'd only been married to her current husband, Jack, for two years. She married him for his money and status in the community. Certainly not for his looks. Jack was five-foot-five and balding. A hundred pounds over his ideal weight.

A marriage of convenience for her, Roki knew. The only inconvenience being her husband's insistence on going to the Bible study. The only reason they were even there was because Roki had manipulated the circumstances. He'd been on the lookout for someone he could use to tempt Roger. He put the word out to other fallen angels. Misty's fallen angel, Boxy, had suggested his girl, and turned out she was perfect. Her eyes had already started wandering from the marriage and a successful, good looking, rich doctor would certainly catch her attention making Roki's job easier.

Boxy explained to Roki how Misty's last marriage ended when she had an affair with her personal trainer at the gym, so she was already open to that possibility and not very good at overcoming temptation. Flirtatious with everyone, Misty was the perfect woman to entice Roger to at least lust after her if not consider a full-blown affair.

When Jack and Misty attended the church the previous week, Roki made sure they got an invitation. It took some coaxing. Roki knew Misty had very little to do with church or religion and had never even been saved. Bob, the associate pastor had been very welcoming to them and had invited them to the study. He'd have to keep his eye on Bob. The man was filled with the spirit and was the biggest danger to his plans.

Meeting that night wouldn't be enough. Roki needed for Roger and Misty to meet outside the Bible study. Now that she'd gotten Roger's attention, he would arrange a chance meeting for them sometime this week.

Satisfied, Roki and Chaz turned their attention to Helen. Misty would do the rest of the work on Roger. Helen was a bigger problem as was the pastor and his wife and some of the other prayer warriors who had arrived with a legion of guardian angels.

The goal of the night was to get Helen through the Bible study without her revealing the doctor's prognosis. Six months to live would incite a flurry of prayers. The longer Helen kept it to herself, the better off they were. If they could keep her isolated in her own fear, they would have more time to embed the disease so deeply in her body that no amount of prayer would work to heal her from it.

Bob opened his mouth and began speaking. "Does anyone have any prayer requests?"

A surge of panic went through Roki and Chaz at the same time.

22

Eighty pedagrams, One pill. Twice a day. The doctor said it would lessen Helen's anxiety and help her to cope. Chaz, the fallen angel assigned to her, didn't want Helen to be able to cope. Demons and spirits assigned to humans spent years cultivating emotional instability in humans, starting at childhood. Over a period of time, the demons could manipulate human emotions almost at any time.

Fear, anxiety, depression, eating disorders, gluttony, guilt, shame, condemnation, anger, resentment, bitterness, and unforgiveness were only a few of the tools in Chaz's arsenal to throw at Helen. With so many fiery darts available to him and Helen in her vulnerable state of mind, he often didn't know which to choose. It had become like a game to him. He could choose almost anything, and it would work.

Even then, demons hated it when their subjects went on medication. They preferred to inflict as much pain and suffering as humanly possible. The medication dulled the pain. It didn't take it away; it just made the person not care about their problems as much. Helen was a good example. She was numb. Almost felt nothing. Even with everything she was going through, she wasn't feeling much pain after taking the pill. She suffered for several days, and Chaz had encouraged her not to take the medication. He probably overdid it with the intensity of emotions. She felt so much pain that eventually, Helen gave in and took one of the pills before the Bible study. The pill worked right away.

The good part about the medication was that humans never really dealt with the real issues that caused them to need it. The guilt, shame, and unforgiveness would just live inside of them for decades, festering and rotting like a piece of food stuck behind a cabinet, or a dead rat in an attic.

While that was good in the long-term, demons and Satan liked short-term victories. They lived in the moment. Only concerned about what was happening in real time. The blastoma diagnosis was a perfect opportunity to hurl fiery darts constantly at Helen.

The downside was that Chaz didn't have years to allow the emotional pain of the sickness to destroy her physically and emotionally. Her diagnosis was six months. He always preferred a long, slow death.

Except for Christians who were really having an effect on the world with their faith. Satan tried to kill them off as soon as possible. Most of the time, they weren't allowed to. That was the ongoing battle. The instructions Satan drilled in his subjects were kill, steal, and destroy.

The guardian angels were there to serve, encourage, protect, and help the Christians to overcome the evil one. A constant and intense battle in the heavenlies. For Chaz, it never let up. He had won more than his fair share of those battles. He'd eventually win this current battle. While he wasn't fully satisfied with his work against Helen, he was certainly making good progress.

The lie that her husband was having an affair was a bonus. The death sentence was hard enough for Helen to deal with emotionally. Add the thoughts of her husband having an affair, and Chaz's job was almost too easy. Helen had become so emotionally distraught in such a short time he was able to manipulate her emotions like she was a puppet. Especially at night. He tormented and haunted her with thoughts of death and betrayal and all the emotions that came with it.

The medication would be easier for her in a way but really would only make it seem like it was helping. Helen didn't realize it would only make things worse in the long run. If she had read some of the potential side effects of the medication, and believed them, she would've realized just how much worse things could become. Fortunately, one of the side effects was sedation. Helen would have a hard time concentrating having taken the pill.

Chaz observed her from his spot in the heavenlies. She sat in the chair with a dazed look in her eyes when Bob had asked, "Does anyone have any prayer requests?"

This was the most anxious moment for Chaz. If Helen spoke up, then a lot of his plans would be for naught. Roger would feel too guilty to have an affair. Bob and others would start praying for her. She might even get healed. Satan wouldn't be happy with him.

I need to do something.

He put a thought in Roger's head. "Look up."

Roger looked up and scanned the room. Misty caught his eye. She smiled at him.

Helen saw it.

Roger quickly put his head down in a guilty manner, or at least it seemed that way to Helen.

Of all the nerve! Helen was appalled. Roger obviously didn't think she noticed. Right there in her home. At a Bible study. Roger was flirting with another woman. A floozy. Bad enough he was cheating on her with his assistant. Now he was doing it right in front of her.

Initially, she directed her rage toward the woman.

Look at how she's dressed. She's obviously trying to get attention. She's not even that attractive.

Then her vitriol turned to her husband.

What a lying, cheating, pig!

Rage was building inside of her, overriding the sedating effects of the medication.

"This is good," Chaz said aloud to himself. Jealousy was a powerful emotion. Led to all types of evil thoughts.

"I just sense that someone has something to share," Bob said in a gentle and loving tone.

Helen barely noticed when Bob asked for prayer requests the first time but did hear him when he asked a second time.

"Shut up!" Chaz shouted, frustrated, knowing no one could hear him except the other angels who were working hard against him.

"Someone is dealing with a sickness. And you need prayer," Bob continued.

A word of knowledge.

Are you kidding me?

Chaz had to act fast. A word of knowledge was a spiritual gift. It occurred when the Holy Spirit spoke to someone and gave them information about something happening in another person that he would have no way of knowing about except by supernatural revelation. Chaz hated it when Christians were walking in the spirit enough to be able to discern something in another person that they were trying to hide. The gifts of the spirit were powerful and could destroy his works if he let them.

He looked around to see if one of the other angels was speaking directly to Bob. No one was. The Holy Spirit inside Bob was giving him the information about Helen. Chaz knew it was coming directly from Christ. Jesus spoke to the Holy Spirit; the Holy Spirit spoke to Bob; and then Bob said aloud what he heard the Holy Spirit say. A powerful and sometimes destructive weapon against Chaz and the other fallen angels when the Christians believed in it. Not so effective, when they didn't.

Helen felt a slight conviction in her spirit. Like Bob was talking directly to her. For a moment, her heart softened. Bob was looking right at her. As if he knew. Chaz knew he did.

"It's embarrassing," Chaz said to Helen. "Don't tell him now. Tell him privately. Not in front of all these people. You'll cry. You don't want them to see you cry."

Chaz grasped for anything to persuade Helen not to speak up.

"You might feel embarrassed," Bob said. "It's okay. You're among friends. We love you and want to pray for you."

Damn him!

"The sickness is your fault," Chaz said to Helen with urgency. "Your sin has caused this. You've been a terrible wife. That's why your husband is cheating on you. Why wouldn't he? His assistant is younger and prettier. Gives him all the attention you never did."

"There is no condemnation to those in Christ," Bob added with authority in his voice.

"Yes, there is," Chaz said to Helen. "These people will tell everyone. You know how big of gossips they are. They will look down on you. So will your husband."

He could feel Helen slipping away as courage rose inside of her.

"I just want to wait another minute," Bob said. "Let's all pray and give the Holy Spirit time to work in our midst."

Helen's heart was softening.

If Chaz didn't do something soon, she'd tell everyone. That would be a disaster. Chaz could sense the power of the Holy Spirit in the room.

Bob began praying. So did the angels in the heavenlies. They were singing and praising God and bringing more strength to the room. Chaz counted five people actually praying.

"Lord, we come against demons, powers, principalities," Bob said slowly and forcefully with power in his voice. "Every evil work that would be present in this room, we command you to leave. We come against sickness, disease, pain, and suffering. By his stripes we were healed. If we were healed, that means we are healed. Your spirit is here among us. Desiring to bring healing to all who are in need. We command every evil force present to flee."

Good. He didn't say in Jesus' name.

"In Jesus' name we pray," Bob added.

I hate you.

Chaz panicked. He could feel the forces tugging against him. The angels were commanding him to leave. He watched Helen closely. If she said amen or agreed with the prayer in any way, he'd have to leave. He could come back if she let him, but it would be harder next time. Everything he'd worked for would be lost. He'd have to start over. Knowing Bob, he might even lay hands on her while he was gone and bring healing to her.

"Look up," Chaz said to Helen and Roger at the same time.

They both opened their eyes. Misty was already looking around. She never closed her eyes. Didn't even know how to pray. She caught Roger's eye. Then Helen's. Misty turned her head away. Obviously, not wanting Helen to see her looking at Roger who quickly lowered his head and closed his eyes.

The damage was done.

The fury returned in a hurry.

Helen would make him pay for this.

Revenge.

Chaz was impressed. He hadn't even put that thought in Helen. It came out of her own evil heart and desires. Revenge was perfect. He had an opening. He knew exactly what to do.

Bob concluded his prayer, obviously disappointed. Chaz could see the demon assigned to Bob, trying to sow seeds of confusion in him. Christian ministers were vulnerable that way. If they spoke out in the spirit with confidence but didn't see an immediate result, they began to doubt if they actually were hearing from the Lord. Bob had no idea how right on his prayer and word of knowledge was. This was a good opportunity for them to sow some seeds of doubt in him. Chaz could hear the disappointment and confusion in his voice.

"Let me read from this passage of Scripture," Bob said. "I will give you a new heart and put my spirit in you, thus saith the Lord."

Chaz turned his attention back to Helen. She was seething. Her eyes glared at Roger with scorn. Her arms were folded. Her fists balled. Determined. The evil thoughts were unleashed in her.

Not resentment. Hatred. Not anger. Rage. Not bitterness. Malice.

She already knew exactly what she was going to do.

The night was going even better than Chaz ever thought possible.

23

I was confused.

Bob had read a Bible verse, "I will give you a new heart and put my spirit in you." Then he read an Old Testament verse. "Guard your heart, for everything you do flows from it." He then spent ten minutes teaching on the heart and the spirit that was in man. One of the verses really confused me.

"The heart is evil above all things."

I had performed many surgeries on the heart. From a surgeon's vantage point, the heart was nothing more than a muscle. Not to belittle it. The heart was the most important muscle in the entire body, but from a surgeon's perspective, it was simply a structure of tissues and cells that came together to form the organ. I'd never seen any evidence that the heart was good or evil.

The tests comparing Mark and Clooney's hearts turned up nothing of importance. Their hearts functioned in exactly the same way. I wanted to ask a question. hoping Bob's knowledge of the Bible might spur a new idea. While his teaching was informative, it was raising more questions than it answered. I lifted my hand to get his attention. He called on me immediately.

"Don't take this the wrong way," I said. "I'm a surgeon. I've performed hundreds of operations on the human heart. While it's amazing what God did in creating the heart, I've seen it firsthand. How come I can't see with my eyes any of these things you talk about in the Bible?"

"That's a very good question," Bob said. "I think when the Bible refers to the heart, it's talking about our spiritual heart. You're talk-

TERRY TOLER

ing about our flesh which is what you can see. The spirit is something that can't be seen with human eyes."

"I understand that," I said. "But shouldn't we be able to see the effects of it. You said that God puts his spirit in us. Where in our bodies is the spirit located?"

"We don't know exactly. It's a mystery," Bob explained. "We may not know until we get to heaven."

I hoped that wasn't true or my whole experiment was for nothing. Not to mention the fate of the world rests on my success.

"Is our soul the same thing as our spirit?" someone else asked.

"Another good question. The soul is separate from the spirit," Bob answered. "The Bible says that God sanctifies us in every part of our being. In our body, soul, and spirit. They are three different things."

"My spiritual advisor says that my spirit is outside of me," Misty said. "And that she can see it. She called it my aura. It's green."

Misty had an unusual voice. Whiny.

"Who is your spiritual advisor?" Bob asked.

"Madame Larue," she answered, excitedly. "She has that place down off of first street. Larue's Crystal Visions. She can tell the future."

I saw Helen roll her eyes and then say, "I've seen that place. She claims to be a psychic. I don't believe anyone can tell the future. She just wants your money."

"Uh-uh," Misty said angrily in a bratty childlike voice. "She told me I was going to marry a rich man. Two weeks later, I met Walter." Misty pinched her husband's cheek.

"Those places are evil," Helen added. "They all are. Palm reading, tarot cards, horoscopes... they are all of the devil. None of those people are Christian."

* * *

Roki had a huge grin on his face. Helen was creating division in the room and was distracting everyone from Roger's questions and Bob's teachings. Helen didn't realize she was wrong. There were people on Saturn who were empowered by evil spirits to tell people their fortunes and predict their futures. Similar to the word of knowledge Bob used earlier when he sensed someone was dealing with a sickness.

Psychics and palm readers were different in that they operated in counterfeit gifts modeled after the gifts of the Spirit in the Bible. Not as effectively and with limited knowledge, but they did have some powers to influence humans. Actually, more effective in most cases, he corrected himself. Most Christians had no idea how to exercise the power of the Holy Spirit even though he was living right inside of them.

"I read my horoscope every morning!" Misty said emphatically. "This morning mine said I was going to meet someone special today." She looked at me when she said it.

Helen glared at me.

What did I do? I wanted to say it out loud, but this wasn't the appropriate time or place.

"The Bible does call those things sorcery," Bob said in a forceful tone. "You shouldn't go to places like that. There are evil spirits just like there are good spirits. The good spirits are called angels. The bad ones are called demons. The Holy Spirit lives inside of us when Jesus saves our souls."

Misty folded her arms and stuck out her lower lip like a petulant child.

"Do dogs have souls?" another woman asked.

Roki was rolling over laughing hysterically. These stupid Christians had totally ruined the Bible study, and he didn't have to do a thing to make them. Now that they opened the door, several spirits of division and strife quickly moved in and were making matters worse.

"Animals don't go to heaven," one of the men said strongly.

"My little Fifi is in heaven. I know it," another woman said with tears forming in her eyes. "I also read my horoscope as well. I don't see anything wrong with it."

Roki couldn't quit laughing. The room was divided almost in half to that question. He would stay out of the debate, even though he knew the answer.

Bob seemed to be trying his best to get everyone back on topic, but the tension and anger was permeating the room. Things had disintegrated quickly. Roki was very pleased with the topic. He knew several in the room read their horoscopes every day. Some even followed them religiously. One of the ladies didn't get on a plane flight because her horoscope that day said that Saturn and Neptune were in the seventh moon. That meant she shouldn't travel during that time. The whole thing was a lie of Satan.

Roki shook his head. *Christians are so gullible*. So easily fooled into believing things the Bible warned against practicing. Bob was right. It was sorcery. Something God hated.

"Back to Roger's question," Bob said. "I think the Bible was referring to the heart because it is the central part of the human body. Inside of us is a spiritual heart. That is the essence of our being. Everything in the spirit flows through our spiritual heart."

I shook my head in understanding even though what Bob was saying didn't help me at all in knowing what to do with Mark and Clooney, which was my only reason for asking.

"Roger, you'll find this interesting," Bob continued. "The Bible wasn't written in our language. So, we have to translate it. I like to go back to the original words and study them for their original meaning. There are a couple places where the word for *heart* is actually the word *liver*."

Everyone in the room laughed.

Misty made a funny face, curling her lips and wrinkling her nose. Helen had a look of disgust on her face. Her smile was obviously fake.

"That's right, liver," Bob said with a wide grin. "A lot of scholars think the heart is in the belly. Some say the heart and spirit are actually in the digestive system and not the literal heart that pumps blood."

That thought gave me an idea.

I can't wait to tell Becca.

24

I helped Helen clean up after the Bible study and was making a half-hearted effort to break through the stone-cold exterior of my wife who was obviously furious with me. I figured the best course of action was to be nice.

"What did you think of tonight? About the Bible study?" I asked in a sweet tone.

"I thought Misty was crazy," she answered smugly.

"Bob was a little hard on her. She's obviously a baby Christian."

"Oh no!" Helen said angrily. "That lady is not a Christian. Far from it."

"You shouldn't judge her," I retorted. "We just met her tonight for the first time."

"Why are you defending her?"

"I'm not. I just think you should give her a chance. She seems nice."

"I bet you do."

"What's that supposed to mean?"

"She had her eye on you the whole night."

"Don't be ridiculous. She's married."

"So are you."

"Right... Whatever you mean by that?"

At that moment, a notification came over my caller. I pulled it out of my pocket and glanced at it. An alarm was going off at my office.

"I have to check this," I said, leaving the room before Helen could object. I went into my office, turned on the artby, and pulled up the

126

camera in the laboratory. One of the machines was flashing a red light. It didn't seem to be anything serious. I was tired and really didn't want to go all the way down there that late at night.

Then the thought occurred to me that the alarm could cause the entire machine to shut down. The alarm had to be shut off within a certain period of time. What was it? *Would it last until the morning?* I couldn't take the risk. Mark's breathing machine could shut off in the middle of the night. I had to go in.

I was torn. I had wanted to spend some time with Helen before we went to bed. The prayer at the Bible study had given me a new resolve to try and work on my marriage. I was thinking that maybe if we talked about it, things might get better. I wasn't willing to give up on my marriage just yet.

I turned off the artby and walked back into the kitchen. Helen wasn't there. She had already gone upstairs. I considered leaving but thought better of it. Instead, I went up the stairs to our bedroom and found Helen in her closet, getting ready to change into her pajamas, which were already laying out on the ottoman in her rather large closet.

"I have to go to the office," I said. "An alarm is going off."

"There's no alarm," Chaz told Helen in her mind. "He's going to meet *her*." Chaz saw Helen's breathing increased. She started fidgeting with her hands. He could see anger building inside of her.

"I'm sorry," I said sincerely. "I wish I didn't have to go back there."

"Yeah right. You'd rather be there than here. That's obvious."

"That's not fair," I said more angrily than I intended. "I'm working on a big project. It'll be over soon, and everything will get back to normal."

I tried to soften my tone. "I'm sorry I've been working so much," I said. "I'll make it up to you when this project is over." Helen hadn't been looking at me. She sat down on the ottoman and started taking off her shoes. She suddenly stood straight up and turned, facing me with a determined look on her face.

"Are you having an affair?" she asked accusingly.

I couldn't believe the words that just came out of my wife's mouth. We were having problems, but I had always been faithful to her. She had no reason to think I was having an affair. Just because I was working late didn't mean I was cheating on her. I resented the insinuation.

"Of course not!" I said emphatically, raising my voice.

"He's lying!" Chaz shouted inside Helen so that it almost reverberated in her ears.

"I don't even know how you could ask me such a question," I said, roughly. "I'm just going to the office. I'll be right back. I promise."

Helen's shoulders sagged as she turned her back to me. I walked over and kissed her on the forehead from behind.

"I'll only be a few minutes," I said. "I just have to check on the alarm and then I'll be home."

* * *

I can't stand this, Helen thought to herself.

Say it out loud, Chaz was thinking. Thoughts could cause a lot of inner turmoil in humans, but the spoken word was where the power of life and death resided. If he could get her to say those words out loud, then she would give them more power.

She did say it out loud. That and several angrier words directed at Roger. She threw her shoes across the closet in disgust. She started taking off her clothes to change into her pajamas when a thought stopped her.

"Follow him," Chaz said to her. "He's obviously going to meet the girl."

An argument was brewing in Helen's head. Chaz was spurring a lot of the negative thoughts countering her arguments.

I don't even know that he's having an affair.

Of course, he is. Why else would he lie about his assistant being a man?

Maybe he has two assistants.

Don't be a fool.

I should trust him.

All men are alike. They can't be trusted. I saw how he looked at that woman tonight.

She was disgusting.

All men cheat. It's what they do. They can't help themselves.

"Roger's not like that. He would never cheat on me," she said out loud.

That's why you should follow him. You need to know.

I'm going to go to his office.

You should take a gun.

Why do I need a gun?

You don't know this lady. She might be crazy like the one tonight.

Chaz knew that two of the side effects of the medication she took were aggressive and violent behavior and also suicidal thoughts. He'd seen many humans have psychotic episodes on the medication even when they weren't provoked. Helen was unstable right now. Though unlikely, the medication might cause her to act irrationally. He'd do everything he could to get her over the edge. Something that would be more likely if she had a weapon. Crimes of passion were easy for him to manipulate humans into, especially when emotions were running high.

Helen went down to Roger's home office and opened his closet door. Inside was a large safe with a number of guns. She picked out a smaller handgun. One that would fit in her handbag. She checked to make sure it was loaded. She'd grown up around guns and knew how to use it.

The drive to the office took less than ten minutes. Traffic was light, and she was driving faster than normal. Tears had started flowing and were running down her cheek faster than she could wipe them away.

Fear was welling up inside of her. Dread.

"Please be alone," she said out loud.

She pulled around the corner and into the parking lot. Her worst fears were realized. Two airmobiles were parked by the entrance. Her husband's and the mobile the woman had gotten into when she saw her the other day.

See, he was lying, Chaz said in her ear.

Chaz already knew Becca was still at the office. He wouldn't have put the thoughts to follow him in her head had she not been. The scene was totally innocent. Roger was coming to the office to shut off an alarm. Helen didn't know that. From her perspective, Roger had lied once more and come to the office to meet his mistress.

A brilliant plan, he would take credit for with the evil one, even though he had little to do with manipulating the circumstances. Chaz had just gotten lucky. Now, if only the medication would kick in and send her over the edge of sanity.

Helen's eyes were wide in disbelief. Shock. Her breaths turned shallow and rapid. Her heartbeat so fast she could hear it in her ears. She wanted to curl up in a fetal position and die, but the rage inside felt like it was driving her insane.

She pounded her fists on the steering wheel.

"I can't believe he would do this to me," she said as she let out a loud scream.

You don't deserve this, Chaz said to her.

"I deserve better!"

They're doing it right now.

Pain shot through her heart like a knife. It stabbed her over and over again. Suddenly the tears stopped. Helen sat up straight. Her shoulders back. Her jaw clenched. She reached into the center console of the airmobile.

She pulled out the gun and held it in her hand, contemplating her next move.

I can't let him get away with this.

25

Becca's airmobile in the parking lot was the last thing I expected to see that late at night. I didn't want to scare her by suddenly entering the building, so I sent her a message from my caller.

I'm here at the office, it said.

Good. I have something for you, Becca responded. A smiley face was after the last sentence.

Sex? I asked.

Yes.

I'll be right in.

When I left the office early that afternoon to help Helen get ready for the Bible study, Becca was hard at work analyzing chromosome data from the DNA sequence that identified the sex of Mark and Clooney. I'd purchased a new machine, a gene analyzer, which had been delivered earlier that day. Extremely expensive and state of the art, it analyzed cell composition at the molecular level. Hopefully, it would give us more insight into the abnormalities we found in their DNA tests. We had nicknamed the machine, Gene just for fun.

The hope was that it would tell us why Mark had the normal male chromosomes markings SXY which signified Mark's sex was male and Clooney's was something unknown SXY-STN. Apparently, Becca had made some progress on determining Clooney's sex which was why she said she had something for me. I was excited to find out what it was.

First, I had to shut off the alarm on Mark's breathing machine. The culprit was a loose wire. One of us had probably bumped it sometime during the day, and it had finally separated just enough to affect the connection. When I first saw her airmobile, I thought Becca had come to the office to turn off the alarm.

She was in her office, staring into Gene's screen. Apparently, she didn't even know the alarm was going off.

"What are you doing here so late?" I asked.

She sat back in her chair and stretched her arms and then rubbed her eyes. "I didn't realize it was so late. Gene is amazing. I've never seen anything like it. There are so many things he can do. I can do mapping. Kyrotesting. Genetic coding. Marking analyses. I didn't want to leave."

She sounded like a kid in a toy store. Her voice could hardly contain the excitement.

"What did you find about Clooney's sex?" I asked.

She motioned for me to come over to her desk. I stood behind her, looking over her shoulder. For a moment, I felt awkward. It probably wasn't appropriate for us to be there alone late at night. Especially after the question Helen had asked me earlier that night. *Are you having an affair?* Those words were still rattling around in my mind.

What gave her that idea?

I suddenly understood. The late nights at work. The animosity between us. Even tonight, I had unexpectedly left after the Bible study. Without really giving her an explanation. What else was she to think? And how would I explain this? A married man, alone with his single and attractive assistant late at night in his office. An assistant I had told Helen was a man.

I don't know why I lied to her about that. I had no reason to hide it. We weren't doing anything wrong then and weren't now. It just came out when she asked me that night. I needed to tell her the truth.

I wouldn't tell her about Becca being here tonight. That didn't look good. I didn't want to give Helen any reason not to believe me.

Even though I hadn't known Becca was there, I could see why Helen would suspect something even if it wasn't true. It would look like I snuck out tonight to be with her.

I'll deal with that later.

My thoughts quickly reverted back to work as soon as Becca started talking.

"I extracted DNA from the cells of Clooney's heart and Mark's heart," Becca began explaining. "Just like we talked about. As I expected, I got the same results. The same DNA marking sequence. Here's Mark's sequence." She read it aloud while I leaned in closer and studied the code on the screen.

"AG IB XY CA OB DC AB MB Y"

"Perfectly normal," I said.

"Right. Seventeen markings. XY in the third marking signifying male."

"Now look at Clooney's sequence."

AC BI STN XY OC YN AS TA AT OA N

"I've never seen anything like this. Much longer." I said, standing straight up.

"I know!" Becca said with emphasis.

"What does it mean?" I started pacing the room.

"STN we already knew about," Becca said. "That is the major anomaly. There are others, though. Look at this," Becca said pointing at the screen. I stopped my pacing and took my place back behind her again.

"Clooney has twenty-three letters," she said. "Every other human on the planet has seventeen, including Mark. Clooney has six more. One is from the STN."

"Or maybe three are from those additional letters."

I counted them out in my head. Initially, I was focused on the STN genetic mutation and hadn't thought about the extra letters. I'd never heard of three letters in a DNA sequence. Now, I realized there were six additional letters. What were they?

"I don't know if it means anything, but the number seventeen in the Bible means victory," Becca explained. "I don't know what twenty-three means, if anything. Six is significant. It represents man and also evil. Three sixes anyway... I'm rambling. It doesn't make sense. I must be getting tired."

She stretched again and started rubbing the back of her neck.

The thought suddenly came in my head that I should rub her shoulders for her. I was standing right behind her in a perfect position to reach them. She had worked hard all day. By my calculations she had been there for nearly sixteen hours. I don't remember her taking a break. She must really be tired.

That would be inappropriate.

Why? I would just be rubbing her neck and shoulders. Nothing more than a friendly gesture. It didn't mean anything sexual.

The argument raged in my head.

Becca was my assistant. The best one I'd ever had. I was a married man. We shouldn't even be there alone at night. My wife doesn't even know her.

I could feel an attraction for Becca rising inside of me. She was an attractive woman. Soft skin. Her hair smelled of lavender, even that late at night. My wife hated me. I hadn't had sex in months. I could almost feel Becca's touch on my skin. I could almost feel her lips on my...

"No!" I shouted to myself. She was only a few years older than my own daughter. I was committed to trying again with Helen. I had to make our marriage work. I tamped down the feelings. That's all they were. I had always prided myself on my self-control and discipline. I quickly put all the impure thoughts out of my mind.

Focus.

I took two steps back from Becca and then walked to the other side of the desk so there was some distance between us.

"Let me see the read-out again," I said. I needed a distraction.

Becca handed me a print-out of the marking sequence.

I studied it. I didn't realize my mouth had flown open, until Becca commented on it.

"What?" she asked with urgency. "What do you see?"

I handed her the paper.

"Look at the last five patterns. Do you see anything unusual?" I asked.

"Everything about it is unusual."

AC BI STN XY OC YN AS TA AT OA N

She stared at the sequence for a good minute.

"I'm not seeing anything."

"Look at the last letters of the last five markings. Read them out loud."

"S... A... T... A..." she read them slowly, stopping before she got to the last letter.

"The last letter is *N*," I added.

"It spells out Satan," she said, her voice fading off as she said it. She looked up at me.

I nodded. "This is the confirmation we needed," I said. "You were right. Clooney is not human. He's some kind of evil being. Just like the Nohelim in the Bible."

"It's like Satan has added his own DNA markings to Clooney," Becca added. "So, he is man in that he has the seventeen genetic DNA markings, but he also has six more. The markings of Satan."

A chill went up and down my spine. An eerie fear. I knew we were on the right track.

"At our Bible study tonight, our teacher said something interesting," I said.

"What's that?" Becca asked.

"In the Bible the original word for heart might have been *liver*."

Becca laughed. "Liver?"

"I know. I laughed, too."

"These samples came from Mark and Clooney's hearts," Becca said. "I'll run some samples from their livers. I'll run them through Gene and see what I find."

"Good idea. But do it tomorrow. It's late. I'm going home. Very good work, Becca. I'm so glad to have you on my team. I don't think I could do it without you."

She stood from the desk and walked over to me with her arms out to give me a hug. I turned to the side, so I wasn't hugging her straight on. I hugged her tightly. It didn't feel inappropriate at all. Just two friends, sharing a moment.

"I am really glad I'm working here as well," she said. "Tell your wife I said hello and that I'm looking forward to meeting her."

"I will," I said.

Although, I wasn't sure exactly how I was going to tell Helen.

I just knew I needed to.

26

Helen sat in her airmobile outside Roger's office, clutching the gun, tears streaming down her face. She wanted to go inside and confront him.

How?

She didn't have a key and catching him in the act was the only way to know for sure. She couldn't just go to the door and knock on it. He'd deny everything. She already had her proof, anyway. Waiting and confronting them as they left would be the best way to do it.

Her hand tightened around the gun.

"Why do I have a gun? What am I going to do; shoot them?" she said.

I can't. My kids would never forgive me.

I should shoot myself.

Helen was sinking into a depression.

I need some medicine.

She didn't have any. The bottle was back at the house.

Images started scrolling through her mind. She pictured her husband having sex with the other woman. Where would they do it? In his office? She'd only been to his office once. He had a couch in it. Probably there, she decided.

Why was what she pictured in her mind so much better than their sex?

Helen was imagining it to be wild and passionate. She could see them kissing... touching. Each image like a dagger in her heart. Each dagger filled with guilt.

Why was I never that way?

What did she expect? She hadn't had sex with him in months. And when they did, it was never like what she imagined it to be like with the other woman. She wasn't young and pretty anymore. She never really liked sex. That's why she never did it much with Roger. This girl obviously did. Younger girls were more expressive and would try new things. That's what men wanted.

It wasn't bad before they had kids. After that, she turned all her energies to raising a family. Taking care of the house. Running the kids everywhere for ball practice, music lessons, doctor's appointments. When did she have time for Roger? By the end of the day, she was exhausted.

He was a man, after all. He had needs. This woman knew how to meet them.

I never made him feel that way.

It's my fault.

Helen took her hand off the gun. Blue lights started bouncing around the car. At first, she thought it might be the rings reflecting off her rearview mirror. She suddenly realized it was a patrolman.

The gun. I have to hide it.

Helen panicked for a moment. She fumbled around, and the gun fell to the floor. She tried to kick it under the seat. The large man in uniform banged a flashlight against the window. Helen rolled it down.

"Hello, Officer," Helen said as she wiped the remaining tears from her eyes.

"Is everything okay?" he asked, in a friendly manner which was a relief.

She wasn't doing anything illegal. Even having the gun wasn't against the law. She was just embarrassed. What if Roger came out of the office right that minute? How would she explain things? Why did she have a gun?

How would he explain things?

She was confused. All Helen wanted to do was get out of there as quickly as possible.

"Yes, Officer. I was just leaving. That's my husband's office." Helen pointed, immediately regretting having linked her presence there to her husband. "He's the director of the center," she added. "Roger Forrester. I'm his wife."

The police officer looked around the parking lot. Helen had stopped a good distance away from the building and was facing the wrong direction if she was leaving it. A fact she suddenly realized.

"I forgot something at the building. And was going to go back when I got a call from my husband. I just talked to him. He's going to bring my handbag home with him. I left it there. I'm going to turn around and head home now. I'm fine."

Helen suddenly realized the handbag was laying on the seat in full view. The man hesitated but then stepped away.

"Okay, Ma'am. I was just doing my job. Checking to make sure you were okay."

"I appreciate that." Helen said. "I'm headed home now."

The officer got back in his policemobile and left. She finally allowed herself to breathe a sigh of relief.

A few minutes later, Helen walked into her house, her hands still shaking. Her emotions were spiraling out of control. She opened a bottle of chilled wine and poured a glass. The cooling liquid was like a salve on her parched throat. One swallow sent a calming effect through her body.

She drank the entire glass and poured another. The first wasn't enough. It barely eased the pain as she couldn't get the thoughts of her husband and the other woman out of her head.

A pill. Take a pill.

They were hidden in her medicine cabinet. Behind some personal hygiene items. They had separate bathrooms, and Roger rarely came in hers. She fumbled with the bottle and finally got it opened.

Should I take two?

She had already taken two that day. The directions were one pill, twice a day. She decided to just take one. The directions were on the side of the bottle, and she had never really read them.

"Don't operate heavy machinery?" she read aloud.

"Okay. I won't." She allowed herself to laugh.

"May cause drowsiness. I hope so. I don't think I'll be able to sleep."

"Don't consume alcoholic beverages. It may intensify the effects of the drug."

"Oops," she said, giggling as she could already feel the effects of the alcohol. She had downed the two glasses pretty quickly. Too quickly on an empty stomach.

"May cause aggressive behavior and suicidal thoughts."

She realized the gun was still in her airmobile.

I'll have to get it in the morning.

Suicidal thoughts.

Why not? I'm going to die anyway.

A number of thoughts flooded her mind. Suicide. The perfect revenge. She should take her own life and cheat death.

Helen laughed at the thought. *How am I cheating death?*

Death wanted to draw the pain out over six months. She could cheat death by saving herself from all the trouble. She'd write a note and leave it somewhere in the house where only Roger could find it. She'd never tell anyone about the blastoma. The note would say she killed herself when she discovered his affair. She'd explain that she couldn't live with the thought of him with another woman. Roger would have to live with the consequences for the rest of his life. Guilt. Shame. Condemnation. Her death would be his fault. Even if the kids found out, they'd blame him.

No one else would see the note. It would be their little secret. A perfect plan.

Should I do it now?

No!

She needed to think through the details. The kids and grandkids would be hurt by her death, and she wanted to say goodbye to them. They wouldn't know it was goodbye. They'll be hurt anyway. This would save them from having to watch her suffer for six months. They shouldn't have to watch her wither away and die a slow painful death. This would be better for them.

Helen changed into her pajamas. Her thoughts still raged out of control. Somehow, the thought of ending her life was easing the pain. Maybe it was the alcohol, or the pill. Either way—a welcomed relief.

She heard Roger returning.

Helen turned out the lights and ran to her bed, pulled back the covers, and jumped in it, pretending to be asleep. A few minutes later, Roger kissed her on the back of her head, turned over and went to sleep.

I want another glass of wine.

Satisfied Roger was asleep, Helen got out of bed and went back downstairs. Roger's phone was on the counter. Still powered up.

A rush of adrenaline suddenly pulsed through her. She picked up the phone. A flashing light indicated a new message.

From Becca.

Now she knew her name.

Thanks. Tonight was good. That was all it said.

Helen scrolled back up to the start of the messages.

I'm here at the office. Sent from Roger to Becca.

Good. I have something for you. A smiley face. Her response.

Sex?

Helen gasped. So loud she wondered if she might wake Roger even though he was upstairs asleep.

Yes.

I'll be right in.

The pain returned like a roaring fire. Betrayal. Jealousy. Rage.

Helen fell to the floor and rolled up into a fetal position. Sobbing. She just wanted to die.

* * *

Chaz laughed diabolically. He hadn't done a thing. He'd just sat back and watched Helen destroy herself emotionally. For nothing. For a lie. He hadn't put a single thought in her head. She'd done it all on her own.

Crazy, how humans are.

Even those with the Holy Spirit.

They'll destroy themselves, if you just let them.

Suicide. That's perfect.

27

Helen woke up early the next morning, laying on the floor, her head splitting in two from the pain. As she pulled herself up with the help of the kitchen counter, her legs wobbled and almost sent her to the ground again. Every joint in her body hurt.

Why was I sleeping on the floor?

Then she remembered, and the pain started all over again. This time powered by anxiety and fear. And jealousy. Images from the last night flashed back in her mind. She had proof now that her husband was having an affair.

The gun.

She went out to the airmobile, got the gun, and took it back inside and put it in the safe.

That was stupid.

I have to think more clearly.

The clock on the counter flashed six. Roger would be getting up soon. She wanted to be out of the house when he did. She made herself a cup of instant coffee. The caffeine jolted her awake after a few sips. With renewed energy, Helen snuck upstairs and into her closet. She got dressed, scribbled Roger a note and left the house.

A few blocks away, she stopped the airmobile. Far enough from the house that she could see when he left but hidden and facing the opposite direction so he couldn't see her.

Thirty minutes later, she saw his airmobile pull out of the driveway and onto the road.

For some reason, she felt an irresistible urge to follow him.

That was Chaz and Roki's handiwork. They had a plan that morning. A chance meeting. They'd thought of it at the Bible study the night before. The plan was in motion. Helen didn't think things could get worse.

They were about to.

* * *

When I woke up the next morning, Helen was gone. The note said she had an early meeting at the salon. Strange, but I felt a hurt in my heart. I wished she was there. I wanted to see her, maybe have a cup of coffee together before I left for work. I wanted to kiss her goodbye, like I used to.

A message from Becca on my caller said she had made an important discovery the night before.

Can you bring some coffee? I worked all night and need some, the message said.

I drove to my favorite coffee shop, my mind torn between two things—Becca's discovery and Helen. I had a renewed determination to work on my marriage. Helen and I had been married for thirty-three years. I couldn't throw that away because we were going through hard times. I made a note to stop and get her flowers on the way home. I wouldn't work late tonight. Maybe we could go out to dinner later. I'd call her after I met with Becca.

My mind was also on the experiment. We were finally making progress. I had no idea what we would do with the information, or where it would lead, but at least we had found something of significance. I was filled with anticipation at what Becca had discovered overnight.

Joe's Coffee and Pastry shop was on the way to the office. It had been my favorite coffee for several years. They knew me by name. Once inside, I didn't see Joe right away. He must've been in the back.

The line was long. It usually was that time of day. I was so distracted I barely noticed what was going on around me. I smiled as an image of Helen flashed in my mind. She had a smile on her face. Back during happier times.

The dual track in my mind continued as my thoughts turned to Clooney. I had information about him that was remarkable. I needed to call a meeting of the Security Council. The Nohelim of the Bible had somehow been resurrected. Satites were cloning men who were giants. Superhuman. Half man, half evil. Fathered by Satan himself. An almost unbelievable discovery. The presentation was already forming in my mind.

Suddenly hands were over my eyes. A rush of fear pulsed through me until I heard a familiar voice.

Misty.

"Dr. Forrester," she said in her whiny drawl. "What a pleasant surprise."

"Hello, Misty." I turned toward her and held out my hand. I don't know why. Just a natural reflex when I saw someone I didn't know very well.

She brushed my hand aside and pulled me into a hug. Her huge breasts were pressed against me. I instinctively hugged her back but barely, awkwardly. It felt uncomfortable and forced. My head recoiled from the strong perfume she was wearing that almost burned my nostrils.

"Do you mind?" Misty said to the person in line behind me. "I'm with him."

I started to object and correct her and say she's not with me, but the young man behind me just gave her a look and said it was fine. What else could he say?

I also looked around for Joe. The people there knew Helen as well. I didn't want them to get the wrong idea.

"I sure did enjoy meeting you last night," Misty said with a wink. "You have a nice house."

"Thank you. I'm glad you and your husband could come."

I mentioned her husband because I wanted to remind her that she was married. She wasn't acting like a married woman. Not that she seemed to care. For the next five minutes, she talked nonstop. And kept touching me. Flirting. She wasn't even trying to hide it. Half of me was relishing the attention, savoring the touch of another woman. The other half of me was disgusted. Appalled that she would be so blatantly forward in public.

I looked her up and down. Not in a lustful way, but in confusion. Misty was not in any way my type. I couldn't understand why I felt any attraction for her.

Helen was my type. Sophisticated. Intelligent. Modest.

Misty was obviously uneducated, flashy, presumptuous, and trying too hard. Trying to be prettier than she was, smarter than she was, and sexier than she could ever be to me. Misty was totally immodest. Something that had always been a turn-off to me.

Modesty was something I found attractive in a woman. Helen had that. So did Becca.

From the looks of it, Misty didn't have a modest bone in her body. She was wearing bright red shorts with a white top, one or two sizes too small. Her chest was almost bulging out of the shirt. It was tied in a knot just above her midsection, so her toned abs and belly button were visible. She wore sneakers, clearly on her way to work out at a gym somewhere. She might've said where. I really wasn't paying attention.

We didn't get to the front of the line fast enough. I ordered two coffees and a couple of pastries. Misty ordered a tall latte with an extra shot of caffeine. She acted like she was already wired with enough energy for the day.

Don't judge, I reminded myself, having sanctimoniously said the same thing to Helen the night before.

The person behind the counter mentioned me by name.

"Your order is ready, Dr. Forrester," she said.

"I'm impressed. You're a celebrity here," Misty said while poking my ribs. I tried to move away from her. My personal space was being invaded and I didn't like it.

For whatever reason, Misty's order was on mine and she didn't offer to pay for hers. I didn't mind. I just wanted to get out of there. I was surprised when she followed me out.

We stood on the sidewalk in front of the shop talking for a couple minutes. Actually, she did most of the talking. I was trying to get away without being rude.

Finally, after one last highly inappropriate hug, I extricated myself from the conversation and was on my way.

Frustrated, because by the time I got to the office our coffee would be cold and would have to be reheated.

* * *

Helen pulled into a parking space across from the coffee shop, just as she saw Roger walk in and the woman from last night, Misty, walk in a minute later.

A sinking feeling sent her into a deep depression.

I can't believe this.

I don't even know him anymore.

Tears formed in her eyes, and she wiped them away. No matter how hard she tried, she couldn't get them to stop. Her worst fears were realized when Roger and the woman walked out of the coffee shop together. They obviously knew each other. They obviously planned this meeting. She thought back over last night. When did they have the chance? It didn't matter.

"My life is over," Helen said aloud.

"Not yet," Chaz said gleefully, proud of himself for having arranged the whole thing.

But it will be soon.

28

"Did you get any sleep at all?" I asked Becca who looked great considering she'd been at the office all night.

"I slept a couple of hours in your office on your couch. I hope you don't mind," she replied.

"I don't mind at all. Other than I hate you had to sleep on the couch."

She waved her hand dismissively while taking a large sip from her coffee. "To be honest, I barely noticed. I was so tired I fell right asleep."

"What were you doing all night?" I asked, barely able to maintain my patience. Last night's revelation was incredible. Hard to imagine what the new breakthrough was. She seemed almost giddy about it but was taking too long to tell me.

"I took a sample from Mark and Clooney's livers," she said, slowly, deliberately.

"Right," I suddenly remembered something she was probably about to remind me of.

"Mark's blastoma is in his liver," she said.

I nodded. I figured she would say that next. That didn't make it any harder to pull a sample of the cells, but it could make the test results more interesting. Blastoma cells were abnormal, genetic mutations.

"Gene has an image enhancer nothing like anything I've ever seen before."

I nodded again. I had read about it in the manual. Gene had more than a hundred functions. Becca could take the samples, put them under the image enhancer and see things never seen before with the human eye. The enhancer could magnify an image up to half the width of an atom. Not that we would ever need that much magnification. It's just interesting that we had that capability in our little lab. I thought I knew where she was going next with the conversation.

"I put Mark's cells under the enhancer and took a picture. Then I did the same thing with Clooney's cells and placed them side by side. The cells were almost identical."

I was wrong. I didn't know that was where she was going with this information.

"Are you talking about clean cells or blastomic cells?"

"The blastomic cells," she replied. "The blastoma has almost entirely overrun his liver. I don't know that I could even find any clean cells in there."

"Okay," I said hesitantly. I still wasn't sure what it meant.

She raised an eyebrow and then rubbed her hands together, unable to sit completely still. Something had her really excited.

"I did the same DNA sequencing I did on their hearts, only I used the liver cells."

DNA sequencing. I hadn't thought of that. "And..." Now, it was starting to get interesting.

"And, here are the results." She handed me a piece of paper.

I looked it over, then sat down in the chair. Stunned. In such shock, I didn't know what to say.

"I know," Becca said. "Can you believe it?"

"I can't believe it. They're the same." I looked at the results again.

Mark: AC BI STN XY OC YN AS TA AT OA N

Clooney: AC BI STN XY OC YN AS TA AT OA N

"They're identical," Becca said excitedly.

I tried to process what it meant.

"So, Mark's blastomic cells have the same DNA sequencing as Clooney's normal cells." I paused to let that information sink in. As much for my benefit as for anything. "Twenty-three characters. STN in the third position rather than SXY. And the last letter of the last five sets of characters spelled out Satan."

"That means that Mark's disease originates from something demonic. Just like Clooney."

"We've always known that the chromosome structure and DNA from blastomic cells were mutations of normal cells," Becca explained. "We just never had anything to compare them to. Now we do. We have the Satite chone. His DNA somehow came from evil. We can see that diseased cells are identical to evil cells."

"What does the Bible say about sickness and evil?"

"I don't know."

"I know someone who does." I took my caller out of my pocket and dialed Bob. He answered right away.

"Bob, it's Roger. Roger Forrester."

"Hello, Doctor. How are you today?"

"I'm good. How about you?"

"I'm blessed. What can I do for you?"

"I'm here in my office, with my assistant Becca Holmes. I'm going to put you on speaker." I mouthed to Becca that Bob was our pastor.

"Hi, Pastor," Becca said. "It's nice to meet you."

"Likewise."

"Bob, I have a question for you. It's related to something we are working on. I hope you can help me."

"I'll do my best. What's the question?"

"Does the Bible say anywhere that sickness comes from Satan?"

I could hear Bob chuckle on the other line.

"You aren't going to ask an easy question are you Roger?"

"No sir."

"Turns out, I happen to know the answer. I wrote a paper in Bible college about that very subject. The paper was more than a hundred pages long."

"Give us the short version," I said jokingly, which didn't match our mood. Becca was sitting on the edge of her seat. I was too. "Our experiment could take a huge step forward depending on his answer to that question."

He chuckled again. "In the Old Testament there is an interesting verse that says..." Bob paused. I could hear pages ruffling.

"Here it is. Let me read it to you. The Psalmist wrote it. An evil disease is poured out on him and holds fast to him."

"That's interesting," I said.

"There's more. There's another translation that says a thing of Belial has attached himself to him and caused a deadly affliction to come upon him."

"What is Belial?"

"The devil."

"Oh my God!" I said to Becca with my hand over the speaker of my caller. Then I uncovered the speaker. "If I understand that verse, it means that the devil put an affliction on him."

"That's what the word *affliction* means," Bob explained. "In the New Testament the Bible says that Jesus healed the afflictions of those who were demon possessed. The word affliction means to experience or suffer evil. Many of the people Jesus healed were suffering diseases put on them by Satan."

"Can you think of anything else?"

"Of course, Satan put boils on the righteous man in the Old Testament. You may remember the story of Boj. Satan asked God for permission to take away everything he had, hoping the men would curse God. The Lord granted him permission, and one of things he did was put a disease on him."

"I'm very familiar with that story," Becca said.

"Bob, I can't thank you enough," I said. "You've been very helpful."

"Before you hang up, how is Helen doing?" Bob asked.

"She's doing okay," I answered. "Why do you ask?"

"I don't know. I've just been sensing in my spirit that something's wrong with her. She's going through something. I could be wrong."

I didn't want to have this conversation in front of Becca. I knew Helen's problem was related to me. I was determined to fix that. It might be good to talk to Bob about it sometime and get some advice.

"Let her know I'm praying for her," Bob said.

"I will," I said as I hung up the caller.

"There you have it," I said to Becca. Proof from the Bible that sickness and disease can come from evil. Actually, comes from Belial. I've never heard of that."

"Neither have I," Becca replied. She ran her hand through her hair and shook it out. I noticed she did that whenever she was thinking.

"This could change how we treat diseases like blastoma."

"Right now, the only thing we know to do is kill all the cells," Becca said. "The good and the bad ones."

The latest treatment was to inject a poison into a person's bloodstream. The poison attacked and killed a person's immune system. Unfortunately, the medicine couldn't differentiate between good cells and bad, so it killed both. It brought the person to near death and then back to life by rebuilding their cells and immune systems. A barbaric treatment that puts the patient through hell.

"It makes sense that if a disease is from Satan, the cure would be from God and not from medicine," I said.

"That's a great point! I wonder if that's true of all diseases."

"I doubt it. But now we have Clooney's markers. We can compare every known disease with his markers and see which come from Satan and which don't."

"This could be one of the greatest medical discoveries of all time," Becca said excitedly.

"We have more research to do, but I think you're right."

"If it's okay with you, I'm going home and straight to bed."

"I don't blame you."

"I need some sleep. I have a date tonight."

"A date?"

Why did I have that reaction? A tinge of jealousy rose up in me. I beat it down with an emotional stick. It was none of my business.

"You sound surprised," Becca said.

"No. I just..." I waved my hands in her direction. "Go. Get out of here. Get some rest. Have fun on your date."

* * *

Roki was in full panic mode. The humans had made a big discovery. Satan would not be pleased. He probably already knew about it. He tried to calm himself. At least they had the date tonight. With the chone. Everything was in place. Becca would be meeting the chone at a restaurant. Now, they just had to be sure he seduced her. If he could mix his seed with hers, then they could bring evil to the Christians, and Satan would be very happy with him.

He flew off to make sure everything went as planned on the date.

I have a lot to do.

29

The hastily called meeting of the National Security Council was about to begin. We were only waiting for the First Minister of Saturn, Elijah Lee, to enter the room. I was to give a report as to the status of the experiment. The timing couldn't have been better. If the meeting had been held yesterday, I would have little to tell them. Today, what I was about to relate to them was going to shake their world to its foundation.

Minister Lee arrived and was now leaning back in the high-back chair at one end of a large mahoak conference table. He called the meeting to order.

I sat on the other end, with my papers neatly organized in front of me. I was the sole topic of discussion as far as I knew.

He abruptly motioned with his hand for me to begin. I wasn't sure if he was aggravated at something, pressed for time, or if he was saying this was my meeting, so get on with it. I was probably imagining things. Either way, it unnerved me for a moment, so I took a deep breath and waited to speak. The gravity of my words caused me to rethink them so they would come out just right, for full effect.

When I was ready, I decided to get right to the point. "We believe the Satite is a Nohelim," I said.

Minister Lee bolted up in his chair, the arm of it banging against the table and sending a loud noise through the room.

I could see everyone else react to the First Minister's actions with alarm as the whole room in unison sat forward in their chairs.

A couple of them gasped. I was certain some in the room had no idea who the Nohelim were. The First Minister obviously did. The rest were taking their cues for alarm from his reaction.

"What makes you think that?" Lee said with his eyebrows raised.

"We ran DNA tests on Mark and then compared them to Clooney."

"Who is Clooney?" he asked, interrupting me before I could continue.

"Oh, sorry," I said, stumbling for my words. "Clooney is the name we gave to the Satite. It's a play on the word chone. Clooney is definitely a chone. However, we believe he was choned from DNA that came from the Nohelims."

"And who are the Nohelims?" Ralph Jones, Minister of Security asked.

I was prepared.

"Let me read you this passage of Scripture from the Old Testament. 'Now it came to pass, when men began to multiply on the face of the earth, and daughters were born to them, that the sons of God saw the daughters of men, that they *were* beautiful; and they took wives for themselves of all whom they chose.'"

"The Nohelim were the offspring of the sons of God and the daughters of men," First Minister Lee explained.

"And who were the sons of God?" Jones asked.

"Fallen angels," Lee replied.

A murmur went through the room as the six other men began talking among themselves.

"Are you saying that demons had sex with humans?" Jones asked, directing the question at me.

"That's correct," I answered. "Let me keep reading. "There were giants on the earth in those days, and also afterward, when the sons of God came into the daughters of men and they bore children to them. These were mighty men who were of old, men of renown.'"

Josiah Matthews, the Minister of Defense, spoke up. "The men we are facing on the battlefield keep getting bigger and bigger.

Stronger. Faster. Deadlier. They don't seem to have any regard for right or wrong. They just kill indiscriminately. They are like giants and unlike anything we've ever seen before.

"Another passage says when they saw the Nohelim they seemed like grasshoppers, and so we seemed to them," I paused to let that sink in. "Our ancestors had to fight the giants and were soundly defeated."

"Are you saying that fallen angels are coming down to Saturn and having sex with Satite women?" Jones asked.

"I don't think so," I said shaking my head. "I think the Satites somehow got DNA from the body of a Nohelim, and they're using that DNA to chone the giants we see on the battlefield today."

"There were reports that Satites discovered a body in a cave," Langston Murray, the Minister of Information, said. "We dismissed those reports as ludicrous. Now, I'm not so sure. We should've taken them more seriously."

"How many giants can they chone?" the Minister of Defense asked.

"Unlimited, as far as DNA goes," I answered. "Practically, they would be limited to how many they can bring to adulthood. They seem to be doing it pretty fast, so I'm thinking they must have an incubation system. There's no way that a human woman today could carry one of these children to childbirth. They would grow too big too fast."

"What's your estimate of how many we may be dealing with?" Lee asked.

"A thousand. Maybe two," I answered. "If they could build that many incubators. Some would die in the process. Also, they must have some way of downloading information. These beings are intelligent. Not enough time passes between the time they are born and when they reach the battlefield to go through the normal growth patterns humans go through."

The Minister of Defense and the First Minister stared at each other, both obviously knowing the ramifications of this information.

"Anything you can do to stop them?" the Defense Minister asked me.

"We don't know of anything yet. But we just found this out yesterday. It's new information. We will start working on that, right away. It would help if I had a live patient to work on."

"Isn't the Satite we captured still alive?"

"Technically yes. But we are keeping him alive artificially. We'll conduct more tests, but I think we need a live subject if we are going to make more progress."

I decided not to tell them about the blastoma discovery. I wanted to keep researching that before I let anyone know what we'd found. It's possible we could even find a cure. Then we could release the information all at once.

"How do we fight these creatures?" Minister of Defense Matthews asked.

"We'll discuss that among ourselves," Minister Lee interjected. "Thank you, Dr. Forrester for all of your hard work."

He gave me a nod of the head which several in the room acknowledged and agreed with. A subtle cue for me to leave. I started packing up my things.

"I will say this before the doctor leaves," the First Minister spoke again. I stopped a moment. "Our battle is not against flesh and blood. The Bible says it's against the forces of darkness. We've always known that. God killed the Nohelim by bringing a flood. The Bible says the battle is the Lord's. If we're fighting a spiritual and evil enemy, then we must fight them in the spiritual realm. With spiritual warfare."

"If God be for us, who can be against us?" the Minister of Defense said as the room erupted in applause.

I gathered my things and walked out, satisfied that I'd done my part. Thankful God had used me. Hopeful that they were right. If God didn't help us, we were in deep trouble.

* * *

I left the meeting with just enough time to run my errands before I went home. I stopped by the store and picked up a beautiful bouquet of roses for Helen and a card. The words on the front of the card were romantic:

I'm so grateful God put you in my life.

You'll never know how much I LOVE YOU and how much you mean to me.

I want to spend the rest of my life, loving you better.

The one thing on Saturn I never want to end is being with you.

You are the love of my life.

The card was red with several hearts on the front. I sat in my airmobile with a writing instrument, thinking about something to say, wanting to personalize it.

I'm going to do better. I need to do better. Just always know that I love you and am here for you. Always and forever. Love Roger.

I parked in front of our house, so I could surprise Helen. I made reservations for dinner at her favorite restaurant. My heart was softening toward her. Tonight was going to be good for us.

I walked through the door and into the hallway and called out Helen's name. She didn't answer.

She must be upstairs.

I arranged the flowers in a vase and sat them on the kitchen counter. On the top of the counter was an envelope. Addressed to me. Helen's handwriting.

Roger.

I opened the envelope.

30

Livid was in a group of about a dozen fallen angels who were being given instructions by Boor in his usual boorish manner. Based on Boor's fiery tone, Livid knew this assignment was important to the evil one. Boor wouldn't be involved if it wasn't. The head over four principalities, Boor had reached the highest rank of ruler, a position Livid aspired to. Perhaps this assignment might propel him further up the ranks. He was basically in charge of it, at a position right below ruler.

He'd once been fairly high up among the angels, back before that dreadful choice. Satan rebelled against God and convinced a third of them to make war with God. Turned out to be a big mistake. Something they all came to regret when they were crushed easily and thrown out of heaven, doomed to a life of separation from God. From what he had read in the Bible, a fiery eternity in hell would be their ultimate fate.

In the meantime, they were to exact revenge against God anyway they could. Something he was more than willing to do and had become good at. The best way to do that was to hurt man, or in this case a woman—Becca Holmes. Livid wasn't sure exactly what she did to draw the attention of such powerful demonic forces, but he was the one chosen to bring death and destruction to her, and he was determined to do so to the best of his ability.

Not in the usual way, Boor had said. He was to get Ed Tansa, a chone, fashioned from the seed of the evil one, to seduce Becca, and get her to have relations with him, thus contaminating the Christian race once again as they had done in the days of the Nohelim. Livid thought God had forbidden the fallen angels from mixing with the humans, but somehow the great one had gotten around the decree and found a way to create a species capable of spreading the evil one's seed on earth. His job wasn't to question the evil one; it was to carry out his wishes.

"Becca Holmes is not your typical Christian," Boor shouted to the group.

Why does he have to be so loud?

The anger... Livid understood. They were all angry. At God. At themselves for not overthrowing God. Too many regrets led to much anger and resentment. He and the other fallen angels had taken the path of evil and that's what they felt all the time. They had come to hate everything that was good.

"Becca is strong in her faith. She will not be easily fooled by the chone," Boor continued interrupting Livid's thoughts. "You must be wily. You must be servants of righteousness, deceitful workers, seemingly workers of faith. Tansa must appear to be as strong in faith as Becca."

Livid started to ask a question but thought better of it. Boor didn't like to be interrupted when he was speaking.

"You must look for the usual openings. The normal human weaknesses. Anxiety, fear, sexual desire to name a few. Wait for Becca to make a mistake. Remember, it can't be just her thoughts. When desire is conceived, it gives birth to sin. We must get her to sin."

"How do we do that if she has such strong faith?" one of the other, less experienced demons asked.

Livid braced for the strong reaction. None came.

Instead Boor said, "Remember, that anything not of faith is sin to a follower of Christ. The Bible says as much. It also says that if a Christian knows what to do and doesn't do it, then it is sin to them. That's the opening. She will know that the chone is bad for her. Nothing you can do about it. The Holy Spirit will tell her. She will know in her heart that the chone is leading her astray. Once she knows it and acts on it anyway, it will open the door for you. Then we will destroy her!" He said the words laughing violently.

We were all together flitting around like bees swarming around a nest. No one could sit still for any length of time. We had to constantly be moving. We'd gathered at a portal looking down on Becca's house in her bedroom where she was getting ready for her date with the chone.

Her caller rang, interrupting Boor's next words.

"Quiet everyone!" Boor said roughly. "That's her mother calling. Let's listen for an opening."

Becca answered the caller on the first ring. She'd expected her mother and her sister to call. They were more excited about her date than she was. Honestly, she'd rather be at the office working on the next experiment. Several ideas had already formed in her head as to what she should do next.

"Hello, Mom," she said in an annoying tone. This was the third time her mom called that day.

"Are you anxious?" her mom asked.

Boor stiffened. The Bible said to be anxious for nothing. Anxiety was one way in which Christians opened the door for a demon to bring further pain and destruction. He motioned for the spirit of anxiety to get ready.

"Not anxious," Becca said. "Just excited."

Boor made a flailing gesture of disgust. "That would be too easy," Livid heard Boor say. Boor told the spirit to stand down.

Becca's caller screen lit up. Another call, this one from her sister Cherry.

"Hold on Mom. Cherry's calling. I'm going to do a three way."

"Hi Sis," Becca said as she hit the button to patch her sister into the call with her mom.

"What are you wearing?" Cherry asked.

"Hold on," Becca said as she snapped a picture of herself with her caller and sent it to her mom and sister.

"You look like you're going to church!" Cherry blurted out.

"I have to agree," her mom added.

"Thanks a lot," Becca said. "What's wrong with how I'm dressed?"

She had on black pants and an off-white blouse that came up to her neck and hung loosely over her pants. Accented by a cross around her neck. A multi-colored sweater was over the blouse and hung down even lower than the shirt stopping just above her knees. She wore two-inch black heeled boots.

"You need to wear something sexier," Cherry said. "This is a date, not a family reunion. Show some skin."

Boor stiffened again. He had been disappointed in how Becca was dressed as well. Not sensual at all. Changing the outfit to show more skin might or might not open a door, it just depended on Becca's motives. It couldn't hurt.

"I'm showing skin," Becca said, waving her arms in front of the caller even though they couldn't see them. "The sweater only comes down to my elbows. My arms are showing."

"Oh please," Cherry said. "How are you ever going to catch a guy dressed like that? You look frumpy."

"First of all, I'm not trying to catch a guy. This is how I dress. If he doesn't like it, then he's not the man for me. Besides, frumpy is my look."

"Honey, I think you look great. But I do agree with your sister. At least put on a lower cut blouse. Show some cleavage."

"Mom!"

"That's how I caught your father," she added.

"We're not having this conversation!"

"Think about it," her mom said.

"I've got to go," Becca retorted. "I don't want to be late."

"Call us when the date is over."

"I'll call you tomorrow," Becca retorted playfully.

"Have fun!" Becca heard them say in unison, and then she heard several smooches right before the call ended.

A large mirror filled up the wall above the vanity. Becca looked at herself in the mirror from almost every angle.

Maybe I do look too frumpy.

She walked into her closet and looked at her options. There weren't many.

I need some new clothes.

One bright pink blouse with a plunging neckline caught her eye. She took it off the rack. Back in front of the mirror, she put the blouse up to her.

It's really low cut.

She had worn it many times but always with a shirt under it. Wearing it would make her feel uncomfortable. She didn't have a peace about it. A verse in the Bible came into her head.

I want the women to dress modestly, with decency and propriety, adorning themselves, not with elaborate hairstyles or gold or pearls or expensive clothes.

Boor had been watching the scene carefully. He quieted the other fallen angels who were scurrying around impatiently.

"This is what I'm talking about," Boor said. "She knows what to do. The Bible says to dress modestly. If she goes against that, then it is sin for her. That creates an opening. A small one, but an opening, nonetheless. Get ready to pounce if she makes the wrong decision."

Becca stood in front of the mirror for a full minute, alternating back and forth between holding up the blouse and then looking at what she was wearing. She walked back into the closet and put the blouse back on the rack.

"What I'm wearing is fine," she said out loud.

Boor slammed his hand against one of the demons sending him flying through space.

"Damn her!" he said, with a loud shout. "A missed opportunity."

"Oh well!" he said. "There will be more."

31

Ed was tall, with sandy blonde hair. Perfectly fit.

Too good to be true.

An engaging conversationalist. Her equal in every way, she thought. Becca hadn't enjoyed the company of another man as much as Ed's in... well, never. Perhaps there was something to this DNA match company after all. Or perhaps there was something wrong with this picture. She wasn't sure which it was, but she was giving her best effort to find out.

For the first hour, Becca had been guarded. Almost standoffish. Ed didn't seem to notice or to mind. As time went on, she let herself relax a little.

She giggled at something he said. She hadn't giggled since she was a teenager. She needed to maintain control of herself and keep her guard up.

If it seems too good to be true, it is.

That's what her dad always said. A nagging feeling inside told her something wasn't right about Ed. What was it? Or was it her? She'd been out of the dating market for a long time. Perhaps, she lost her edge and her discernment skills. Or maybe she'd been on so many bad dates, she was the one who was no longer too good to be true. Maybe she wasn't the good catch anymore. Hopefully, Ed would feel that way and this would be their last date.

"I love that," Becca said about the bite of food she just took as she felt the tension leaving her body with each passing moment. Ed had brought her to *Madoras*, the most famous and expensive restaurant in all of Noh. She regretted insisting they both pay for their own meal. It would be expensive.

The restaurant overlooked the beach of the Sea of Capra on the east side of Noh. The rings of Saturn and its moons were shimmering off the water. Seventeen moons were visible from their vantage point, sitting on the upper floor, next to one of the large windows that provided a 360-degree view of the mountains to the north, the sea to the east, and the most colorful part of the rings to the south.

"I wish my mom would call me more," Ed said.

"Really," Becca laughed. "I wish mine would call me less."

Becca coiled her shoulders back. That was a strange thing for a man to say. Was he serious or trying too hard? Was he a momma's boy? The last thing she wanted was someone who was more in love with his mother than he was her.

A major red flag.

Why? The argument continued in her mind. She'd been back and forth all evening on how good the date was going in her head. Over-analyzing everything. *So, he loves his mother.* The Bible says to honor your father and mother. Becca thought she was really getting picky in her old age. She was dismissing the perfect man because he loved his mother too much. *I'm pathetic.*

It wasn't that. It just sounded like a lie, a line. Something he said to impress her. Surely, he didn't mean it. She finally decided to give him the benefit of the doubt.

Ed had a slight tic. Very indiscernible. She noticed it because she was a doctor and was trained to pick up on that type of thing. The medical handbook of symptoms scrolled in her head as she tried to determine the cause.

He's not my patient.

"You look really nice, tonight," Ed said sweetly.

"That's the third time you've said that."

"Oh sorry. You're just so beautiful."

"That's the fourth time you've said that."

"You don't take compliments very well, do you?"

"I'm sorry. I'm just not used to them."

"I'm not used to giving them. To be honest, it's been a long time since I've been out with someone as pretty as you."

"I find that hard to believe. You're a good-looking guy. I'm sure a lot of girls would be interested in you."

"Not really."

"Now look who's the one who doesn't take compliments very well."

Ed laughed and brushed back his hair.

I like his laugh. And his smile.

I should laugh more.

Why do I like him so much?

This wasn't normal. Becca was trying to control her emotions which were raging out of control. She felt an instant attraction to him. Something she never felt before. An intensity. Deep desire. Seriously. *Am I that needy?*

Livid, the fallen angel, had the ability to intensify feelings in humans. Very few humans realized that. He had done some work in Becca the moment she met Ed, by making her have an instant attraction. Once she accepted it, the attraction became a seed inside that he could cultivate. The lust of the flesh was easily magnified by demonic forces when a human opened themselves up to it. That's really what temptation was. A feeling intensified by the devil. If humans understood that, they'd be less likely to fall into it. Fortunately, for him and his fellow fallen angels, humans were susceptible to the power of intense emotions, both good and bad.

Ed smiled at Becca.

"What?" she said, feeling uncomfortable. His looks were endearing. Ed's eyes were piercing. Soft at the same time. Gentle. Blue. Every once in a while, they flashed mischievously.

Devilish.

Why would I think that?

"How come the waiter hasn't brought the check?" Becca asked, looking around, trying to ease the discomfort of him staring at her.

"It's taken care of," Ed said.

"When did you do that?"

"I have my ways."

"I said we were going notch."

"You can get the next one."

"Will there be a next one?"

"I hope so. Will there be?"

"I haven't decided yet."

"Oh. Playing hard to get."

Becca saw it. A flash of anger came across his face when she said she hadn't decided yet. His jaw clenched slightly. She thought she saw his veins bulge in his neck. His smile was tight lipped.

You are overanalyzing this.

Emotions were raging inside of her. Both good and bad. Probably good and evil if she analyzed it closely. It felt like temptation. Why would it be temptation? She wasn't doing anything wrong.

But the attention was sparking desire. No question she was attracted to him. *What's wrong with that? We are two grown adults. This was how people fall in love.* They seemed to hit it off. She thought he felt the same way.

Something wasn't right. She just couldn't put her finger on it.

It's the first date. He's probably nervous. So am I.

Livid wasn't happy with the way Ed was performing. He could be doing better. They needed to go outside, where it was dark, so she couldn't see his face as clearly. Becca was very observant. Ed was about to blow the whole thing. *Stupid chone!*

He put the thought to go outside in Becca's head.

"Let's go outside," Becca said, standing up abruptly.

They walked out on the veranda, down the steps to a trail that walked along the sea. The rings of Saturn were filling the night sky with a kaleidoscope of colors bouncing off of the sea. Almost blinding, even though late at night. Becca took Ed's arm and they walked slowly down a path that ended at an overlook.

The pace of the conversation slowed as Becca's heart started beating faster. She could feel the strength in his arms. Desire was building as well, as she was close enough to hear him breathe, and could feel his steady, calm, confident strength. He rubbed his hand down her arm, and it sent chills through her. He turned and faced her.

Is he going to kiss me?

Should I let him?

This was the best date she'd ever been on, she decided.

Livid was sending her all kinds of thoughts. She had opened the door with her desire. The Holy Spirit had been warning her throughout dinner. Her guardian angels had been frantically trying to get her attention. Livid could see them hard at work. He had counteracted their every move by increasing her desire.

Becca had a strong need for male companionship. She was a confident and strong woman, but she was a woman who liked to be romanced, even if she hadn't let herself feel anything for another man in a long time. Once she let her guard down even further, Livid could do a lot more manipulation of her emotions. If she would let him kiss her, that would really open the door.

The setting was perfect. Romantic. A cool breeze came off the sea, and each rippling wave sent a chill down Becca's spine. She shivered slightly. Ed took off his coat and put it around her shoulders.

How sweet!

"I know you're not going to like me saying this, but you are so beautiful. Even more so in the ringlight." Ed said it so sweetly, Becca could feel her heart melting.

"I guess it's okay for you to say it one more time," Becca responded by gently patting him on his chest. Nothing but hard muscle met her hand. She pictured him without a shirt on and could feel her face blush.

Where did that thought come from?

Get hold of yourself. This is a first date.

"Have I convinced you I'm not a murderer?" Ed asked.

What a strange thing to say? Becca pulled back slightly, releasing his arm.

"I'm joking. Sometimes people don't know when I'm kidding. It's just that you're here all alone with me. No one's around. It's a good thing I'm a nice guy."

Becca wanted to run away as alarm bells were going off in her head. Before she could do or say anything, his lips were on hers. Forcefully. He pulled her toward him with the full power of his arms. For a moment, she couldn't move. Trapped.

"Give into it," Livid said. "Enjoy it."

Becca tried to pull away, but his hands had moved to the back of her head and were holding her against him. She could feel his warm breath. Feel his passion.

It felt good.

You need to stop.

Ed loosened his grip, his kiss not quite so forceful. Their lips parted. Seconds later, they were together again. This time the kiss was gentle, slow, and long.

Perfect.

Becca had never felt such passion. Such intensity. She'd never been kissed like that. She didn't want it to stop.

It is perfect, Livid thought to himself. Becca was falling for him.

The plan was working.

32

The envelope was on the kitchen counter addressed to me, obviously from Helen. Just as I picked it up to open it and read it, my caller erupted with a notification of an air message. I sat the envelope back down and pulled the caller out of my pocket.

The message was from Misty.

Loved seeing you today! I'm there every morning. Same time.

A red heart and a smiley face stared back at me. I didn't respond and made a mental note to avoid the coffee shop at that time of the morning.

I should delete the message.

After the question Helen had asked me that morning about having an affair, the last thing I wanted was for her to see that message. One click, and it was gone.

"Helen," I called out louder, sitting the caller down on the counter.

She must be upstairs.

I thought about reading what was in the envelope but couldn't wait to see my wife, so I picked up the flowers in the vase and carried them upstairs to our bedroom. Excitement pulsed through my body as I was genuinely looking forward to being with her tonight. I felt almost like I did when we were first dating.

I called out her name again.

"Helen. I have a surprise for you."

Seven red roses, which signified *love* on Saturn were in the flowery display. The vase was red as well, and the roses were arrayed with various green stems and carnations. Helen's favorite flower.

All was quiet in our room. One lone light on the table next to our bed was on. I called out her name again, but she didn't answer. An eerie stillness permeated the room.

Strange.

I went back downstairs, remembering the note, thinking she must have gone out to the store or something. Maybe she was working late. Although that would be highly unusual. There were probably less than a dozen or so times over the last year when Helen was not home when I got home from work.

Was I taking her for granted?

Back downstairs, I opened the envelope and pulled out the note addressed to me and in her handwriting.

Roger, I've gone to visit my grandkids. I'll be gone for a week. Don't call me. I need some time alone to think about things. Helen.

I ripped the note in two as rage overcame me before I could stop myself. With my right hand, I backhanded the vase with the flowers, sending them off the counter against the pantry door where the vase shattered with a loud crashing sound. The flowers scattered across the floor in a puddle of water and broken glass. My heart, that only seconds before was filled with love and anticipation, was now filled with anger unlike anything I'd ever felt before.

She didn't even have the courtesy to call.

I suddenly regretted not having called her. I wanted it to be a surprise. *Stupid.*

"My grandkids," I said aloud. "They're *our* grandkids!" The intensity in my voice increased as the anger returned with a fury. Helen always referred to everything as hers. Never ours.

"Don't call me? I'm your husband. I can call you if I want," I said out loud with extreme sarcasm as if Helen was actually in the room and could hear me.

I will call her.

The caller was still on the counter, so I picked it up and started to dial the number of our daughter, Cheryl. That was most likely where she's gone. I hesitated. I needed to calm down. It wouldn't be good to get into a shouting match with our daughter and grandkids listening.

I suddenly regretted destroying the vase and flowers. My gesture of love was a pathetic mess on the floor. The guilt washed in like a flood. That wasn't me. I wasn't a violent person. Usually, I had better self-control than that. Everything seemed so out of control, including my emotions. What did the note mean? She needed time alone, to think about things. What was there to think about?

I'm her husband. She's my wife. We can work this out.

Not if she's not here.

I don't know if I even want to work it out anymore.

Tonight was a huge rejection. I made the effort. More than she had done in years. I bought her flowers, came home early from work, and she doesn't even appreciate it. In her defense, she didn't know about the flowers, or the restaurant, or the date.

But that's no excuse! *Whose fault is that? She didn't know.*

Every time I started to soften my heart toward her and defend her actions, my mind came up with a better counterargument.

She should've been there. A wife's place was with her husband. If she wanted to get away, then we should've talked about it. Springing it on me like that was rude and inconsiderate.

I had some things to think about as well, I decided. Maybe I wouldn't be here when she got back.

That'll show her.

I'm not going to call her. I laid the caller back on the counter. Having the house to myself for a week sounded like a good idea. I wouldn't have to deal with her cold, icy, and frigid looks and comments. I could let the house go. Helen was a perfectionist. Everything had to always be in its place. No dish could be left in the sink. No towel on the floor. Even my own private space had to be kept perfect.

As those thoughts entered my head, I realized how resentful I had become of Helen. She had been controlling me for years. I didn't even recognize who I was. That was going to change.

Emboldened, I cleaned up the mess on the floor and threw the flowers into the trash in disgust. They were symbolic of our marriage. It belonged in the trash heap.

Maybe we should get a divorce.

I wondered if that was what she was thinking as well. This might be a permanent separation. Suddenly, intense pain filled my heart. I wasn't ready for our marriage to be over. If she had just been there when I came home and had waited one more day before going away, maybe our marriage could've been saved. Tonight would've been a turning point for us. I was determined to get her to fall in love with me again. That dream was now gone.

She doesn't love me anymore. It wouldn't have worked anyway. She would have rejected me.

The pain deepened. That's what it was—Helen didn't love me. She certainly hadn't shown me love in years. The realization hit me like a ton of logs falling from a truck, crushing the life out of my body.

Why did I care?

Thirty-three years, that's why. I had given her the best years of my life, and now they were all wasted. Every one of them. Even in my anger, I couldn't imagine life without Helen. It's all I had ever known. I'd been with her longer than I had not been with her.

Divorce. What does that mean?

I'd known couples who had divorced. It was always contentious. I never thought I'd go through that. The house. Furniture. Airmobiles. How did we divide everything? My business. Her business. It would be so complicated. Insurance policies. Our callers were on the same plan. So were the utilities. I was overwhelmed just thinking about it, much less actually doing it. I could see why the Bible says we were one flesh. Helen and I shared everything.

Where would I live? Who would stay in the house? I liked our house. I didn't want to move out. She should move out. She's the one who wants the divorce.

Maybe she already has a place to go!

There's someone else. Helen has a boyfriend.

No! That's not possible. Not Helen.

That would explain a lot of things, though. Helen wasn't strong enough to leave me without having someone else on the side. She needed a man to take care of her. Helen hated sleeping alone. I remembered her saying that when I traveled.

That's why she asked me if I was having an affair. She's the one seeing someone else.

I bit down so hard on my lip I could taste blood. My shoulders tensed and my jaw clenched. I suddenly felt embarrassed. What about our Bible study group? We seemed like the perfect couple. Everybody was going to know we weren't. We're supposed to meet next week at our house. Would Helen be back in time? We couldn't meet here anymore.

I need to talk to Bob.

Why? This is Helen's fault.

Who gets to stay at the church? Probably Helen. I liked Bob, though. *Would we stay friends?*

The kids. Has she talked to the kids?

The kids would be devastated. They had always said that we had the model marriage. When my oldest son got married, at the wedding reception he said, "I hope we find the same happiness that my parents have found. You are my heroes." Braydon, our son, had lifted a toast to us.

I guess I won't be his hero anymore.

I wondered if Helen had already told them. That wasn't fair.

We should tell them together.

I went into my office and slumped in my chair.

How did it come to this?

* * *

I, Roki, the fallen angel assigned to Roger, slung thoughts as fast as I could into him. It got so hectic, I couldn't tell which of the thoughts were coming from Roger's evil heart and which were his ideas. They were all a jumbled mess.

It didn't matter where the thoughts came from, I'd get the credit for all of them. Everything was working out perfectly. Beyond what I could've ever hoped. Roger and Helen and their marriage were being sifted like a shaft of wheat. I could taste victory. A broken marriage. A suicide. A life of guilt. Pain. I could see Roger's future, and it wasn't good.

When I told Chaz, Helen's fallen angel, what Roger had planned for the evening, we'd both panicked. In his brilliance, Chaz had devised a plan to get Helen to leave. The excuse of visiting her grandkids, and saying her last goodbyes, worked perfectly for our aims and also kept Helen on the path to suicide. I manipulated the timing so Roger would find the note the same day he got home with the flowers.

We were right. Roger was devastated when he read the note. The hope and anticipation of a great evening of reconciliation with his wife were dashed, shattered on the floor like the flowers.

I could see Nahum, Roger's guardian angels trying to console him and remind him of Bible verses, but Roger was ignoring them. Nahum couldn't get through with all the emotional turmoil going on inside of Roger.

He was over the edge, and the emotional stage was set. I could bombard Roger all night long with dark thoughts of betrayal. Making him think Helen was having an affair was a stroke of genius. I wished I'd thought of it. Roger came up with that on his own. Helen would be having the same thoughts that night. I was certain of that. This was so funny to me. Both Helen and Roger would have a miserable night from the pain of their spouses having affairs, even though it was all a lie!

Humans are so ridiculous. Hard to believe they were made in the image of God with the way they acted sometimes.

I really wouldn't have to do that much. All I needed to do now was keep fanning the flames of unforgiveness, resentment, anger. Roger's thoughts and broken heart would do the rest.

I'd have to be strategic. What worked for Helen wouldn't work for Roger. I'd focused on deep emotional heartache and pain for Helen. But with Roger, I'd focus on the anger. His manhood had been violated. Opposite of what the Bible said the Christian were supposed to always feel. They were to be content in all things.

This was a perfect opportunity for the lust of the flesh to kick in. Discontent was a powerful and evil emotion. Discontent, lust, an affair. This had been a pattern, the evil one had perfected over tens of thousands of years and dozens of planets.

By the morning, Roger would be so racked with bitterness and resentment, he might not ever forgive Helen and would be open to an affair.

A new opportunity had emerged. *Tomorrow morning.* A new plan had formed in my mind.

I have all night to make it happen.

In the morning, I have to get Roger to the coffee shop.

33

The next morning, Roki screamed Roger's name in his head so loud he woke up startled.

"What was that?" I said. It sounded like someone was calling my name. I rubbed my eyes and tried to focus. My heart was pounding, and I was breathing hard. I must've been dreaming. The room was still dark, but I could see well enough to know that no one was there. Helen's side of the bed was empty, still perfectly made, just like she left it. Funny how I slept all the way over on my side of the bed, even though she wasn't there. A habit, I guessed.

I felt a twinge of hurt. It's weird waking up and my wife was not lying next to me.

"I guess you'll have to get used to it," Roki said to Roger. By the grimace on Roger's face, Roki knew the fiery dart had hit its mark.

The clock showed ten minutes to seven, a little early to go in to work. I gave Becca the day off since she had a date the night before, just in case she was out late. Plus, she worked all night the previous day. I intended to sleep in myself, but I tossed and turned all night. Getting Helen and our problems out of mind was impossible.

Who was Becca's date with?

My mind was still groggy. I wasn't awake yet. Even then, why did I go there so fast? Was I jealous? No, I decided after some introspection. I just wondered.

I need coffee.

I suddenly remembered the text I had gotten the night before from Misty. She would be at the coffee shop at eight. Her usual time.

I'm not going there. That girl is trouble.

After a quick shower, I was dressed for work and downstairs making myself a cup of coffee.

Joe's Coffee is better.

Why did my thoughts keep going there? I had no interest in Misty whatsoever. That was the last thing I needed to concern myself with. Yet I felt this attraction. An urge. It felt like a temptation. It was stupid. Misty wasn't the least bit attractive to me. Her whiny voice and constant flirting were obnoxious.

An image of her flashed across my mind. A picture of her in *Joe's Coffee*, wearing that skimpy outfit kept appearing in my mind with alarm bells going off in my head every time I thought of her.

She does have a nice body.

Get your mind out of the ditch, Roger. Flee temptation.

I laughed out loud. The coffee shop was several minutes away. No temptation to flee from in my kitchen.

Roki laughed as well. Typical human. They don't see temptation when it's right in front of their eyes. Roger didn't need to be with Misty to be tempted by her. Jesus said that even lust was adultery. But Roki wasn't satisfied with just mental lust. He saw an opening in Roger. He wouldn't be satisfied until he got him and Misty together. It seemed like a challenge that might take a while. Roger genuinely disliked Misty. However, Roki knew the power of lust in a man starved for affection.

It won't be that hard to get him to go to the coffee shop.

When I opened the trash bin to empty the coffee grounds, what I saw sent a sharp, stabbing, pain through my chest. The flowers. Wilted. In with the other trash to be discarded. My good intentions along with my feelings, had been unceremoniously discarded by Helen as well. For thirty-three years.

"I wasted twenty rings on those flowers. Just like the thirty-three years I wasted with you, Helen." I was surprised at the vitriol coming out of my mouth. So unlike me to be so angry.

Roki laughed again. Another typical trait in humans. A little adversity and they over exaggerate. Roger was discounting all the good times they'd had over thirty-three years as if he didn't even remember them.

He saw Nahum, Roger's guardian angel trying to get Roger to take those negative thoughts captive. Roki felt good about his chances. Roger wasn't in a good state of mind to be listening to the Holy Spirit or affected by Bible verses. Evil was overcoming good at the moment, both in Helen and in Roger. The evil one would be pleased.

Upon seeing the flowers, the anger came back inside Roger like a raging inferno.

Roki added some intensity just for good measure.

"Why shouldn't you go to the coffee shop, Roger?" Roki said.

Why shouldn't I?

"It's just coffee with a friend," Roki continued barraging Roger with thoughts.

It's just coffee. I was considering it.

"Helen left you. Your marriage is over." A low blow, Roki knew. All's fair in love and war, the evil one always said.

A few tears welled up in my eyes.

Helen's having an affair, why can't I just have coffee with a friend?

"Because you're married," Nahum interjected. "Stay faithful to your wife and your vows."

Because I was married. And so was Misty.

"You're not going to be married that much longer. You'll be single soon," Roki said.

I didn't know how much longer I'd be married, but for now, I had a wedding ring on my finger and a wife, kids, and a reputation to uphold.

I'm not going.

The coffee was too hot to drink. I poured it into a thermal cup to take it with me to the office.

"Goodbye, Helen," I said aloud, angrily, dripping with sarcasm and smothered in resentment as I walked out of the house.

I don't think I've ever been this mad at her before.

* * *

The moment I got in the airmobile, I felt an overwhelming urge to drive by *Joe's Coffee*. Not go in, just drive by to see if Misty was there. The shop was one block over from my normal route to work.

"I'm not going to," I said aloud. "Just keep driving," I told myself.

"Time to ramp up the pressure on Roger," Roki said mostly to himself. If the timing was right, Roger would drive by just at the exact same time Misty arrived.

Yep! There she is.

I saw Misty before she saw me. I tried to speed past her, but she waved. *I didn't want her to see me.*

I have to go back. I had no choice. It would be rude if I didn't.

I parked and went into the shop. We ordered coffee and sat down in a booth this time. After a few minutes, Misty became suddenly very attractive to me. It seemed weird. How did I develop feelings for her so fast? We talked for more than an hour. I didn't know she was so funny. She kept touching my arm and hand. Every time she did, it sent waves of desire through me. I was wrong about her. She was pretty, and sexy.

She kept calling me dear, honey, and sweety instead of calling me Roger. It felt good for someone to talk nice to me. Helen was always so cold. Helen never touched me. Rarely kissed me. I wondered what it would be like to kiss Misty. I wasn't even trying to control the thoughts anymore.

"My husband's out of town on business," she said.

"My wife's out of town as well," I said before I could stop myself.

"Roger," she said hesitantly. "I think we should get together for dinner."

"I don't know if that's a good idea."

"I'll be a good girl. I promise."

"I'm not sure I want you to be... a good girl." I couldn't believe the words coming out of my mouth.

Roki couldn't either. Roger had just thrown the door wide open. The evil desire and lust were bubbling to the surface like a volcano. All Roki did was intensify it. A fallen angel couldn't make a human do anything. They had free will. Roger could walk away at any time. Once the words were spoken, it became harder for the human to walk away from temptation. It didn't seem like Roger was going to.

Misty was the perfect choice. She was attracted to Roger from the moment she saw him. Roki couldn't believe she was having this effect on Roger this fast.

"Why wait until tonight, sweety?" Misty said with a wink. "Let's go to my place now."

"Not your place," I said without hesitation. "That would be too weird. Not my place either. We can go to a hotel."

"Sounds good to me."

"Do you know the Hotel Segara? It's on the other side of town."

"I'll meet you there."

"I'll walk out first," I said. "Give me a couple minutes and then you can come out. In case someone sees us. I'll meet you in the lobby of the hotel in fifteen minutes."

I knew I shouldn't do it. I should walk out the door, get in my airmobile, and never see Misty again. I just couldn't help myself. I really wanted her. I could tell she wanted me. She told me all about Walter and how horrible he treated her. She was in just as bad a marriage as I was in.

I paid for the room with rings, so there was no record on my charge card.

It was the best sex I've ever had.

34

"Watch this," Roki said to Azza. They were looking through a portal into Saturn and were watching Roger come out of a hotel room having just committed adultery with Misty. Azza was an apprentice fallen angel assigned to Roki for advanced training. Boor believed Azza had potential and had instructed Roki to teach him everything he knew and make a recommendation if and when he was ready to move up in the ranks.

"What am I watching for?" Azza asked.

"You'll see."

Roger was walking down the hall with a bounce in his step and a huge smile on his face.

"He looks so happy," Azza said.

"Not for long," Roki replied. "Humans don't understand how the lust of the flesh works. It feels good when they are in the sin and living in the moment. Once they are out of it, they feel miserable. Roger is about to find that out firsthand. Keep watching."

Roger went down to the parking garage and was walking toward his airmobile.

"Is he whistling?" Azza asked.

Roki chuckled. "He's in for quite a shock in less than two minutes. Wait for it."

"Now," Roki said in a commanding voice.

Immediately, the spirit of lust left Roger and flew out of his body back into the heavenlies and stood next to Roki.

"Why did you do that?" Azza asked.

"He's not with the girl anymore. I don't want him to feel anything good about what just happened. Don't worry. I can send the spirit of lust on him any time I want. He's opened the door. I don't think we'll even need the lust anymore. The damage has been done."

"That doesn't make sense," Azza replied. "I think you should keep the lust on him for a while longer."

Roki's face contorted into a serpent as his eyes burned like coals of fire. He grabbed Azza by the throat and thrashed him back and forth.

Azza's eyes were wide with fear.

"Don't ever question me!" Roki shouted.

He threw Azza to the ground, violently. Azza staggered for a moment but finally regained his footing.

"I'm sorry, ruler."

Roki ignored him.

Roger was in his airmobile. The smile had left his face.

"Go!" Roki commanded. Five demons rushed through the portal onto Saturn into Roger's airmobile and into his heart. The evil spirits were guilt, shame, condemnation, anxiety, and regret.

"Watch and learn, Azza. Keep your mouth shut and watch how it's done. Our job now is to make Roger as miserable as possible."

* * *

I sat in my airmobile, confused, dazed almost, in a state of shock. I couldn't believe what I'd just done. It happened so fast. One minute, I was driving to work. Four hours later, I've ruined my life. Helen will never forgive me.

I pounded the steering wheel with my fists. Just moments before I felt so happy. Now, the guilt washed over me like a tsunami. Before, I could be mad at Helen. The breakup of our marriage was her fault. Now it was mine.

"I'm such a horrible person."

The words flowed out of my mouth like vomit. I couldn't stop myself. Tears welled up in my eyes. Suddenly, the thought of Misty repulsed me.

"I don't even like her."

Roki slapped Azza across his head. "Did you see that? Did you hear what the vermin said? Roger is realizing he doesn't love Misty. He can't even stand her now. You know why? Because I removed the spirit of lust. That was the attraction. He never would've slept with her or been attracted to her if he hadn't been deceived."

Roki raised his hand to hit Azza again.

"I get it now. I understand. You were right," Azza said, cowering down, covering his head to protect it from another strike.

"That's how sex works in humans. When it's immoral and evil against God's plan, we enhance it. Lust of the flesh always seems better than it is. We have to make sure the human's pay a huge price for the sin."

"His wife wouldn't have sex with him. Is it really his fault?"

Roki could barely control his anger. He wondered what Boor saw in Azza. He'd send him away immediately except he would be the one who looked bad, not Azza. The failure would be on his record. He had to get through to this imbecile.

"No mercy! Ever! Don't ever feel sorry for humans. They do it to themselves. It doesn't matter the excuse. Roger knew what he was doing. So, I lied to him. I blinded his eyes so he couldn't see clearly. He opened the door. God gave him a beautiful wife and marriage. God blessed them with riches. Look at their house and their airmobiles. They have kids and grandkids. They are both to blame. Helen wasn't a good wife, and he wasn't a good husband. It's both their fault. They wasted what God gave them. We have permission to destroy their lives. They gave it to us. I intend to take advantage of it."

"What do you intend to do to them?"

"Watch and learn, Azza." Roki's eyes were ablaze again. Flames of fire were coming from his mouth.

Roki balled his fists and clenched his jaw. His voice bellowed and echoed throughout the heavenlies.

"I'm going to crush him," Roki said, his voice filled with hate. "I won't stop until everything he cares for is destroyed. Roger will rue this day. He will regret having ever met Misty. He'll regret being born."

* * *

I sat in my office, unable to concentrate on my work. I kept getting out of my chair, pacing around, confused, double minded, not sure what to do next. Thankfully, Becca had taken the day off. I was a nervous wreck.

I prayed and begged God to forgive me, but peace never came. I wanted to call Helen but didn't know what to say. An airmessage was on my caller. It had been there for several hours. It was from Misty. I didn't have the courage to answer it, until now.

I had fun! Misty said in the message.

Me too, I wrote back.

Do you want to come over tonight?

I stared at the message for a good minute before answering.

Are you trying to kill me? I thought I'd try to be funny.

LOL.

That was a weird thing for me to say. Part of me wanted to die. I could feel myself slipping into a depression. Maybe, being with Misty would make me feel better. I just wanted to be with Helen. To hold her. Ask her to forgive me. I knew that was impossible. She could never know what happened.

Misty would make me feel better.

I'll come over. There it was done. I was all in.

I can't wait.

I need to go home and change.

If I was honest with myself, I wanted to go home and take a shower. Wash my clothes. Somehow wash the stain of my sin off of me and my clothes.

Then why was I going over there again?

I can't help it.

I had to do something to take away the pain. Being with Misty would do it. I was sure of it.

I left the office and headed home. The music in the airmobile made me feel better. My favorite worship songs were playing. I remembered a sermon I heard recently about God's forgiveness. The woman caught in the act of adultery was brought to Jesus and laid at his feet. He told her he didn't condemn her. "He who is without sin, cast the first stone."

"That's right," I said. "I'm forgiven. Jesus doesn't condemn me."

A new resolve was building in me. Did I have the strength to not go over to Misty's?

I should take a cold shower.

I pulled into my driveway and opened the garage door. My heart felt like it had leaped out of my chest.

Helen's airmobile was in the garage. She was home. Panic and fear shot through my veins like an electric current. My thoughts raged out of control

Do I smell like Misty? She was wearing too much perfume. Was it on my clothes?

Is there makeup or lipstick on my shirt? I frantically looked in the mirror for any signs.

How do I hide my shame? Helen would see my guilt. I looked in the mirror. I couldn't hide it. The moment Helen looked at me, she would know something was wrong.

What about the house? Did I leave anything there that was incriminating?

I made my side of the bed. The flowers were still in the trash. I had not taken the trash out. Helen would be mad about that.

That's the least of my worries.

I realized Helen would wonder what was taking me so long. She would've heard the garage door open. I needed to go in and face the consequences. Whatever they were. I opened the door and walked in, slowly, hesitantly.

Good, she must be upstairs.

I sat my work case on the table and my phone, wallet, and keys on the counter. I got a drink of water from the refrigerator to soothe what was suddenly my dry and parched mouth. My breathing was shallow and quick. My heart was beating faster than I ever remember it. So fast, it felt like it was going to leap out of my chest.

I found the courage to go upstairs. Just as I started to leave the kitchen, an envelope caught my eye.

To Roger.

Another note lay on the kitchen counter in Helen's handwriting. I looked up at the ceiling wondering if I should go upstairs first or read the note. I decided to read the note.

I opened the envelope. It wasn't a note. It was a letter. Two pages front and back. I leaned back on the kitchen counter and began reading.

Dear Roger. I know about the affair...

35

Helen sat at Roger's desk, tears streaming down her face, the tears dripping onto the paper of a note she had just started to write to him.

She'd returned home from her trip a few hours before. She went to her daughter Cheryl's house, spent the night, and said her good-byes to the kids and grandkids.

The next day, she drove an hour and saw her son, his wife, and their two kids. They played together, laughed, and had a good time.

She tried to be strong and not give them any reason to believe anything was wrong with her. On the way there, she felt a pain in her side. Evidence the blastoma had begun to rear its ugly head and had started her on the slow march to a long and painful death. The pain in her side only gave her more resolve that she was doing the right thing.

Telling her son and daughter was not an option. There would be so many unanswered questions for them, and she hated that. Why would their mom kill herself? It wouldn't make any sense. If they knew about the blastoma, they'd understand. If they knew about her husband's affair, they wouldn't blame her.

But she didn't want them to hate their father. If she told them about his affair with his assistant Becca, a woman he worked for, they would blame him for her death. She only wanted Roger to suffer the humiliation. He's the one who betrayed her. He would get the note. He would understand why she did it. She couldn't put the kids through any more pain than they were already going to feel. It would be hard enough for them to lose one parent. As much as she hated Roger, she didn't want them to lose both of them. That's why they could never know.

She began writing.

Roger, I know about the affair...

For two pages, front and back, she poured out her heart. Helen tried to filter out the anger and resentment. She had tried many times to forgive him. The whole drive there and back, she wrestled with doing the right thing. Forgiving him was the right thing to do, but she couldn't bring herself to do it. The struggle was real. The Bible story of the prophet who wrestled with the angel and broke his hip came to mind. That's what it felt like. She felt like she was fighting with God.

The right thing was to forgive Roger. And live. Until she died of the disease. They wouldn't stay married, of course. But God let the disease come on her, she decided, so maybe she should just take the punishment, accept it, and suffer.

But the thought of facing blastoma alone was too hard to bear. She didn't have the strength. How could she live with the pain of the disease and the betrayal? Maybe she was strong enough to handle one of them, but not both. No person should have to go through that.

It's better this way.

* * *

Helen was sobbing as she neared the end of the letter. Chaz was watching intently. Feeding her thoughts occasionally. He wanted her to really get angry and let Roger know how much he hurt her. Helen was tempering his recommendations. It didn't matter. The letter would serve its purposes.

The spirit of depression was heavy on her and over the entire room. Chaz made sure of that. Also, a spirit of deception. Helen didn't think there was any way out. That was a lie. Chaz had been feeding Helen lies on the drive all the way to her kids and back. God said there was always a way out. He promised to always work everything together for good to those who love him and are called according to his purpose. Chaz knew the verses well. So did Helen, but she was ignoring them right now, much to his delight.

Chaz saw her guardian angels mostly standing on the sidelines. They tried to comfort Helen, but she wouldn't receive it. The medicine had numbed Helen to the point she was oblivious to anything the Holy Spirit or the angels were trying to tell her.

Chaz had done a good job of convincing her the situation was hopeless. He just had to make sure she killed herself before Roger got home and could stop her.

I can't stand the thought of you in the arms of another woman.

Helen was weeping so hard she could barely breathe as she wrote those words on the paper. The tears were soaking the sleeve of her dress as she tried to wipe them away. Her favorite dress. That's what she wanted to be wearing. Black. Appropriate.

I wonder what they'll say at my funeral. I want them to sing Grace So Amazing.

She panicked for a moment, wondering if anyone knew that. She had told Roger once, but he probably had forgotten. *Typical man,* she thought angrily. She kept writing.

I'm sorry I wasn't a better wife.

That line was hard to write and hard to admit to. The tears ebbed as some anger fought its way through the depression.

We both have to live with our mistakes. I can't live anymore with yours. Please understand why I have to do what I'm going to do. It's better this way.

Helen doubled over in pain. From the blastoma or from the hurt of the betrayal? She wasn't sure. It's what made ending her life easier. No person should have to go through both.

But now you are free. Free to be with Becca. Free to live your life. Free of me.

This is goodbye. Forever.

Love, Helen.

She started to scratch out the word *love*. Was that how she wanted to end the letter? She did love him, she suddenly realized. More than she ever imagined. He was the love of her life. The only man she had ever been with. The only man she'd ever loved, ever would love. Why did it take getting to the end of her life to realize it? If only she'd realized it sooner, maybe things would've been different.

So many regrets.

P.S. Know that I really did love you and that I forgive you.

There she did it. She forgave him. She felt more at peace.

Chaz didn't try to stop her from writing it. It might be heartfelt, but it wasn't complete forgiveness. If Helen really forgave Roger completely, she wouldn't be taking her life. She would trust God and work it out with him. God would even heal her of her disease. Their marriage would be reconciled. Even with the affair. The one she didn't know about.

Chaz couldn't help but laugh. Helen was killing herself over an affair that didn't happen and a disease that God would heal her from. She would kill herself over a lie that had now become reality. Helen's worst fears had happened. Roger did have an affair. As a reaction to her abruptly leaving and turning her heart away from him by believing the lies. Not that it was her fault. It was both of their faults. Not that Chaz cared. Better if they both shared the blame.

Chaz had been doing this for thousands of years on dozens of other planets. Humans were the same. They destroyed their lives because they didn't believe God and his Word and didn't listen to the Holy Spirit who lived inside of them.

His thoughts were interrupted by a fallen angel informing him that Roger was on his way home and would be there in about twenty minutes.

"You need to hurry," Chaz told Helen. "Roger will be home soon."

Helen wiped the tears away from her eyes, folded the letter, and stuffed it into an envelope addressed to Roger. After a deep breath, she left his office for the last time and placed the note on the kitchen counter and went upstairs.

The pills were on the bathroom counter where she had unpacked them earlier. She was amused at how carefully she had unpacked and folded her belongings. She had gone through the entire house and cleaned it. People were going to be in her house. EMT's, the coroner, maybe police detectives investigating her death. She wanted the house to be presentable.

Twelve pills were the right number to take, she had decided. One for each apostle. She laughed, trying to release the tension as she remembered how she came to that number. Turns out, there were exactly twelve left in the bottle. A sign from God. Another confirmation she was doing the right thing.

A wave of fear suddenly came over her as she took the first pill. What will it be like to die? Will God forgive me? A preacher once said that anyone who killed himself would go to hell. Another said he wouldn't. She didn't know who to believe. It didn't matter. Her mind was made up.

The rest of the pills went down easily with a drink of water after each.

Helen walked out of the bathroom and into the bedroom where she laid down on the bed to die. Roger had made his side of the bed. That made her smile. She had fixed it because it wasn't done right, but she appreciated his effort. At first, she wondered if he had even slept there. Maybe he stayed at his lover's house. She was relieved to find the evidence that he had been there overnight.

A weird feeling came over her. Then intense pain. Searing pain. In her stomach. Then between her shoulder blades. She tried to sit up, but the room started spinning. Helen cried out for help. The pain started running down her arms and legs. She felt numb, like she couldn't move.

She tried to stand, but her legs wobbled and wouldn't hold her weight. She fell and hit her head on the side of the nightstand as she reached for something to grab onto. With her hand she managed to grab the lamp which she pulled off of the table onto the floor.

The room suddenly went dim, but she was still alive. Her heart was racing. Fear was pulsing through her almost in unison with her heartbeat that was pounding in her ears.

"God help me?" she cried out. "I don't want to die!"

Her breathing became labored. She no longer had the strength to speak. She lay on the ground in agonizing pain, her vision blurred, unable to talk, as an eerie silence filled the room.

She heard a sound downstairs. *Roger.*

She tried to call out to him but couldn't get the breath or the strength to muster the words. All she could do was lie there in agony. Mercifully, after ten long and horrifying minutes, everything went black.

36

My heart sank when I read the words, *Dear Roger, I know about the affair.*

How could she know?

All kinds of questions were swirling in my mind. Did she follow me this morning to the hotel? Was she really out of town? I read further, searching for answers.

I read the text messages from Becca, Helen wrote in the note.

Becca?

What did Becca have to do with it? My mind wasn't processing what Helen meant.

I can't believe you would have an affair with your own assistant. Now I know why you lied and said she was a man. Did you think I wouldn't find out?

I looked up from the note and stared across the rooming thinking. Relieved that Helen didn't know about Misty but confused as to why she would think I was having an affair with Becca.

What text messages?

I set down the note, grabbed my caller off the counter and scrolled to the messages from Becca. There weren't many. I gasped audibly and put my hand over my mouth as I read what she must've been referring to.

I'm here at the office. I had texted that to Becca right after the Bible study. At my office when I went to check on the alarm. I didn't want to frighten her.

Good. I have something for you. A smiley face. I remembered she had news about her testing.

Sex? About the sex of Clooney.

Yes.

I'll be right in. I went in. I turned off the alarm. She showed me her discovery. I left and came home. Nothing happened.

"Oh Helen," I said aloud, chuckling nervously. A sense of relief came over me. I could explain the text message. I would introduce Helen to Becca, and everything would be fine. Then I realized things would never be fine. I did, in fact, have an affair with Misty. And I lied about Becca being a man.

Yeah, but Helen doesn't know about Misty. I can keep that a secret. It's over anyway. She'll be mad about Becca, but she won't leave me over it.

Then I realized I told Misty I was coming over tonight. That obviously couldn't happen. I started to send Misty a message but hesitated. Helen was obviously reading my airmessages. I needed to be more careful.

Finish reading the letter.

Not that the rest of the letter mattered. I could fix this. I scanned it quickly, not reading every word until I got near the end. A rush of panic jolted me back to reality as I realized it was not a letter at all. It was a suicide note!

I can't stand the thought of you in the arms of another woman... We both have to live with our mistakes. I can't live anymore with yours. Please understand why I have to do what I'm going to do. It's better this way.

"What... what does she have to do?"

I don't want to live anymore. This is goodbye.

"No!" I shouted. "She can't mean it."

I looked up at the ceiling. Surely, Helen didn't mean what I thought she meant.

But now you are free. Free to be with Becca. Free to live your life. Free of me.

This is goodbye. Forever.

I dropped the note on the floor and bolted up the steps. I burst into our bedroom. Helen was lying on the floor in a pool of blood. The lamp light was on but lying next to her having somehow fallen off the table. I rushed to her side and knelt beside her.

She had a faint pulse, but her breathing was shallow. I turned her over, gently. The blood was coming from a gash in her head. White foam was trickling from the side of her mouth.

What was that substance?

The scene wasn't making sense. I inspected the source of the blood. The gash on Helen's head was bad, but not bad enough to cause these near-death symptoms. She probably had a concussion, I concluded, but why was she barely breathing? I stood and went into her bathroom to get a wet washcloth. In my rush, I almost didn't notice the empty pill bottle. When I did, I picked it up and read the label.

Predoxarin. For anxiety. The bottle was empty.

I had to hurry. That was the source of the white substance coming out of her mouth. Helen had taken an overdose of a pill that was deadly in volume.

I rushed back to her, lifted her head from the floor, and placed it on my lap. I opened her mouth and stuck my finger to the back of her throat to induce vomiting. At that moment, Helen began to seizure. I removed my finger just before she would have bitten down on it. The jerking motions convulsed her body. I turned her to her side so her airway would stay clear. I pulled a pillow off the bed and propped it under her head and then gently laid her on the floor. I had to get her help, and fast.

I ran back downstairs where my caller was on the counter. My hands were bloody, so I wiped them on my shirt but still left blood on the counter and on my phone. I dialed three nines.

"What is your emergency?"

I went into doctor mode.

"I have an unconscious female. My wife. Helen Forrester. Her breathing is shallow. Faint pulse. She's overdosed on Predoxarin and is near death. I'm a doctor. There's nothing I can do for her here. We have to get her to the hospital right away or she's not going to make it."

"Someone is on the way," the lady on the line said and then confirmed our address.

"What's your name?"

"Dr. Roger Forrester."

"Stay on the line. Help is on the way."

"I'm hanging up now. I'm going to have to take emergency action to keep her alive until they get here. I'm going to need both hands. Just hurry."

I started to run back upstairs but then saw the note on the floor. I put my hand over my eyes, confused as to what to do.

No one can see the note.

I picked it up off the floor and tore it into little pieces and sent it down the garbage disposal in the sink. Then I ran to the front door and opened it and rushed back up the stairs. I didn't want to leave Helen's side to come down and open the door for the emergency workers.

When I got upstairs, the seizure had stopped but so had Helen's pulse. I began chest compressions and then alternated with forced breathing, trying to get air into her lungs. I inspected the gash on her head again, not sure exactly what had caused it. She probably hit it on the nightstand.

I frantically continued the compressions and breathing. I could tell I was keeping her alive. Nothing more. She wasn't responding to anything. A few minutes later, I heard the emergency personnel call out from the front door. I yelled for them to come upstairs. I stopped the compressions for a moment and just held Helen. I squeezed her close to me and prayed.

"God please don't let her die. Please. Helen, I'm so sorry. I love you so much. Will you ever forgive me?"

Tears were soaking my shirt and wetted her hair as it was against my chest. I didn't even hear or see the two men come into the room until one of them pulled me away from her.

I composed myself enough to explain her condition and what I thought had happened.

"I'm a doctor. This is my wife. Helen. I think she had an accidental overdose of Predoxarin. Not accidental," I corrected myself. "I think she took a lot of the pills. I have no idea how many. I've been doing compressions and breathing. She's not responding."

"We'll take it from here," one of them said as they loaded her on the stretcher, took her downstairs, and into the emergency vehicle. I followed them all the way to the ambumobile.

"Take her to Mercy Medical. Tell them it's Doctor Roger Forrester's wife."

I went back in the house and retrieved my phone, wallet, and keys, got in my airmobile and headed to the hospital, not able to fully comprehend what had just happened. I couldn't believe Helen had tried to take her life. Probably did take it. I knew from my experience that her chance of survival was slim. I used to work in the emergency room at Mercy Hospital. I saw many cases like hers. If anyone could save her life, it would be them.

I dialed Bob's number. He answered right away.

"Bob, this is Roger. Something terrible has happened to Helen. The ambulance is taking her to Mercy Hospital right now. I'm following them. It's bad. I don't know if she's going to make it."

"I'll be right there," Bob said. "We'll send out a message through the prayer chain. Hang in there, buddy. Trust God for a miracle."

"It's going to take a miracle," I said as I hung up the phone.

When I arrived, Helen was already back in a room, hooked up to a breathing machine and heart monitor. I went right through the double doors before anyone saw me and found where I suspected they had taken her. They wouldn't let me stay there, even though I was the husband, and even though I was a doctor. I understood.

Hospital procedures. I could tell from the monitor that she'd flat-lined. Her face was blue and cold. Some patients who were dying looked peaceful. Helen looked troubled. I knew why. She had no pulse and very low blood pressure. I wanted to help them, but there was nothing I could do for her.

All I could do was go back to the waiting room and pray.

* * *

Bob and I had been in the waiting room for a good hour and still no word from the doctor. Not hearing anything was actually a good sign. I knew that at least there was a chance she would make it. They would work on her for thirty minutes, and if there was no response, they would declare her dead. Maybe thirty-five minutes since she was my wife. They might make the extra effort. The fact that it had been an hour was a sign she was still alive.

Bob had been a great comfort to me. So had the hospital staff. A nurse brought me a doctor's uniform so I could change out of my bloody clothes.

"Any idea what happened?" Bob asked.

"No. I just came home from work and found her lying on the floor in our bedroom. There was blood on the floor. I think she hit her head."

I hadn't told him about the pills. I didn't want Bob to know she had tried to take her own life. That would be hard to explain. As far as Bob knew, everything was okay between us. I rationalized that it was for her benefit. If she lived, she would be embarrassed. If she died... I couldn't even let my mind go there.

Finally, the doctor emerged from behind two huge double doors and came and sat down next to us. I tried to anticipate what he was going to say by the look on his face. I had done the same things many times for many families. The best doctors kept the same expression whether it was good news or bad news.

Dr. Jeremy Grisham was a good doctor. I had known him for a long time. I wasn't surprised they called him in to assist with Helen.

The hospital would do anything for me, and for that I was appreciative.

"Roger, she's alive," Jeremy said.

"Praise the Lord," I heard Bob say.

I didn't respond. I knew there was more from the tone of his voice.

"Barely," he added.

I didn't say anything. He would get to the details. I just put my head in my hands for a moment, rubbed my face hard and prepared for the worst.

"She's not breathing on her own. We have her on a ventilator. We pumped her stomach. She took a lot of pills."

Bob looked at me with a strange face. His lips were contorted to the side.

"I think she had an overdose of some medication she was taking," I explained. I looked at Jeremy and gave him a look as to not say anything more. This was a private matter. He must have understood because he didn't say anything else about the overdose.

"Jeremy, this is Bob," I said. "He's Helen's pastor. Our pastor."

They shook hands.

"You can go back and see her in a few minutes," Jeremy said. "Read her chart. That will give you all the details."

I nodded as Jeremy stood to his feet, and I did the same. I held out my hand, and he shook it. He even pulled me in closer for a half hug. He slapped me on my back. I knew from his tone he didn't have much hope for Helen.

"Thanks Jeremy. I can't tell you how glad I am that you are taking care of her."

"One other thing," Jeremy said.

"What's that?"

"How long has Helen had blastoma?"

"I didn't know she did," I said, as the words hit me in the gut like a punch.

It took me a moment to grasp what he had just said. I was dumb-founded. I had no idea. That must have been why Helen had the anxiety medicine. It dawned on me that it was a common pill for blastoma patients. Helen must've been petrified. Why didn't she tell me? That would explain a lot of her behavior.

"Glionolonic hypoblastoma. Stage four," he said.

I couldn't believe what he was saying. I slumped back in my chair overwhelmed with every emotion I could imagine. Mostly guilt. She killed herself because she thought I was having an affair. How alone must she have felt to choose suicide over talking to me about it? The pain of my betrayal was almost more than I could stand. I wished it was me laying in that hospital bed. Helen didn't deserve this.

"What is it, Roger?" Bob asked me.

"Helen was sick," I explained. "She never told me. My guess is she only had four to six months to live anyway."

Jeremy nodded.

My phone erupted in a loud sound. An airmessage.

Misty. *"Where are you?"*

As if things couldn't get any worse.

37

The heavenly portal overlooking Becca's apartment was abuzz with activity. Thousands of demons had gathered to watch the night's events unfold. A sense that something big was about to happen had brought some of the most powerful rulers of principalities to the scene. Some to watch—some to bring their evil power to bear on the situation to ensure victory for the evil one.

Boor was there, and Livid. Even Chaz had flown in to watch, although he was taking a back seat in the preparations. His subject, Helen, was comatose and essentially brain-dead, lying in a hospital of no threat to anyone. That allowed him the freedom to come and observe the battle that was about to ensue.

Ed was sitting in an airmobile outside of Becca's apartment. Becca was inside making dinner in anticipation of what would be their second date in as many nights. The goal of the forces of darkness were to get Becca to have relations with Ed and mix the demonic seed inside of him with her own, bringing the power of the Nohelims back to life through a Christian virgin. A diabolical plan, if it would work.

In typical God-like manner, only two guardian angels were present, Esra and Boza. Esra had watched over Becca all of her life and knew her well. He was confident she wouldn't give in to the lust of the flesh and have relations with the evil seed. Boza was less experienced and there to be mentored by Esra and to assist him in any way he could. His inexperience caused him to be less optimistic.

"We are outnumbered at least a thousand to one," Boza said, while looking anxiously over at the demons who kept giving him evil looks.

"Do not fear," Esra retorted. "Greater is he that is with us than he that is with them. Have faith in God and trust our dear Becca to do the right thing."

"How can she with so much against her?" Boza said cautiously. "Boor is here. Every demon spirit is here working against her. It's just us. She's going against all those armies of demons."

"Though an army encamps around me, my heart will not fear," Esra said emphatically quoting one of the Scriptures. "Though a war breaks out against us, we will keep the trust in God," he continued, quoting another.

Boza started to respond but was interrupted by Esra speaking with more animation in his manner and urgency in his voice.

"Come on, Boza! You know the Scriptures as well as I do. You've seen what God can do with insurmountable odds over the eons. He parted the sea at just the right moment to deliver his people. The walls of the great city fell, and an entire army was defeated. Remember when God defeated an entire enemy army with only three hundred men?"

"Ed is a descendant of Nohelim," Boza countered. "He is powerful. What if he forces himself on her?"

"Remember when Cassie killed a Nohelim giant with nothing but a pebble. Our God is mighty! Don't ever forget it. Ed can do nothing to Becca that God doesn't allow."

"But if Becca gives in voluntarily..."

"God's will be done," Esra said in a loud, commanding, and booming voice. Loud enough for the demons to hear him and respond with rage. They were wailing and gnashing their teeth, growling at Esra and Boza. Slinging fiery darts at them. Flying over their heads, dripping venom and spewing evil words, cursing them.

Esra easily deflected them away and ignored the verbal assault.

"Jesus," Esra said with authority, and the demons cowered and scurried away. Esra could've made them all leave by taking even more authority over them, but it wasn't God's plan. This was Becca's fight. Esra was there to help her. To give her strength. She was the one with the real power to overcome even thousands of rulers, demons, and principalities. It was up to her.

Esra was just toying with them for his own amusement. He was looking forward to the glorious day when they would be out of all of their lives forever and thrown into the lake of fire. God had promised a huge gulf would separate heaven and hell, and no one would have to worry about them anymore.

In the meantime, they were in constant war.

"What do you think is going to happen?" Boza asked.

"There's no way to know," Esra replied. "Becca has free will. God insists on it. We cannot force her to do anything."

"The demons will lie and say anything to get her to sin. She's going to be under an attack unlike few humans have ever encountered. She's already opened the door. Look at how she's dressed."

Becca had on the low-cut blouse. The one she had rejected the night before, choosing modesty over trying to entice Ed with sexual desire and lust. The demons had bombarded her with lust and desire and convinced her to wear the more sensual blouse, without a shirt underneath it. Consequently, Becca had already compromised some, which had opened the door.

Esra just prayed she didn't open it all the way to destruction.

Becca's caller rang, and the heavenlies suddenly grew quiet as everyone crowded in to hear what was going on.

"Are you ready for your date?" Cherry, her sister, said excitedly.

"I'm ready. I cooked him his favorite meal. I hope he likes it."

"You really like him, don't you?"

"I think he may... be the one." She hesitated as she said it.

"Girl!"

"I know, right."

"I've never heard you say something like that before," Cherry said.

"I've never felt this way before. It almost doesn't seem real."

"It's not," Esra interjected, but Becca was already on to her next sentence.

"At first, I was really skeptical about this DNA site. I wasn't even going to go on the date, but you know Mom, she wouldn't take no for an answer."

"Be careful, sis," Cherry said. "Don't move too fast. Make sure he's the one God has for you. Don't kiss him right away."

"I..."

"You kissed him! On the first date!" Cherry said in an excited voice. "Haven't I taught you anything?" Cherry was Becca's older sister by four years. Even though older, Cherry loved her little sister and they were inseparable. Growing up, Cherry taught Becca everything about how to become a young woman, including how to handle boys. Wait until you're engaged to be married before you kiss a boy, were her instructions.

"I know. I shouldn't have," Becca responded meekly. "What does it matter if we're going to be married?"

"Married! What are you talking about?" Cherry said. "You barely know him."

"The DNA says we're a perfect match."

"Just don't sleep with him."

Becca didn't say anything.

"You slept with him!"

"No! I didn't sleep with him. We just kissed. Several times," she added sheepishly, "That's all. I promise."

Growing up, Cherry was emphatic that Becca should wait to have sex until she was married. Becca was thirty-seven and a virgin with every intention of keeping that promise. Although the night before, the thought had occurred to her that if they were going to be married anyway, it didn't really matter.

Livid, Becca's fallen angel, turned to Boor and said proudly, "I put that thought in her."

Boor didn't seem impressed.

"I'm not going to have sex with him," Becca said. "It's just dinner."

"Play it by ear," Livid said to Becca. "Be open to anything. Ed is the one. God brought him to you. God won't mind if you have sex with him."

"Just be careful," Cherry said. "I love you. Call me if you need me."

"Why would I need you?"

"I don't know. I suddenly have a bad feeling about this."

"Don't worry. I'll be fine. Love you."

Becca hung up her caller, confused. What did she mean by "bad feeling?" She suddenly felt it as well. Esra was speaking to Becca in a still small voice.

"He's not the one God has for you." Esra said.

"That's of the devil!" Livid responded.

Satan's trying to trick me, Becca thought to herself. Satan wants me to be afraid.

"Fear not," Livid said in a loud voice erupting in Becca's thoughts.

"They're using Scripture," Boza said to Esra excitedly. "They can't do that. They're trying to make Becca think God is speaking to her. She's resisting what you're telling her. She thinks it's not of God, even though it is."

"She knows the Scripture," Esra responded. "The Scripture says that the body is not for fornication, but for the Lord. If she is deceived, it will be her own fault. She knows what to do. Just believe in her and God. She will do the right thing."

"It's not fair," Boza retorted. "Our hands are tied. They can lie all they want. They can put any thought in her they want. We just have to sit back and let it happen. It's frustrating. We know the truth."

Esra just smiled. "Satan is the author of lies. He disguises himself as children of light when it will get him what he wants. The Holy Spirit will not let it happen without warning her. He will speak to her. He lives inside of her."

Becca got on her knees and prayed.

"Dear God, thank you for Ed. I know he's the man you have for me. I've prayed for so long for a husband. I rebuke any work of the enemy to try and convince me he's not the one."

"Do something," Boza said. "She is believing the lies. She's rebuking us!"

"Have faith, Boza. I still believe in Becca. I've watched her grow in her faith. She will do the right thing."

"Dear God," Becca continued. "You say you will give me the desires of my heart. I desire Ed. I ask you to give him to me. Amen."

"Do you still believe in Becca?" Boza asked.

"I believe in God. That's what I believe in, Boza. I also believe in Becca. She will do the right thing. I know it."

Or at least I hope so. All of Saturn depends on it.

* * *

Ed was in an airmobile, outside Becca's apartment, talking to Eval, the director of choning for the Satites.

"Tonight's the night," Eval said. "You must get the girl to have relations with you."

"Don't worry, sir. You can count on me."

Eval had brought Ed back to the lab that morning and put more downloads in him. Ed recounted the previous night's conversations, and Eval realized there had been a few glitches on their date. Several times, Ed made comments or mistakes that could have cost them the entire mission. Not everything was fixed in him because there wasn't enough time, but Eval was confident Ed would perform better.

"Remember, you have two main goals," Eval said strongly. "To get her to mix her seed with yours and to get inside their lab. I've got to get the chone back."

"What should I do if she won't have relations with me?" Ed asked.

"Then force yourself on her. I don't care. Do what you want to her. Just don't kill her. We need her to let you into the lab. It's better if she will sleep with you voluntarily. So, don't force it right away. Give her time. Seduce her. Turn on the charm. You have plenty of it in your downloads. She's a woman. With needs. She'll give in."

"Can I kill her after I get in the lab?"

"Yes, Ed. You can," Eval said.

Eval laughed to himself. Ed was choned to be a killer on the battlefield. It was his nature. Those downloads hadn't been taken out of him, just overridden by new software. Deep down, Ed knew who he was and was itching to let his real nature out. Eval couldn't wait for that time as well. In fact, all of the Nohelim giants were getting closer to being released on Saturn. He'd found a way to speed up the process. The four thousand would be ready for harvest earlier than first thought. When they were, they would bring devastation to Saturn, and the Christians would be destroyed.

Tonight was an important night to those ends. They could speed up the process that much quicker if the Nohelim seed could be mixed with a Christian virgin. That would bring unspeakable evil to all of the Christians and start an entirely new race of people. For a scientist like Eval, the possibilities were endless.

If Ed does his job.

* * *

Ed got out of the airmobile, walked up the sidewalk and knocked on the front door.

Becca answered with a huge smile. She threw her arms around Ed's neck and gave him a big kiss.

The demons in the heavenlies burst into action with a flurry of activity.

One of the biggest spiritual battles in the history of Saturn was about to begin.

38

After we got Helen settled into her room, I finally had a chance to catch my breath and reflect on the whirlwind events of the day. Bob had gone down to the cafeteria to get us something to eat. I refused to leave Helen's side. I'd have to eventually, but now was too soon. For all practical purposes, she was brain dead. Without hope of recovering, although Bob said more than once that all things were possible with God. At some point, a decision would have to be made to take her off life support. For now, we'd keep believing for that miracle.

My caller buzzed for what seemed like the hundredth time in the last two hours.

Misty.

I scrolled through her messages. Four messages, four missed calls. The airmessages were going back and forth between angry and needy. I didn't listen to the voicemails.

I have dinner ready.

Dinner's getting cold.

I miss you.

Why aren't you here?

You could at least call!

I've been busy! I wanted to shout into the caller. This morning was a nightmare I wanted to forget as soon as possible. It was over between us. It had to be. I should've never started it. If I could go back and change it, I would. I wished I'd never met her. I wanted Helen back.

I wasn't sure if I should respond. Then I decided she wouldn't quit calling and messaging me until I did. I thought about calling her but decided to send a message instead.

I'm sorry. Something bad has happened. She had no idea how bad.

I knew it. I've been worried about you.

I'm at the hospital.

Did you have a wreck?

No. It's Helen. She's on life support. They don't expect her to make it.

Tears streamed down my face as I wrote those last words. Misty didn't respond right away. I buried my face in my hands. I didn't look up until I heard the notification that I had another message.

That's great. Now we can be together.

I stared at the screen, unable to even process how unbelievably cruel and evil that message was.

I angrily typed in the words. *Don't ever contact me again!*

I erased her messages and deleted her voicemails without listening to them and then blocked her from my caller so her number couldn't get through to me. Bob walked in just as I angrily shook my caller in the air as if somehow, I was hurting Misty by doing so.

"Are you okay?" he said.

I just looked at him with tears in my eyes.

"Of course, you're not okay," he said. "That's a dumb question."

"I just had to deal with something from work," I said dismissively.

"Have some food," Bob said, sitting a tray in front of me.

"I'm not hungry."

"You need to eat something. When was the last time you ate anything?"

I didn't remember. I tried to think, but my mind was a jumbled mess. It was when Misty and I had ordered room service at the hotel. About twelve hours ago. I suddenly felt nauseous. Thinking of anything related to her disgusted me.

A knock on the door interrupted my thoughts as I pushed the tray away. I did take a huge swig of the coffee, hoping it would give me some energy.

The door opened and a man in a suit stood in the doorway.

"Hello, Dr. Forrester, my name is Hick Stone. I'm a detective with the police department. Mind if I come in and ask you a few questions about tonight?"

"No. I don't mind," I said. I expected a detective to arrive. When I worked at a hospital, standard procedure was to contact the police department when a suicide victim arrived. They investigated just to be sure no foul play was involved.

"Maybe I should step out of the room," Bob said.

"You're fine," I retorted. "Stay and finish your meal. Detective Stone. This is Bob. He's our pastor."

Bob stood and shook hands with the detective and then offered him his chair.

"I'll just stand," he said. "I'm sorry about your wife," Stone added sincerely. "I hear the prognosis is not good."

"Thank you. No, it's not," I responded. "This has been quite a shock. I'm still trying to process all of it."

"Can you tell me in your own words what happened?"

Stone adjusted his lapel on his coat jacket.

"I came home from work. I found Helen unresponsive upstairs in our bedroom. I checked her vital signs, and they were weak. She was near death." My voice cracked as I said it. I took a deep breath.

Fighting back the tears I said, "I went downstairs to call 999. I went back upstairs and performed chest compressions and mouth to mouth breathing to try and keep her alive until the paramedics came."

"Do you know how your wife got that gash on her head?" he asked.

Helen was lying in the bed just a few feet from us. It seemed strange talking about her as if she wasn't there. A huge bandage covered one side of her head. I assumed he'd been briefed by the doctor before he came in to speak to me.

"I don't know. She was laying on the floor in a pool of blood when I found her."

The images came rushing back into my mind like a flood for the first time jolting my system. *The blood was everywhere.* It was a deep gash. She needed forty-three stitches.

"Do you know why your wife would try to take her own life?"

"She has blastoma. Stage four. That means she only had about four to six months to live. I didn't know about it. She never told me." I got choked up again.

"Take your time," Stone said. "Did you know, Pastor?"

Bob shook his head no and shrugged his shoulders as if to say he had nothing to add.

"For whatever reason," I continued, "she didn't want anyone to know. I guess she didn't think she could handle going through it. I mean... I'm a doctor. She's seen the toll that disease takes on people and their families. I guess she didn't want to put us through it."

"Did she leave a note?"

The note! A jolt of panic flashed through me like a bolt of lightning.

I can't tell him about the note.

"No. She didn't leave a note."

I wasn't sure if my indecision showed on my face. It must have by his next question.

"Do you have a life insurance policy on your wife?"

"I don't. We used to, when we were younger. We are self-insured now. So, we don't need it."

I thought I saw a flash of disappointment go across the detective's face.

Was I a suspect?

The gash on her head. Did he suspect me? My fears were realized when he started probing further with more questions.

"Tell me what you did today," he said.

"Like I said, I was at... work today," I stumbled with my words.

"You were at work all day?" he asked.

The images of the hotel and Misty flooded my mind. I had to lie. *Would Misty say anything? Did the detective already know about her? If he did, would lying make me look guilty? Of murder?*

I couldn't believe the mess I was in. I started fumbling with my hands and caught myself. I didn't want to seem nervous, even though anxiety was shooting through me as fast as a shooting star.

"Yes sir. I was at work all day."

"Anyone else there with you who can verify that?"

"No. There are only two people who work in our office. Just my assistant and me. She was off all day today. Helen was out of town, visiting our kids. Like I said, I came home from work and found her. I don't know what happened to her head, and I wasn't there when she took the pills. It was a suicide attempt, though. I know that for sure."

I was sounding defensive. I knew it. It made me look bad. The detective was making me angry.

"I have one last question for you," he asked in a serious tone.

"Go ahead."

"Have you ever killed anyone?" he asked.

I almost came out of my chair. Bob almost did as well as he bolted straight up and let out a gasp.

The image of Clooney flashed through my mind. Between images of Helen, Misty, and the chone now seared in my memories, I wondered if I would ever have a normal life again.

"Of course not, detective," I said angrily. "I've invested my whole life saving lives. Do you have reason to believe Helen was murdered?"

Stone waved his hand.

"The questions are just routine. I hope you understand. Just doing my job. I have to cover all the bases. Again. I'm very sorry."

He walked to the door and opened it. He turned back around and said, "Do you mind if we go to your house and have a look around?"

"No, I don't mind. Just let me know when so I can be there."

"Is 5:30 tomorrow okay?"

"Of course. Have a good night."

He nodded to Bob and then left.

I slumped back in my chair, trying to settle my nerves and my heart that was beating out of my chest.

Bob looked at me with his lips twisted into a slight frown.

I wondered if he believed me.

* * *

Detective Stone drove back to headquarters. Before he went to his office, he stopped at the desk of James White, his assistant detective. He unhooked a wire off of his lapel that ran down the inside of his suit jacket and into a recorder attached to his belt on the back of his pants. The department had recently invested in a new lie detector machine that could detect deception from a person's voice inflections.

"Run this through Lily and bring the results to me." Lily was the name of the machine. "I'll be in my office."

Twenty minutes later, he had the results.

Dr. Forrester lied three times. First was when he said he was at work all day. The second was when he said there was no note. The third was the most disturbing of all. He lied when he said he had never killed anyone.

He called James White into his office. When James entered, he nodded for him to take a seat across from his desk. He leaned forward with his elbows on his desk and said, "The good doctor lied to me. I want you to find out everything you can about him. What he did today? Where he works? Who he works with? He says he has an assistant. Talk to her. Who does he hang out with? Who are his friends? Does he have a girlfriend on the side? Does he put cream in his coffee?"

White laughed. "I get your point. You want the works on him. I'll get right on it."

"Get back to me as soon as you find something."

White turned and left the room.

"Why would the doctor lie? Why would he kill his wife?" Stone asked himself, right before he answered his own question.

Because he's got a girl on the side. It's always a girl.

39

The demons were almost gleeful about how well things were going in Becca's apartment. At least to the extent demons could be gleeful, considering their total depravity and miserable existence. Not to mention, the fiery eternal fate that awaited them. Esra knew the demons would win many of the battles in the world, but God through Christ would have the final victory. They could be giddy now, a better way to describe it, but they would get theirs someday.

I can't wait.

Even then, this battle for Becca's soul and body was one Esra intended to win. Even though it wasn't looking good, Esra was doing everything in his power to warn and help Becca, but Livid wasn't making it easy. If it continued the way it appeared to be going, drastic measures would be needed. Esra was going to give Becca every opportunity to overcome her flesh, before he tried a supernatural intervention.

Not knowing if she would give in, he had a backup plan if it looked like she was going to. He told Boza the plan beforehand, and Boza was prepared to execute it on his cue, should it come to that. In the meantime, they'd fight the battle with everything they had.

"Livid is outnumbering our thoughts, ten to one," Boza said. "Look. Deception is all over the room."

"I know," Esra replied.

"They will fight against you, Becca, but will not overcome you. Thus, saith the Lord," Esra said to Becca.

Livid countered.

"Didn't God say he'd provide you with a husband someday? Ed is an answer to prayer."

"That's not fair!" Boza said. "The enemy is using the same thoughts we use when we're trying to get someone to follow God's will."

"That's a good lesson for you, young Boza. The evil one will use anyone and anything to destroy a Christian. No lie is off limits. No deception too great. He has nothing restraining him except God and the power God has given us. Even then, Satan had considerable power over Saturn. Man has given him his authority when he fell into sin in the garden. It's just how things were. They had to do the best they could. Fight the enemy with the truth of God's word."

Ed and Becca's conversation turned more intimate.

"How come you've never been married?" Becca asked Ed.

"I've never met anyone worth marrying," he replied. "Actually, I'm embarrassed to say it, but I've never actually been in a serious relationship. I've never even had sex before."

"You're a virgin?" Becca said with surprise in her voice. "So am I."

"I've never met anyone worth marrying, until now that is."

Becca blushed as she took her last bite of food. "That's sweet. I feel the same way."

Not only was Livid at the top of his game, Ed was doing much better than he had the night before. Eval, the director of the chones, had downloaded a program into Ed that was working better than it had yesterday. The major glitches seem to have been corrected. The new program focused on wooing her romantically and seducing her by playing on her emotions, and Ed was functioning very well from the enemy's perspective. Coupled with the lust of the flesh attached to Becca's emotions when she gave in and put on the sexy blouse, she was starting to fall into the chone's deception.

"I want you to be..." Ed said gently.

"What," Becca said expectantly, not sure what he was going to say.

"I want you to be my first."

A flash of desire sped through Becca like a rocket. Livid added the intensity for effect. Becca would never feel enough desire on her own to forsake her commitment to wait for marriage. She was too strong in her faith. Livid had to enhance the feelings so they were magnified in intensity, and then he had to deceive her in some way. The best way was to blind her with what she thought was love but was really lust.

Is this what love feels like? Becca asked herself.

"Ask him if he believes in Jesus," Esra said to Becca. He wasn't going to sit back and let Livid control the situation.

Becca hesitated. She didn't want to offend Ed by asking.

Why? That's the most important thing. Becca was angry at herself for even hesitating. She knew she had already compromised to some extent, but she wasn't going to give up all of her values just for a man.

Livid was panicking. That was one conversation Eval had not downloaded into Ed. Eval had no knowledge of God or how to be saved anyway. He wouldn't have had any idea what to get Ed to say to convince Becca he was a Christian. She'd see right through it. They had hoped the issue wouldn't come up. They downloaded a fall back program just in case. Livid hoped it worked and Becca was fooled. He'd soon know.

"Do you believe in Jesus?" Becca asked.

"Yes," Ed said.

That answer was downloaded in him. The only one. If she probed further, Livid knew they'd be in trouble. So did Esra.

Becca started to drop it. That was all she needed to know. She could never be with someone who wasn't saved.

"Ask him if he's born again," Esra said.

He must be. Obviously, he is.

"Ask anyway." Esra's words were getting through, but Becca was being double-minded. The Bible said that a double-minded person was unstable in all of their ways. Becca was certainly unstable. She

SATURN: THE EDEN EXPERIMENT

was on the verge of making the biggest mistake of her life. One she would pay a huge price for.

Becca decided not to ask. Esra sent Boza away with a sense of urgency. "Go! Hurry. We don't have much time. Execute the plan. Can you do it?"

Boza nodded with a determined look on his face. He flew away rapidly and disappeared in the heavenlies.

"Are you born again?" Becca finally blurted out.

"Good girl," Esra said.

Ed hesitated. He tilted his head to the side, a sign he was confused. Becca became concerned as her eyes narrowed, the discernment starting to cut through the attraction and overcome it.

Why did he hesitate? Becca asked. *Oh my God. He's not a Christian. What am I doing?*

"Don't worry. You can get him saved," Livid said in case the fall back download didn't work.

"Are you?" Ed said with a grin.

"Yes, I am," she said emphatically.

"Well, so am I!" Ed said just as strongly as they both burst out laughing.

Livid breathed a huge sigh of relief. The download had worked. Ed gave the perfect response. When he was confused, he was just supposed to ask her that question and agree with whatever she said to answer it. That wasn't a fool-proof plan, but it had worked this time.

"I'd like to see your work sometime," Ed said, changing the subject.

That wasn't possible. The Eden Experiment was classified. No one could come into the lab. She'd just have to dodge the question. She did so by asking him a question.

"Where do you work?"

That question started a ten-minute conversation as they finished their meal and then got up from the table and went to the couch where they snuggled together. Not before Becca had turned the lights down.

They were quiet for a good minute or two. Then Ed started kissing Becca. Lightly at first. Gently. Almost with hesitation. That made Becca desire it more. She took the lead and became more aggressive physically. Passions were burning inside of her. Intense desire. She was trying to hold them back, but it was like trying to hold back a wild stallion with small reins. Soon, she wouldn't be able to control herself.

His hand started to wander from her waist to her thigh. A bolt of fear jolted Becca back to reality. She stood up from the couch and went to her bathroom, making up some excuse to leave the room.

"What are you doing?" Becca asked herself in the mirror. "You need to stop this now, before you do something you'll regret."

"Did God really say you couldn't have sex with someone who was going to be your husband?" Livid said to Becca.

"Don't be yoked with an unbeliever," Esra said.

"He said he was born again," Becca said.

"That's not what he said," Esra retorted. "He never answered your question."

"I'm so confused," Becca said, rubbing her eyes roughly.

"You're not confused," Esra retorted. "You know what to do."

"Yes. This is what love feels like." Livid interjected. "You are in love with him. He loves you."

A warm feeling came over Becca.

He loves me. I think I'm falling in love with him.

"It's only been two days," Esra said. "It's not real love."

"He wants you," Livid countered. They both knew this was the defining moment. "How long has it been since a man wanted you? Don't you want him?"

"I don't even remember the last time," Becca said, soberly.

"What fellowship does light have with darkness?" Esra said more strongly.

"Everybody does it. God will forgive you," Livid said even stronger.

"Be sober," Esra said. "Be watchful."

Livid was trying to speak over Esra.

"Silent," Esra bellowed in the heavenlies. "In the name of Jesus."

Livid stopped speaking. Esra knew this was his last opportunity with her. He wanted to speak his words unencumbered by Livid interrupting them. That would work for a moment. Becca had freewill. He couldn't make Livid shut-up completely. Becca was the only one who could do that. And Jesus, of course.

"He is your adversary," the Holy Spirit spoke to Becca in a still small voice. "Resist him. Be firm in your faith."

Becca felt a sudden resolve. She took a deep breath.

"I'm going to send him home."

She walked out of the bathroom. Ed wasn't there. She scanned the room as anxiety rushed over her.

Did I say something to offend him?

She heard a noise. In her bedroom. She walked down the hall and into the room. Ed was laying on the bed. He had a flower in his hand. Becca could feel her heart melting. His smile was showing the huge dimples on his cheeks.

He patted the bed next to him.

"Come lie with me."

Becca looked around the room and at the door she had just walked through. Torn. Part of her wanting to flee. The other part was wanting him.

Livid and Esra weren't saying anything. Just watching in anticipation. The choice was Becca's. They had both done all they could. It came down to this moment of temptation. What would she choose?

Why am I so nervous? I'm a grown woman. Thirty-seven-years-old.

"Okay," she said as she jumped on the bed, laughing.

A somber look came over Esra's face as Livid was dancing with glee along with the other demons.

"I hope Boza hurries," Esra said to himself. "Before it's too late."

40

The heart monitor echoed Helen's heartbeat in the room, piercing what would otherwise be an eerie silence. Seventy-two beats a minute. The lung machine that kept her breathing sent a rhythmic sound throughout the room as well, and I found myself inhaling and exhaling almost in unison with it. The doctor had just left. His words still lingering cast a deadly pall over the room.

"There is no brain activity," Dr. Gresham had said. "I have no hope that there will be."

The words had crushed my spirit. Bob was doing everything he could to encourage me, and it was helping to some extent.

"God will work all things together for good, Roger, if you just believe," Bob said. "You have to trust him and believe that God's will be done."

Helen's spirit left her body and was hovering over the room. It continued upward until she saw a great light. A moment, a year, a second, she didn't know, but suddenly she was in the presence of Jesus. His hands were outstretched, and she ran into his arms. Tears of joy streamed down her face.

Everything was calm. Peaceful. Unspeakable beauty all around her. She felt an overwhelming joy.

Jesus took her hand and led her back to the room. The demons in the room and in the heavenlies all fled, including the spirit of death that had been over the room, just waiting to pounce at the right time. They fled at the presence of the Lord and watched from a distance.

"The choice is yours, Helen," Jesus said.

"What choice do you mean, my Lord?"

"You can return to Saturn. Your life doesn't have to be over. Or you can come and be with me. What do you want to do?"

Helen looked down upon the scene. Her lifeless body lay on the bed. Roger sat in the chair next to her, clutching her hand. His eyes were red from obviously crying. Bob had his hand on Roger's shoulders. They were praying for her.

"Your work on Saturn is not done, if you want to go back," Jesus said.

"Will my body be healed?"

"If you will receive it."

"Will my marriage be restored?"

"If you will forgive Roger and be the wife, I've called you to be for him."

Helen thought about what it would be like to return to Saturn. She could see her grandkids grow up. Maybe God did have a greater purpose for her. Then she remembered where they had just come from. When Jesus came to meet her, the Pearly Gates were right behind him. She could see a shining city in the distance. Heaven.

Jesus's hand was in hers. She never wanted to be away from him again.

"I don't want to go back," she said emphatically. "I want to stay with you."

"It is not yet time, but will be shortly," Jesus said. "Return to your body, and I will come for you in just a few days."

* * *

"Did you feel that, Roger?" Bob said.

"Feel what?" I asked.

"I felt the presence of the Lord in the room."

"To be honest, I'm having a hard time feeling anything at the moment. I have a hard time feeling or hearing from God anyway."

"It comes from your heart. That's where you will feel it and hear him speak."

"I don't understand about the heart," I said, standing and stretching. "We talked about that at life group. But I'm still confused. Tell me what the Bible says about the heart."

"It's with the heart man believes," Bob replied. "The Bible says to trust in the Lord with all your heart and lean not on your own understanding. In other words, it's not your own thoughts, but what's in here." Bob tapped two fingers on his chest near where his heart would be. "The Bible says to guard your heart because everything flows through it."

"Call Becca!" Boza shouted to Roger, but he wasn't paying attention. He was too engrossed in his conversation.

"Like I said, I've seen the heart and held it in my hand. I don't see how everything flows from it. I know blood does. Oxygen. Cells. Everything flows through it. But I think you're talking about a spiritual flow, not physical attributes. Am I wrong?"

"You're right. The Bible says that God's attributes are invisible to the human eye. But they can be seen through his creation."

"Which means I should be able to see them with my eyes, right?"

"We can look around Saturn and see God in creation. Look at the rings for instance. How do they stay in perfect alignment around the planet? Have you ever done a hula hoop?"

I laughed. "That's a strange question to follow that sentence."

"Follow me on this," Bob said. "You put a hula hoop around your waist, and it doesn't fall to the ground as long as you keep it up with the force of your hips."

"You obviously have never seen me try to do a hula hoop. I can't keep it up for longer than one or two turns."

We both laughed as tension was leaving the room slightly. I liked talking about spiritual things with Bob. A bond was forming between us.

"That's my point. The rings are kept in perfect alignment by God. If you stop wiggling your hips, the hula hoop will fall down to the ground, because of gravity. If God wasn't holding the universe in place, then everything would fall into chaos."

"I see what you mean. So, you can see God through the order of the universe."

"Roger! Roger! Roger!" Boza shouted as loudly as he could. "Call Becca now."

Call Becca. Why? That's strange.

I'll call her tomorrow. It's late. She's probably sleeping.

"No!" Boza shouted.

Suddenly, God appeared.

Boza bowed down before him. "Thank you. I'm so glad you're here. I can't get through to Roger. Becca's going to have sex with the demon creature. That will be a disaster for Saturn. Esra sent me here to get Roger to call Becca to get her to come to the hospital. He won't listen to me." Boza was talking so fast his sentences were running together.

"Do not fear," God said. "I'm going to do great things through this man."

"Through Bob?"

"No, Roger."

"Do you know about his adultery?"

"Of course."

"And you are still going to use him?"

"He is forgiven through Christ. All of his sins. The sins of the entire world were placed on Christ. And he has repented and turned away from his sin. I chose the weak things of the world to bring shame to the strong. What Satan intended for evil with Roger, I am turning to good."

"Well, you need to hurry. We don't have much time."

God laughed.

"You know what they say on Saturn," God said. "God is never late, but I miss a lot of opportunities to be early."

Boza looked at God with confusion.

"Never mind. We have time."

God lifted Boza up to his feet from his kneeling position.

"Tell him again to call Becca, except this time in a quiet voice. Don't shout. He can hear you. I have given him ears to hear."

Bob and I didn't say anything for a good five minutes. The heart machine kept the steady beat. I just kept staring at it. Beat after beat.

Call Becca, I heard a still small voice say, in my spirit. Not in my mind. My caller was laying on the table next to Helen. I picked it up and looked to see if I had a message from Becca. I wondered if she was in some kind of danger. Nothing. I looked at the clock. The time had flown by as it was about to strike ten.

I laid the caller back down on the table. Becca was probably asleep. It was too late to call her.

Helen's heartbeat seemed louder. Stronger. Perhaps the fact that it was the only sound in the room was magnifying it. I couldn't stand listening to it. On the one hand, her heart was still beating which meant she was alive. On the other hand, it kept reminding me of why she was in that condition. I needed to keep talking. To drown out the sound of her heartbeat.

"We did some experiments on liver samples," I said.

Bob seemed confused.

"Remember. You said that the word for heart in the Bible could be translated as *liver*."

"Oh yeah. I remember," Bob said.

"We made some interesting discoveries in our lab. I don't think the liver is the heart though."

"Me neither," Bob said. "I was just saying that. I try to take the Bible literally whenever I can. I think if it says heart, it means heart."

"Could it mean our mind? Could the spiritual heart be somewhere in our brains?"

"I don't think so, Roger. The Bible talks about our thoughts. It says that we are transformed by the renewing of our minds. But Jesus said that even evil thoughts come from the heart."

"Thoughts are in our brains. How do they come from our hearts? I also remember you saying that life and death is in our tongues. The heart definitely can't be the tongue, can it?"

"I don't think the Bible would use the term *heart* over and over again if it wasn't somehow related to the physical heart. Not the brain. Not our tongues. But the heart. The Bible is so accurate with everything. I can't imagine God didn't use the word *heart* on purpose. Somehow the invisible attributes of God and all the things mentioned in the Bible that flow out of the heart, literally come from man's physical heart. It's just a mystery we don't understand."

"Say that again," Roger said, sitting up in his chair.

"It's just a mystery that we don't understand."

"No. Right before that. What did you say?"

"I said something to the effect that the invisible attributes of God have to flow out of the physical heart in some way since the Bible uses the term over and over again."

I think I had the answer.

I fumbled for my phone.

I dialed Becca's number.

* * *

"I'm going to step in the restroom," Becca said. "I'll be right back. I promise."

Things were getting very passionate on the bed. She didn't leave to stop it; she genuinely needed to use the restroom. When she went back, she was ready to give herself to him. She'd thought about it and now was the time. He was the right guy. Everything was coming together in this one moment.

Her caller rang in the room startling her. She decided to ignore it. Her mom, or Cherry was probably calling to find out how her date went. The caller went silent after four rings.

She laid back down on the bed.

"Where were we?" she said with a loving smile.

The caller rang again.

Becca stood up and crossed the room and picked up the caller from where it was laying on the dresser.

That's how Esra had gotten the idea. When Becca sat her caller down on the dresser, Esra devised a plan to have someone call and interrupt them right before Becca gave in. He had hoped that if she did, it would be in the bedroom.

Roger.

It must be important.

"I need to take this call. It's my boss," she said to Ed right before leaving and walking back into the living room so she would have privacy.

"Roger. Is everything okay?"

"I need to talk to you. I've made an important discovery about our experiments."

Becca's mouth flew open as anger rose inside of her.

"Roger. It's ten o'clock. Can it wait until tomorrow?"

"No. It can't wait."

"I'm in the middle of something."

"I'm sorry. It's important. I'm not at the office, though."

"Where are you?"

"I'm at the hospital."

"Hospital! What's wrong?"

"It's Helen. She's dying. She's on life support."

"Oh Roger! I'm so sorry. You should've said something. Of course, I'll be right there. Which hospital?"

"Mercy."

"Okay."

"Are you coming right now?"

"Yes. I'll leave this minute."

Livid was panicking. Twittering around frantically waving his arms shouting, "What do I do, what do I do?" He hadn't planned for this contingency. He saw Becca on the phone and heard her say she was leaving right away for the hospital. This was not the plan. They were so close. He kept throwing thoughts at Becca, but they were bouncing off.

He watched in horror as she rushed Ed out of the house, gave him a kiss goodbye, and told him she'd call tomorrow.

"Resist her, you fool," he was shouting at Ed. "Take her. You don't need her permission."

Ed seemed confused. Dazed. Not sure what to do. He got in his airmobile and drove away.

Livid saw Becca do the same thing moments later.

He looked Esra's direction.

He was smiling. A wide grin of satisfaction was on his face.

"I'll get you for this," Livid said. "You may have won this one, but it's not over yet."

I'm sure you'll try, Esra thought to himself.

41

"Follow my logic," I said to Bob and Becca. She had arrived a few minutes before and we were sitting in a circle in Helen's room.

"According to Bob, the Bible says that we are transformed by the renewing of our minds. He also quoted the verse that life and death are in the power of the tongue, and everything that has to do with spiritual life is generated from the heart. We are saved when we believe in our hearts. Are you with me so far?"

They nodded. Both were sitting on the edge of their seats. I wasn't tired at all, considering the day I'd had. My adrenaline was pulsing through me either from the excitement of where the conversation was going or the two cups of coffee I drank before Becca arrived.

"Did I say that correctly, Bob?"

"Yes, Roger. We're with you so far."

I stood, unable to contain the excitement.

"The mind, the tongue, and the heart are three very important parts of the body when it comes to spiritual things. Am I right?" I said using my hands for added emphasis. Standing allowed me to be more animated.

They both nodded.

"This is what made me think of it. Helen is connected to a heart machine," I said. They both looked over at her and then to the machine as I said it. "We can hear every beat. We don't hear her heart itself, but we hear an artificial noise that is replicating the beat."

I was choosing my words carefully. I didn't have a lot of time to put this together into a presentation.

"Right," Becca said. "But the heart does generate sound waves when it beats."

"Exactly!" I said pointing my finger at her in acknowledgment.

"What does that mean?" Bob asked.

"Those three parts of the body, the mind, the tongue, and the heart are the three areas of the body that generate either sound waves or electrical currents in our body. The mind sends electric currents to move muscles, instructs the organs to function, and sends other messages like telling the immune system to heal a wound on our skin. The tongue, more specifically the vocal cords, vibrate when we speak, sending sound waves through the body."

"The entire universe was created through the spoken word," Becca added.

"Becca has a degree in biblical studies. Along with being a noted physician and researcher, she's also a Bible scholar," I explained to Bob.

"I wouldn't say I'm a scholar, Roger. But I know a few things about the Bible," Becca said.

"Bob is a powerful man of God," I added. "A strong man of faith who believes in healing and deliverance."

They smiled at each other, still not knowing where I was going with this.

"I read somewhere once that the universe has a heartbeat," I said.

"I read that too," Becca said excitedly. "Scientists have discovered a pulse in space. It's been described as a ripple in space-time. The sound waves travel throughout the universe. They haven't been able to figure out what the sound wave is."

"What if the sound waves are from God telling the universe what to do? Sound waves are like when you throw a rock in a lake. The ripple goes out in every direction. In rings. Like Saturn's rings."

"Like the rings of a tree," Bob said. "You know what I mean? When you chop down a large tree, there are rings. The smallest is in the center. It tells how old the tree is."

"Right," I said. "The spirit has to communicate to the body in some physical way. The Bible says it all comes from man's heart. When the heart beats, it sends sound waves through the body. What if those sound waves are the way in which the Holy Spirit communicates through our heart to every part of our body? Just like sound waves communicate to the universe what God is commanding it to do."

Bob's mouth was wide open as he was considering it.

Becca's eyes were as wide as I had ever seen them as she was contemplating the same thing.

"What if the mind sends electric currents to the heart based on what we believe by faith?" Bob said.

"Yes!" I said in agreement.

He continued. "If we think negative thoughts or have negative emotions, or give in to temptation and lustful thoughts, those are sent to the heart in the form of an electrical current. In the same way, positive thoughts, and a renewed mind send currents to the heart with messages of faith."

"The heart might then respond to the rest of the body by the direction of the Holy Spirit through a heartbeat," I said.

"The tongue also gets involved," Becca said. "The Bible says to call that which is not as if it were. The vocal cords send sound waves through the body, vibrations if you will, when we speak the words of faith. I wonder if those vibrations are different when we speak negative words of unbelief."

"What if the heart responds to those vibrations?" I asked. "If so, then the heart is sending sound waves through the body through a heartbeat based on the messages it has received from the mind and the tongue. The heart is then the center like the Bible says, because it is the center of faith for the body."

"I'm not a medical doctor, obviously," Bob said. "But that's why you should guard your heart. If the brain is sending negative thoughts or emotions to your heart, then evil can come out of your heart and permeate throughout your whole body. If you speak life or death, that message is sent to the heart through the vibrations, and the heart responds accordingly."

"What does all this mean?" Becca said.

I had to be careful. Bob didn't know about the experiments. "Bob you believe in physical healing of the body, right?"

"Absolutely."

"So, do I," Becca said.

"Okay. We all do. What if the sound waves could be replicated?" I asked.

"I don't understand, Roger," Becca said. "Do you mean, can you replicate the sound waves from a heartbeat that comes out of faith?"

"Yes!"

"I don't think that can be done," Becca said. "We don't even know if the sound waves coming from the heart are always the same."

"No, but it's not that hard to find out. We can do it in our lab. We can create experiments. What if we tested Bob's heartbeat and mine and compared them? He is more of a person of faith than I am. What if we compared Bob's heartbeat to an unbeliever's?"

I had Clooney in mind but couldn't say it.

Becca flashed a look of recognition to me and gave me a nod of the head.

"I can order a software for our lab that records sound waves," I said, excitedly. "We can get a base reading. Then Bob can speak positive words of faith. I can speak negative words. We can record the sound waves and see if there is a variation in the heartbeats."

"We can do all kinds of controlled experiments," Becca said excitedly. "Like flashcards. Movies. Music. How does the heart respond with different stimuli? For instance," she paused obviously thinking. "If we showed a subject a picture of a demon, how would the sound waves, coming from the heart change, if at all? We have no way of measuring the brain waves, but we can measure the heartbeat."

"Would you be willing to help us with this experiment?" I asked Bob.

"This is way over my head. But I'm happy to help anyway I can. But what's the end goal?"

Of course, Bob couldn't know about the Satites and Nohelim and our quest to discover a way to kill them unless I brought him into the project, and he signed a confidentiality agreement. But he could be a subject in our lab.

"If I'm right, and that's a big *if*, the applications could be vast," I said.

"Let's say for instance that the Holy Spirit uses the heartbeat to send messages throughout the body," Becca said. "Just for the sake of discussion. Suppose those messages are based on the electrical currents it receives from the brain and the vibrations of the vocal cords. Those are based on how much the person's mind is renewed by the Word of God and also by the words of faith."

"I like it," Bob said.

She paused, and I took that time to walk back around my chair and sit down and lean forward on the edge of the chair, close to her.

"So, a patient is sick," she continued. "Has blastoma or something?"

Becca saw me wince because she stopped talking.

"Helen has blastoma," I explained. "Stage four. We think that might've been why she tried to take her life."

"I'm sorry," Becca said, putting her hand on mine.

"You didn't know. It's okay. Finish your thought."

"What I'm saying is that if we were able to capture the sound waves of the heartbeat at that exact moment, it might be possible to send those sound waves through a sick patient, and the body may respond in supernatural healing."

"Whoa!" Bob said, raising his voice. "That sounds like you're playing God. Healing comes from faith and from hearing the Word of God. I would think the individual has to exercise their own faith, not someone else's to receive healing."

"How is that any different than going to the elders of the church and asking for their prayer for healing?" Becca pushed back. "The Bible says the prayer of faith will restore their health. If they could do it on their own, why do they need the prayers of the elders? This is the same thing."

"Or what if someone is like Helen and is comatose," I said, looking at her, feeling the intense pain of the loss. "She's sick but can't express her faith," I continued, my voice shaking. "You just laid hands on her a few minutes ago and prayed for her healing. We are expressing faith for her."

"I see what you mean," Bob conceded. "I'll still help you with the experiments. I just want to know how it's going to be used."

"Fair enough," I said. "We are way ahead of ourselves. That's okay. As researchers, we try to see the end to make sure the effort is worth it. It won't take long to find out if this theory is correct. Can you come to my lab tomorrow at one?"

Bob took his caller out of his pocket and I saw him pull up a calendar.

"One works for me," he said.

"I think it will take all afternoon."

"I'm good," Bob said.

"So am I," Becca added.

"I'd really like to have one more person in the experiment as a subject."

"I'll do it," Becca said.

"No. I need you to work the machine and take the readings."

"My boyfriend mentioned tonight that he'd like to see where I work. I could ask him."

"Boyfriend?" I said, pushing Becca's shoulder playfully. "I thought you just had a date with him. I didn't know it was that serious."

"Maybe," she said shyly. "We'll see. His name is Ed Tansa."

"Sure. Invite him. The more the merrier," I said.

42

Bob, Ed, and Dr. Jeremy Gresham arrived before one o'clock, and it didn't take long to get everyone hooked up to the sound waves. Jeremy was one of Helen's doctors, and we had worked together at Mercy Hospital. When I explained the research testing and what we were going to do, he agreed to be part of the experiment. This way Becca and I could both run the experiments. A cardinal rule of research was to not insert yourself into the experiments. It helped us maintain objectivity.

We spent the entire morning developing protocols, creating flashcards, and updating the sound wave software that would be used to record each of our heartbeats. It turned out that Gene had the capability of doing everything we needed with only some minor adjustments.

We were all in the conference room which was off of the lab. That kept everyone a good distance from the surgical lab where Mark and Clooney were being kept. Gene had been moved into the room, and each of the three subjects were sitting on the same side of the conference table with their shirts unbuttoned. Becca had shaved a spot on their chests, just below the sternum and had adjusted a node with a recording device directly onto their skin. Three wires, one each, connected the nodes to Gene. Everyone was ready.

I explained the first procedure to them.

"We call this machine, Gene," I said. "The node taped on each of your chests is a recording device. The wire runs to Gene. The first thing we're going to do is get a base reading. Just relax. You don't need to do anything other than just sit there."

"Roger, the artby is getting a good reading and connection from all three of them," Becca said. "We're good to go from my vantage point."

We had tested the software that morning on Clooney and Mark and the results were promising. Their sound wave recordings were different. We didn't know why, although we guessed it was because one was a Christian and one wasn't. But as scientists, we didn't guess. We dealt in facts and probabilities. More evidence was needed. I was confident we'd learn more in just a few minutes.

"The test will run for about a minute," Becca said. "It doesn't take long. Just breathe normally. Are you ready, Roger?"

I nodded yes.

"I'm starting the recordings now."

Becca handled the input into Gene.

I was monitoring the results.

Gene hummed into action. The software had the ability to process up to twelve recordings at once. We only needed it to do three. Gene was a powerful artby. It had more than a hundred thousand core speed capability and could process sixty-million megaflops of data in one second. We would never utilize its full potential but having it in our lab was beyond what we could've ever imagined working with. Even with that speed, Gene was only the twentieth fastest artby on the planet.

The three subjects sat quietly, looking around curiously. Ed seemed nice. Something about his eyes, though, reminded me of the first time I met Clooney, that first day when he was brought to the lab in chains. I dismissed the thought. Becca really seemed to like him, and he had a big grin on his face like he was enjoying the experience and was eager to help. I saw her give him a smile which he returned. I was happy for her.

When the first results came across my screen, they surprised me. Jeremy and Bob's readouts were virtually identical. Ed's was different. There were several unexplainable variations to his test results.

Similar to what I had seen in Clooney's results earlier that morning. I checked his connection to make sure it was on securely and had Becca run the test again with the same result.

It didn't necessarily mean anything. We were just trying to get a baseline starting point, so I decided to move on to the next experiment. Becca began explaining it to them.

"On the second experiment," Becca said, "we're going to have you read a Bible verse out loud. Turn over the first flashcard in front of you. You will each read one at a time. Starting with you Jeremy, then Ed, then Bob."

Becca asked if I was ready, which I was.

"Jeremy, start reading when you're ready," she said.

"I can do all things through Christ who strengthens me," Jeremy said.

Becca hit a key and ended the recording, saving it to the file for analysis. The results popped up on my screen. Definitely a variation from his first test. I had no idea what it meant, just that there was a difference. More confirmation that my theory might be correct.

"Go ahead, Ed."

"For God so loved the world that he gave his only begotten so..., that... whosoever, believe... the." He was stumbling over his words.

I looked at Becca.

She shrugged her shoulders.

"I'm kind of nervous," he said.

"Stop the test," Becca said, with frustration in her voice. "It's okay, Ed. But we have to start over. Just read it again. Ready, read."

"For so loved the world that he gave his only begotten, that whosoever, believeth should not perish but have everlasting life."

He had omitted the word God, son, and him. I wasn't sure if Becca caught that.

Strange.

When the results of Ed's test came up on my screen, every wave was scrambled. Instead of a normal flow, the chart was like a seismograph registering a quake. The lines were close together and going up and down the screen in fast progression.

"Thank you, Ed. Bob, your turn," I heard Becca said, although I was distracted by Ed's results and his omission of the words. *Was it on purpose?* Becca obviously hadn't caught it.

"Heal me, O lord and I shall be healed. Save me and I shall be saved," Bob said as I turned my attention back to the work at hand and put the other out of my mind.

For the next twenty minutes, they each read various cards. For another ten minutes, they looked at flash cards of various objects. Some strange anomalies kept showing up on Ed's tests. Especially if he read or saw anything that had to do with the Bible. I had to be sure it wasn't an equipment malfunction.

I changed the node. Then replaced the wire and plugged it into a different connection. Each time I kept getting the same unusual results. Ed's readouts were clearly different from Jeremy's and Bob's. Theirs were different as well. I attributed it to the possibility that my theory was really correct. Bob was further along in his faith. His printouts were significantly different, depending on what they read or saw on the flash cards.

On a whim, I pulled up Clooney's print out and compared it to Ed's.

That's strange.

They were identical.

Fear rose up inside of me.

I had an idea. A different experiment came to mind. I didn't want anyone to know what I was doing.

I went into the kitchen area and got three glasses and a pitcher of water. Back in the lab, I poured each of the three a drink of water, telling them we were taking a break. I poured a glass for Becca as well.

Then I took the glasses back to a workstation. I extracted Ed's DNA from his glass and put it onto a swab that I inserted into

Gene. The results popped up almost immediately.

I printed them out and took them back to my office to analyze them. I then went back to the lab to get Becca.

Becca and Ed were sitting at the table, holding hands. Bob was on his caller, and Jeremy was looking through the flashcards, clearly bored.

"Becca can I see you in my office for a minute?" I asked.

"You got it." She jumped up from the chair with a bounce in her step.

"Have a seat," I said, after closing the door to my office.

I handed her a printout.

"What am I looking at?"

"What do you think you are looking at?"

She studied the paper.

"Clooney's DNA results."

"Those aren't Clooney's results. They're Ed's."

Becca gasped and then put her hand over her mouth.

"They can't be. There must be some mistake. How do you even have his results?"

"I became suspicious, and I extracted DNA from the glass of water. I ran the sample through Gene, and these are the results."

"That means... Oh my God!"

"Yes."

"Ed's a chone!" Becca slumped back in her chair as the gravity of the situation obviously hit her.

"And to think I almost slept..." She stopped her words in mid sentence.

Her mouth flew open again.

"What?"

"His last name is Tansa. Those letters spell out Satan. I can't believe I didn't see it."

"He's obviously been sent here by the Satites to get close to you. Now he's in our lab."

"I'm so sorry. What are we going to do? I trusted him."

"I've called the First Minister's office. They are sending soldiers over right now. We just have to keep him occupied between now and then. I think we should send Bob and Jeremy home to get them out of harm's way."

"I agree. I still can't believe this. I'm in shock. I can't believe I was so stupid."

"It's not your fault. You didn't know."

"I did know. I just ignored the signs. I thought I was falling in love."

"It happens. The main thing is that we caught it in time. Before he could do anything to hurt any of us."

"We should get out there before he suspects anything," she said.

I stood up from my desk and opened my safe.

"What are you doing?"

I pulled out a gun and checked it to make sure it was loaded.

"Roger!"

"Just in case. Let's pray I don't have to use it."

43

"Wait, Becca," I said. "Don't go out there yet. I have an idea."

We'd just learned that Ed was a Nohelim chone with evil seed in him. He had no doubt been sent to seduce Becca and infiltrate our lab to find Clooney, which we had unknowingly let happen. Ed, Bob, and Jeremy were in the conference room still hooked up to Gene. Every minute we left them alone with Ed put their lives in danger, but we couldn't go in there without a plan.

Ed was a trained killer, just like Clooney. I had already had one physical confrontation with a chone that almost ended in my death, and I didn't want another. I might not be so lucky the next time.

"What's your idea?" she said.

"Ed is hooked up to Gene," I said. "So, we know the signal is flowing through the wire from Ed to Gene recording his heartbeat. Can it be reversed? Can we send a heartbeat from Gene back to Ed, and will it send the soundwaves throughout his body?"

"We can reverse the signal," Becca said. "But I don't know what effect the sound waves will have on his body because it's external, not internal."

"Is there any way to get the signal inside of Ed, without having to open him up like we did Clooney?"

Becca paused, obviously thinking.

"It might work, if he just heard it," Becca finally said.

"What do you mean?"

"The Bible says faith comes by hearing and hearing by the Word of God."

"Ed already heard the Word of God when Bob was speaking it. It had no effect on him."

"That's because he doesn't have the capability of faith. An unbeliever can hear the Word and respond by faith. Ed can't. An unbeliever can also hear the Word and ignore it because they don't have the faith to receive it."

"Then it won't work externally," I said reluctantly, still seeking a solution. "We need to find a weapon to use on the battlefield. There's no way we can cut open every Nohelim."

"I don't think we have to," Becca responded. "We could just play the heartbeat. Ed heard the Word but didn't respond. What if he hears the heartbeat that has already responded to the word by faith? His body won't know the difference."

"I see what you mean," I said with renewed enthusiasm. "We bypass his mind and go straight to the heart." I thought about that for a moment. That was the theory we thought might work from a positive standpoint. We could bypass people's faith, and they might receive healing from a heartbeat that wasn't theirs, if their body didn't know the difference. Would the opposite work? Could evil be defeated by a heartbeat of faith?"

"But how will Ed's heart react?" I said. "It's pure evil."

I saw Becca grimace. It's hard to turn feelings on and off that easily, I realized. She now knew that Ed was evil, but that didn't make her romantic feelings for him instantly go away. She must've been having tremendous regrets. I knew what she was feeling. I had my own regrets. Although for me, any feelings for Misty were long gone. If there ever really were any.

"I have no idea how his heart will respond," Becca recovered and said. "We'll just have to see. But I think it would cause his entire body to malfunction. He's a chone. Ed doesn't have normal brain and body functions. All of his soul, mind, will, and emotions have all been programmed into him. I think if we play Bob's heartbeat, especially when it's related to a verse about coming against the enemy, I think Ed will die."

"I hope you're right. Which of Bob's recordings do we want to use?"

"I'm not sure which would be best."

"Do you remember when Ed was reading a Bible verse, he could not say the name of God or Jesus?"

"I don't remember that," Becca said, looking off in the distance.

"You were busy making sure everything went smoothly with the recordings. But I remember it. He could not say the name of Jesus. Let's play one of Bob's recordings that mentions Jesus several times."

"Why don't we make a new one? One about defeating Satan with the power of Jesus."

"Do you have one in mind?"

"I have a good one," she said after thinking for a few seconds. "The God of peace will crush Satan under your feet. The grace of our Lord Jesus be with you."

"That's perfect. We'll go in there and get Bob to read it. Record Bob's heartbeat as he says it. Then reverse the signal and send it through Ed's node. If that doesn't work, then play it through the speaker and into the room so Ed can hear it. Wait to play it for Ed until we get Bob and Jeremy out of the room. I don't want to put their lives in any more danger."

"Sounds like a plan. I hope this works. You know, it could have the opposite effect," Becca said. "It could turn Ed into a raving lunatic. You may need that gun anyway. Are you prepared to use it?"

"I am. I just hope I don't have to."

* * *

When we got back to the conference room, in typical Bob fashion, he was witnessing to Ed, explaining the things of God to him. Trying to get him saved. He must have discerned that Ed wasn't a Christian and certainly didn't know that Ed was incapable of salvation. I couldn't explain it to him. The program was classified. Ed just sat at his place with a blank stare on his face. Unresponsive. Bob didn't seem to mind. He'd probably seen it all.

You've never seen a Nohelim, I wanted to say to him. Bob would probably be fascinated if he knew who Ed really was.

Becca forced a smile when her eyes caught Ed's. The charade had to continue a little while longer. I saw contempt and disgust on her face when she looked away. I felt bad for her. If we did manage to kill Ed, I wondered how it would affect her to watch him die right before her eyes. Better than seeing him kill us, I reminded myself and would remind her later; although, she probably had already come to the same conclusion.

Becca took charge in a very matter-of fact-manner. We both knew time was of the essence. Ed could turn on us at any moment. Hopefully, he was biding his time, waiting for a better opportunity.

"Jeremy, you can go ahead and go," I said. "We aren't going to need you anymore. I appreciate all your help." I walked over to him and unhooked his node. He let out a yell when I ripped the node patch off his skin.

"Sorry, buddy," I said, allowing myself a slight grin. In my hurry, I removed it a little quicker than I might normally. He would've appreciated it if he knew the real reason. I was relieved when he finally left and was safely out of the room.

"Bob, we need for you to read one more thing," Becca said. She had handwritten the verse on a flashcard and handed it to him. Bob looked it over.

"Give me a second and start reading on my cue," Becca said.

"Look at that verse, Bob. Do you believe it?" I asked.

"I believe every verse in the Bible," Bob retorted. "But yes, I do believe it. With all my heart."

Just the answer I wanted to hear. "Then I want you to say it like you really mean it. Like you were speaking directly to Satan himself. Which you are, in a way."

"Anytime we are speaking the Word of God, the enemy hears it," Bob said. "Let me practice it."

Bob took a deep breath and got a serious look on his face. A similar look to when he was in the pulpit preaching at church.

"The God of peace will crush Satan under your feet. The grace of our Lord Jesus be with you," Bob said with strength and authority.

Ed started to squirm in his chair. I could see him balling his fist and clenching his jaw.

"Say it again," I said.

"The God of peace will crush Satan under your feet. The grace of our Lord Jesus be with you."

Ed squinted his eyes together. His lips were pursed. When Ed opened his eyes, I could see a shift. To evil. They were no longer gentle and loving eyes. His dimples had disappeared. His face had contorted into a frown. His eyes were like Clooney's eyes that day he tried to kill me.

"Again! Louder, with power," I said, imploring Bob. Urging him to apply all his faith, knowing we would need it. I also touched my gun just to reassure myself it was there.

"The God of peace will crush Satan under your feet. The grace of our Lord Jesus be with you." His words echoed through the room. I could feel the power of the Holy Spirit flowing through Bob. Something I had never felt before in my life.

I was emboldened. I said the words. "The God of peace will crush Satan under your feet. The grace of our Lord Jesus be with you." I looked right at Ed when I said it.

Suddenly Ed bolted from his chair and charged toward me. I whirled away from the threat and reached for my gun, but it was too late. He struck me on the shoulder, sending me sprawling onto the floor. The gun skirted out of my pocket and flew to the other side of the room, out of my reach. Becca screamed. Bob hesitated, not sure how to react.

I hope Becca got the recordings.

Before I knew it, Ed was on top of me, pouncing like a cat, straddling me. I had my hands over my face as he pummeled me with punches. I blocked most of them, but some got through, stunning me. For a moment, I saw stars. I had to do something.

I threw a punch his way, but it just glanced off of him. Bob grabbed him from behind and tried to pull him off of me, but Ed swatted him away like a fly. Undeterred, Bob was back on him, this time with more resolve. Enough to where Ed turned his attention to him, and I rolled away, out from under him.

Out of the corner of my eye, I could see Becca typing away on the screen. That told me she had captured the recordings and was trying to send it into Ed. It wouldn't work. I had Ed's wire in my hand. I had ripped it off of him in the struggle. I think Becca saw me holding the wire and then throwing it aside. She went back to furiously typing.

It was two against one, but Ed was completely dominating us. I was on the floor, on my knees, at his feet, from behind, trying to pull his feet out from under him. The only thing it was doing was keeping him from getting a strong enough footing to hit Bob with a debilitating blow.

Everything around me intensified. My senses heightened. I could hear the sounds of Ed and Bob huffing, inhaling and exhaling rapidly, almost panting. Bob was suddenly on the floor, stunned, dazed. I hadn't seen the punch, but I heard the crunching sound. Blood was trickling from Bob's nose. His hand was instinctively at his face, catching the blood, holding his nose.

Ed turned toward me. Hatred filled his eyes with rage.

I started crawling away, backward.

He was spewing saliva and curse words as he took his time to come over me like a lion moving in to finish off his prey.

He pulled me to my feet by my shirt. I tried to run away, but he grabbed my arm and pulled me toward him. I had no strength to get away. He was behind me and wrapped his massive forearm around my neck and began squeezing. My body panicked as the flow of oxygen was suddenly cut off. I flailed my legs. My arms were on his, trying to pull them off of my neck. They were too strong. I was too weak.

He's going to kill us and then rape Becca.

This is how I'm going to die.

Ed laughed maniacally, but the sound was fading as I was slowly drifting into unconsciousness. Bob stood to his feet but staggered and fell back down.

A noise suddenly permeated the room. A heartbeat. Quiet at first. Then the volume increased. The heartbeat was steady and strong. Ed loosened his grip slightly while letting out a slight scream.

The blurred vision went away as blood started flowing and returning to my brain.

Everyone in the room had stopped moving. We were listening. A beautiful sound of life. A heart beating words of faith.

Just as quickly as it had started, the heartbeat stopped. I was now completely free from Ed's grip. I was able to wiggle out from under his arm. I started coughing, trying to catch my full breath. I bent over with my hands on my knee. Ed regained his composure and started toward me again.

The heartbeat started again and stopped him in his tracks.

The gun.

I looked around. When I spotted it, I ran to it and picked it up, cocked it, and turned it on Ed. I didn't fire. What I saw caused me to pause.

Ed's body was contorting like he was having a seizure, even though he was still standing. He shook his head from side to side, violently. His hands were over his ears. He took them off when the heartbeat stopped.

I pointed the gun at him, but he barely acknowledged it. He looked confused. The heartbeat started again. Apparently, Becca had recorded all of the times Bob had said the verse and was playing them in rapid succession. She had turned up the volume again. It was almost deafening.

Ed put his hands to his ears again as his body re-contorted. I ran for him and pulled one of his hands off of his ears with my free hand. He wasn't as strong. I easily held his hand away from him.

It played again. This time the heartbeat was even stronger. It must've been the last time, when Bob was talking the loudest and the strongest and with the most faith. I suddenly realized it was probably my recording. I felt Ed's body completely relax. His eyes rolled to the back of his head. He let out a huge breath. Then collapsed in a heap on the floor.

I checked his pulse. Nothing. He had stopped breathing.

Did my recording cause his death? Did I have that much faith? I certainly felt like I did in that moment. I looked at Becca, then at Bob.

"He's dead," I said. "Ed's dead." I saw Bob slump back to the floor in exhaustion and relief.

Becca buried her head in her hands.

44

The soldiers from the First Minister's office arrived ten minutes later. Ed's body was already in a black body bag. I unhooked Clooney from the machines and had them take his dead body away as well. They would go to another lab for autopsies and further research.

Bob was sitting at the conference table, staring at a confidentiality agreement.

"I need to explain what happened," I said. "But you have to sign that first."

"Why?" he asked skeptically. "What's going on? Why didn't we call the police? I don't want to be a part of a cover up. It was self-defense."

"I know," I said. "It doesn't make any sense, but it will after I explain everything to you."

There wasn't much legal jeopardy for him at this point. We had made the discovery we needed. I was convinced we found a way to kill the chones in the battlefield. I had Bob's recordings, and we could use those, but I had another idea that I needed Bob for. I really hoped he signed it.

"I had a lot of questions at first too," Becca said. "Is what we're doing really a good thing? I wouldn't be doing it if it wasn't. I can assure you of that."

Bob's eye was starting to blacken some. He had a broken nose. I had reset it, and he had an ice pack against it while he was reading through the agreement.

"How will this be good for Saturn? I don't understand," Bob said.

I couldn't tell him about Ed or Clooney without him signing the agreement, but I could tell him about Mark. Not everything, but some things. At least what I had in mind.

I looked at Becca and she smiled back, reassuringly.

After a deep breath, I said, "We have another person on life-support in the back. In our surgical lab. He's dying of blastoma. We are keeping him alive to do our research. I think a heartbeat could heal his disease. If it does, we could bring healing to thousands of people on Saturn. Think of everyone we can help."

I saw Bob's eyes brighten.

"How will a heartbeat heal him?"

"The same way the heartbeat killed Ed. Except that Mark is a Christian." I realized that I shouldn't have said his name. *Oh well.* That would make it more personal for Bob. Maybe make it more likely he would help us.

"Mark already has the Holy Spirit living in him," I explained. "For whatever reason, his faith is not strong enough to overcome the disease. So, his own heartbeat, the electric currents from his brain to his heart, and the vibrations from his vocal cords, are not filled with enough of the word and enough faith to activate the healing from his heart. If it were, his heart would send sound waves through its beats that would bring healing to him."

"Where do I come in?"

"You do have that kind of faith," Becca said. "Like the apostles. They laid hands on the sick and they recovered. They could bring healing just from laying hands on someone. You remember the man who was healed from just the apostles' shadow.

"If Mark can hear the heartbeat of faith, and the sound waves travel through his body, God will heal him of the blastoma," I added. "We can take him off of life-support, and he can live a normal and healthy life."

"Why do I have to sign this?" Bob asked.

"These experiments are not sanctioned by the government. But the First Minister himself is the one who authorized it."

"I met him once. Heard him speak at a Bible conference. He seems to be a real man of faith." Bob sat down the ice pack, picked up the pen, and tapped it twice on the paper. Then signed it.

"There, it's done," I said reaching out my hand which he reluctantly shook.

"So, tell me about Ed," he said. "Who is he?"

"Ed was a Nohelim chone," I said.

I thought I was going to have to reach across the table and steady Bob as he almost fell out of his chair.

* * *

We were back in the lab, standing around Mark's bed. Bob had already laid hands on Mark and prayed for him, but nothing happened. I could see Bob's compassion for the sick coming across his face and manner as he was obviously moved by Mark's condition. I didn't tell him everything, just what he needed to know for what we were doing.

Bob recorded a verse, "I will restore you to health, and heal your wounds, declares the Lord."

We had moved Gene back into the lab. Becca captured the recording and had the heartbeat ready to play in Mark's ear.

"Is everyone ready," she said.

"We're ready," I replied.

Bob nodded.

The heartbeat started. Steady. The sound of a beating heart had become like music to my ears. My spirit was strengthened every time I heard these heartbeats. I had no idea if it would work on Mark, but I was optimistic and filled with faith.

I was a different person. I could tell it. I would never go back to the man I was. My main regret was that I found out too late to save

Helen. Maybe God could use it for my good. My life was now in his hands to use in whatever way he wanted.

The recording stopped, and there was a silence in the room. We were all leaning forward, our eyes wide in anticipation. I held my breath. The others might have been as well, because I didn't hear a sound coming from either of them.

"Play it again, Becca," I said quietly.

The heartbeat began, this time a little louder as Becca turned up the volume.

I thought I saw Mark's eyes twitch, but I think it was my imagination. Maybe even my mind trying to will him to be healed.

After several attempts, we gave up. A solemn mood came over us. As if Mark had died all over again.

"What if the words aren't exactly right?" I asked.

"God knows the desires of our hearts," Bob said. "I don't think we have to say everything perfectly in order for someone to be healed."

"What did God say when he created the world?" I asked, showing my ignorance of the Bible. Something I was committed to change in the coming months.

"Let's read it," Becca said.

"I have the Bible on my caller," Bob said.

He began reading the account of creation.

"God began everything with the words 'Let there be.' I said. "The very first verse says, 'Let there be light, and it was so.'"

"I see what you're saying," Becca said. "What if we made recordings based on the same words?"

"Let there be healing of blastoma," Bob said.

"Yes!" I was excited. My spirit jumped when he said those words.

"Let me hook you up," Becca said.

"Did you hear what you said?" I said to Becca.

"What?"

"Let me hook you up," I repeated her words. "Even our everyday speech starts with the word *let*, many times. Let's go to dinner. Let's spend the night home watching a movie. Let's go to church."

"Let God arise, and his enemies be scattered," Bob added. "Let the peace of God rule in your hearts."

"Let not your heart be troubled," Becca added.

"There are several verses that connect *let* and the heart," I said. "I think we are onto something."

Bob made several recordings so she didn't have to start and stop them, and they could continuously run in Mark's ear.

"Everyone be quiet," Becca said. "I'm starting the recordings now."

The heartbeat sounded different to me. Again, it might have been my imagination, but I felt power in each beat. When Mark didn't awaken, the disappointment almost overwhelmed me. I almost expected that he would.

Everyone else seemed extremely disappointed as well.

"Let not your heart be troubled," Bob reminded us. "We need to keep the faith. Jesus raised a man from the dead. So did the apostles. They didn't even need a recording of a heartbeat to do so. Let's just keep praying."

"Becca, can I speak to you for a moment alone. Bob stay here and keep praying."

We walked to the other side of the lab so Bob couldn't hear what we were saying.

"Bob's frontal lobe is completely destroyed," I said. "By the poison. God can heal that. We all know that. But I don't think he can hear the words or the heartbeat because of the damage to his frontal lobe."

"That makes sense. That's probably why it's not working."

"What if we stopped his heart and then played the recording internally? The soundwaves from the heartbeat would go through his entire body."

"If we stop his heart, we might not be able to get it restarted."

"What does it matter? We should probably take him off life-support anyway. His life is over unless God heals him."

"It's worth a try," she said.

We walked back over to where Bob was still praying over Mark.

"We are going to try something different," I explained to Bob. "We're going to stop Mark's heart. He may die. He will die, actually. But we are going to play the heartbeat inside of him and see if it brings healing. You don't have to watch if you don't want to."

"I want to," Bob said. "We're in this together. I want to see God do a miracle. I'm believing for a miracle."

"Okay. Becca turn off Mark's heart machine."

She turned the switch to off, and Mark's heart stopped beating immediately.

An eerie silence filled the room as we could no longer hear his heartbeat.

* * *

Mark's spirit left his body. He saw a bright light, and immediately he was in the presence of Jesus. He bowed down before him and began praising the Lord.

All around him was peace. Bright shining lights reflected off the gold streets and the large mansions that lined the streets. People were singing and dancing and rejoicing everywhere. The colors were fantastic. Like the Saturn rings, only more vibrant. Mark had never felt more alive.

"The choice is yours, Mark," Jesus said.

"What do you mean?" Mark replied.

"You can return to earth. Your life doesn't have to be over. Or you can come and be with me now. What do you want to do?"

Jesus took Mark's hand and led him back to the portal overlooking the laboratory. Mark could see his lifeless body on the table. Dr. Forrester was standing over him with deep concern on his face. A woman was placing some kind of device inside of him. Another man was next to his bed and appeared to be praying. His head was bowed, and his hands clasped.

"Your work on Saturn is not done, if you want to go back," Jesus said.

"Will my body be healed?"

"I have made provision for your healing," Jesus said.

"I want to go back, either way," Mark said. "You said my work on Saturn is not done. If you need me on Saturn, I'll return. I'll be with you for an eternity. At the right time."

"Let it be done."

Mark's spirit immediately returned to his body.

Becca placed the amplifier inside Mark's body near his heart. She held it in place with one hand and turned on the recording with the other.

The sound of the heartbeat started immediately, although more muffled for us in that it was inside of his body.

Becca jerked her hand back.

"What happened?" I asked.

"I felt a vibration," she said.

A heart beat! Mark's heart was beating!

His eyes fluttered. He coughed.

"Turn off the breathing machine," I yelled to Becca. "He's breathing on his own."

His eyes opened completely, and he started to sit up. I held him back down.

"Don't try to sit up, Mark. Your chest is open."

"It's a miracle!" Bob said with his hands raised high in the air.

I had to hurry.

"Becca get everything we need for surgery. I've got to close him up."

Becca sprang into action.

Bob moved away from the table.

"Mark. Everything's going to be okay. I'm going to take care of you. You're alive, buddy. God has healed you."

I gave Mark a mild sedative to put him to sleep. I scrubbed my hands for surgery and stood over him ready to close his chest.

Just as I was about to begin, Becca said, "Let's do a biopsy on his liver. Since we have him opened up."

"That's a good idea. Go get a tube."

I removed a small scraping from the outer edge of Mark's liver. From looking at it, his liver looked perfectly normal. No sign of blastoma at all.

Becca took the sample and put it on to a swab and placed it in Gene.

Becca let out a scream.

"What?" I said.

"The test results are already back."

"Are you going to tell me?" I said with urgency even though I already knew.

"The blastoma is completely gone from Mark's liver!"

"I knew it! Praise God," I said with exuberance. "Go tell Bob the good news. Tell him Mark is completely healed."

45

Mark had wanted to surprise his family, so I didn't tell them why I wanted them to come to my office. It probably wasn't a good idea, since his wife fainted when she saw him and almost hit her head when she fell to the ground.

And his youngest daughter was terrified and started yelling, "It's a ghost! It's a ghost!" It took several minutes before she would even let Mark near her. She might have some nightmares over it. After the hysteria died down, they had a tearful and very satisfying re-union. I was glad how it all turned out.

"Do I get to keep the rings?" Mark asked. His family had been paid a million rings for his participation in the project.

I laughed and told him he could. That he earned every one of those rings and then some.

Mark left my office in perfect condition. Completely, one hundred percent, blastoma free. Better than when he arrived, except for the huge scar on his chest that ran from above his sternum to just above his belly button. Aside from struggling to walk from having lain in a bed immobile for several weeks, I knew he'd be fine in no time.

Mark said that when he died, he went to heaven and saw Jesus. He described him and heaven in detail. When he described seeing us standing near his bed, almost in detail, I became a believer. Who was I to doubt his story? Miracles had suddenly become a big part of my life in a big way.

"You should write a book," I told him.

I wanted to see another miracle that night. We were taking the recordings over to the hospital to see if they would work on Helen. I didn't know why they wouldn't. It would take some time to get Gene ready for travel, loaded up, and over to the hospital. So, I decided to go home and take a shower and get cleaned up before I met Bob and Becca at the hospital. Becca said she'd take care of getting Gene to the hospital and would have it set up by the time I got there. I called the hospital and asked them to give us an operating room to work out of and to move Helen there. They asked some questions but mostly they were accommodating.

On the way home, the caller in my airmobile rang. *Unknown caller*, the read out said.

"This is Roger," I answered.

"Dr. Forester, this is detective Hick Stone. From the Westminster Police Department."

"Yes, detective," I said, slapping myself on the forehead. I had forgotten he wanted to meet me at my home that afternoon at five-thirty. I didn't need that right now. I wondered if there was any way to get out of it.

"I just wanted to confirm that we are meeting at five-thirty," he said.

I might as well get it over with.

"Yes, sir. I'm on my way home now. I'll see you then." I hung up just as I pulled into our garage.

I ran up the stairs, stopping at the door to our bedroom before going in. This was the first time I'd been back home since I left with Helen to go to the hospital. I prepared myself for the shock of seeing the blood on the floor by our bed. I opened the door and flipped on the light. The blood was gone. There wasn't even a stain. I blinked twice, just to make sure what I was seeing was correct.

The maid.

I'd forgotten today was her day to clean the house. I imagined she must've been shocked to see the blood on the floor. She probably tried to call Helen's caller and didn't get an answer. I don't know if she even knew my number. At any rate, she cleaned it thoroughly. The smell of bleach still lingered in the air.

The thought suddenly hit me, *What will Detective Stone think?*

Did that make me look like I was trying to hide something. It wasn't my fault. I didn't tell the maid to clean up the stain. But would he believe it?

No time to worry about it. *What's done is done.* I jumped in the shower and let the hot water ease the tension in my head, neck, and shoulders. I scrubbed the dried blood off of my body and from under my fingernails. When I looked in the mirror, a bruise had formed on my neck from where Ed had wrapped his massive forearm around it and tried to squeeze the life out of me. There were scratches on the side of my face as well. I wasn't sure how they got there. They had to be from the struggle.

Would Stone notice them?

Of course, he would. They were right in plain view. I couldn't think of a good excuse for why they were there.

I dressed quickly, just in time, as the doorbell rang as I finished putting on my shoes in time to rush down and open the door.

The person standing at the door was not Detective Stone.

Misty.

The thought of seeing Misty standing there sent waves of rage and shock through me. Not only from my intense dislike for her, but also the timing. The detective could arrive at any minute.

"What are you doing here?" I said roughly as she walked past me and into my house, uninvited. "You can't come in here," I said, but she ignored me and was already well into the living room.

"I had to come. You won't return my calls," she said sharply as I closed the door.

"I blocked your number," I said rudely.

"Why?"

"You know why. What you said about my wife was cruel and totally insensitive. And wrong. I never said I wanted to be with you. It was a one-time thing. I wish it never happened. But it's over now."

"Do you think I'm some kind of trash that you can just use and throw away whenever you want?"

I wanted to answer yes. But as much as I couldn't stand the sight of her, I didn't want to be as cruel as she'd been. I was still by the door with one hand on the knob. Mostly to keep my distance from her and also to let her know she wasn't staying. She needed to leave and right away. The sooner the better.

"Look. It never should've happened," I said in a nicer tone. "It's my fault. Blame me if you want. But it can never happen again."

"I went to the hospital," Misty said.

"What?" I was so mad I wanted to hit something. "You had no right to go down there."

"I saw your wife. The nurse in her room said she wasn't going to make it. I'm sorry about that. I really am. But I want to be with you." Misty walked my direction and tried to put her arms around me. I pushed her off, roughly.

"Don't be mad," she said. "You just lost your wife. I get that. But I know you feel the same way about me."

"You stay away from my wife! I don't feel that way about you. I never did. It was just sex. That's all. It didn't mean anything." I pushed her away from me as I said it. She folded her arms and turned her back to me. I grabbed her arm roughly and jerked her around, so she was facing me. "Don't ever come near my wife, my family, or me ever again. Do you understand?" I was shouting at the top of my lungs.

Suddenly, the doorbell rang again. I put my hands to my head in disbelief.

"Just go!" I said in a whisper. "Go out the back door." I took her by the arm and led her to the back door with some resistance. "You can go around to the front. But leave now. Before someone sees you."

"Call me," was the last thing I heard her say as she scurried onto the back deck and into the back yard.

I tried to calm myself as I walked back to the front door. I took a huge breath and opened the door, wanting to get the detective in the house quickly so he wouldn't see Misty come around from the back.

"Is everything okay?" he said. "I heard shouting."

"Probably just the airscreen." We both looked at the screen in the center of the room which was dark, and I realized how dumb an answer that was considering the airscreen wasn't even on.

"It sounded like a woman's voice."

I shrugged my shoulders. "Come on in. I'm really pressed for time. I have to get to the hospital."

"Why don't we start with you showing me where you found your wife's body?" Detective Stone was looking around the house, his eyes darting back and forth, as we walked through the main room, past the kitchen, and to the stairs. When we got to our bedroom, I pointed to a spot next to our bed on the door side of the room.

"I thought you said, she was lying in a pool of blood."

"She was. Helen was on her side, with her arm above her head. Blood was coming from the gash on her forehead."

"How did she get the gash on her head?"

"I think she hit her head on the end table." I pointed to the sharp edges.

"How come there is no blood on the carpet? And none on the table?"

"The maid came today," I said. "She must've cleaned it all up."

"Do I smell bleach?" He lifted his nose in the air and sniffed loudly, twice.

"That's probably what the maid used to get the stain out of the carpet."

"Why were you in such a hurry to get the stain out?"

264

"I wasn't. I didn't even know the maid was coming today. I haven't been home since the incident."

"Where were you staying?"

"I stayed at the hospital with Helen. Then I went to work today."

The detective was at the nightstand end table inspecting the broken lamp.

"How did this lamp get broken?"

I shrugged my shoulders again.

"I don't want to speculate about things I don't know," I said. The detective was clearly suspicious. I had to admit that it looked bad.

"Where did you get those scratches on your face and the bruises on your neck?"

"I don't know." Each question was raising the level of panic in me. I couldn't tell him what had transpired at my office. I was under total secrecy. Even as bad as it looked, I couldn't say anything in my defense. Then I thought of an argument.

"You saw me last night at the hospital," I rebutted. "I didn't have them then, so I obviously didn't get them from Helen if that's why you're asking."

"The room was dark. I couldn't really see your face. Anyway. You're probably right." The detective talked in a slow, monotonous voice. A steady drawl. I could see why he was a good interrogator. He could easily get someone to let down their guard with his friendly, hick, manner. That's probably where he got his name, Hick Stone. I might've asked him under different circumstances.

"Are we done here?" I asked.

I started walking back out the door and he followed me, so I kept going down the steps to the front door where I opened it and glanced out front to make sure Misty was gone.

"One final question," Stone said. "I don't know if I asked it yesterday or not."

"Go ahead," I said with a sigh.

"Have you ever killed anyone?"

"Not today," I said laughing. He didn't crack a smile. "I'm joking. You did ask me that question last night."

"Oh. I must've forgotten. Anyway. Have a good night."

I closed the door behind him. I wanted to slam it. I thought I did okay, considering the circumstances. I had logical explanations for everything. Misty had gotten out of there without the detective seeing her, which was the main thing. Now I could focus my energies on helping Helen.

I just pray that the heartbeat works.

If it did, Helen could explain everything to the detective and tell him that I didn't try to kill her. I'd have to confess my affair to her. I had already decided I would. Not really an affair, I rationalized. Just a momentary lapse in judgment. One-time thing. She would forgive me.

I hope to God she gets the chance.

* * *

Detective Stone got in his airmobile and drove around the block where his assistant was parked. In his backseat was a woman. Stone rolled down his window.

"Who's the woman?"

"I saw her sneaking around from the back of Forrester's house. I pulled her over and was holding her. I figured you'd want to talk to her."

"Good job. Take her back to headquarters and put her in a holding room. I want to question her." He took the lie detector device off of his lapel. "Take this in as well and run the results and bring them to me. I'm going to grab a bite to eat and then I'll be right there."

An hour later, Stone was sitting in his office. He hadn't questioned the woman yet. He wanted to let her sit in that interrogation room for a while. Let the anxiety build and let her squirm from not knowing what was going to happen. Also, give her time to try and get the story straight in her mind. The detective knew that the more time passed for someone who intended to lie, the more intricate their lies became and the greater the opportunity for inconsistencies.

His assistant walked in the door with a piece of paper in his hand, interrupting his thoughts about what questions he would ask the woman. "I have the results," he said. "The doctor lied about three things."

"What were they?" Stone said.

"He lied about the shouting coming from the airscreen."

"I already knew that. I heard a woman's voice. Very clearly. They were having a pretty heated argument. I'm sure it's the lady in the holding room."

"He lied about not knowing how he got the scratches and bruises on his face."

"That was obvious as well. Who doesn't know how they got cut up that badly?"

"You're not going to believe the next one."

"What?"

"He lied when he said he hasn't killed anyone today."

46

"What is dark matter?" Bob asked Becca and me.

Becca had just said to me that Gene had the ability to run a dark matter test on cells. She was excited to explore that further.

"There exists a force of attraction between masses in the universe," Becca explained to Bob.

"You mean gravity?" Bob asked.

"Sort of. You might say yes. Like gravity is a better way to say it. Gravity does hold mass in place. But scientists have discovered that the universe is expanding faster than the strength of gravity."

"What does that mean?" Bob asked, looking more confused.

"The mass of the universe still stays in place," I answered. "So, the theory is that dark matter is a power stronger than gravity that holds everything in place. It's estimated that ninety-six percent of the entire universe is made up of dark matter."

"That's obviously God," Bob said.

"Maybe not God, but something he created. Some people call it the God particle, although many scientists don't acknowledge the higher power, so they try to attribute the power to a theory that can be explained without faith in God," Becca said.

"The Bible mentions dark matter," Bob said, while taking his caller out of his pocket. Becca sat up further in her seat. I was standing but reacted almost as strongly. Helen was on the table in the operating room of the hospital, ready for us to begin trying to bring her back to life. I was anxious to get started, but I also wanted to hear this.

"Here it is, Roger," Bob said. "By faith we understand that the worlds were framed by the Word of God, so that the things which are seen were not made of things which are visible."

"Wow!" Becca said. "Dark matter is the thing not visible that made the things that are and holds them in place,"

"Why don't they call it light matter?" Bob asked emphatically. "The Bible says that God is light, and in him is no darkness at all. Leave it to secularists to call God the opposite of what he is.

I chuckled as did Becca. He had a good point.

"You are so right," I said. "From now on we will call it light matter."

"What's interesting, Roger," Becca said, "is that when I compared Mark's cells with Clooney's, Mark's had a lighter tint to them. Clooney's cells were darker."

"That is interesting," I said, although my mind was wanting to focus on Helen. We could have this conversation later.

Bob interrupted that thought. "The next verse after the one I just read says that God upholds all things by the Word of His power. That word *upholds* could mean "holds *together*." Bob paused for a minute and then his eyes suddenly widened. "I just thought of something. Oh! This is huge."

"What are you thinking, Bob?" Becca asked, matching his excitement.

"In creation, the very first thing God created was light. On the first day. Remember, he said, 'Let there be light.'"

We both nodded in agreement.

"Go on," I said.

"Roger, God didn't create the sun until the fourth day!" Bob exclaimed.

"How could there be light without the sun?" I asked.

"What God created on the first day was light matter?" Becca said. "It makes perfect sense. Before God could create anything else, he made light matter to hold everything he would create over the next five days in place."

"And this light matter isn't visible to the naked eye," Bob added.

"But you can see the effects of it." I said. "Across the entire universe. You can even see it in the cells as Becca said."

Becca's eyes lit up and her eyes widened more than Bob's had. "Normal cells stay where they belong in the body. As if a higher power was... is," she corrected herself, "holding them in place. Lung cells stay in the lungs. Liver cells stay in the liver. How do they know to stay in the right place?"

"Light matter," I said. Bob said the same thing in unison with me.

"Yes. But blastoma cells don't do that," Becca explained. "They move around the body, indiscriminately. That's why people die of blastoma. The bad cells travel to other places and other organs and multiply, and a person gets overrun by the unhealthy cells. Why do they not obey the light matter?"

Becca paused and looked up with her hand on her chin like she was deep in thought.

"You look like you're about to say something else," I said.

"Think about this, Roger. The blastoma cells are odd shapes, and they're darker than normal cells. The darkness is because they have excess DNA. Remember how Clooney had twenty-three DNA markers and a normal human only has seventeen?"

I nodded, knowing where she was headed with it.

"The excess DNA in blastoma cells might very well be from something evil. Maybe Satan himself. That's how he brings sickness on people. Creating abnormal DNA like he did with the Nohelim. That's why the cells disobey the Word of God in the light matter telling them what to do."

"Fascinating," Bob said. "I have no idea what you are talking about, but it sure sounds interesting."

"I think you do know what we're talking about," I said to him. "Probably more than we do. This is a spiritual concept we are trying to explain in human terms. Blastoma cells have an evil presence in them and rebel against light matter which is the power of the Word of God that controls the universe and holds everything together, including something as small as the cells in our bodies. The same light matter that holds planets together keeps our body functioning in perfect harmony. Light matter is like glue that holds everything together. Blastoma cells don't obey the light matter and leave sickness and disease in their wake."

"That's why our battle is not against flesh and blood," Bob said. "It's not against blastoma. It's against the evil that is working within them. It's like the blastoma cells are actually rebelling against the light matter that is trying to control it. Just like Satan rebels against God and was thrown out of heaven."

"Exactly!" I said. "It's definitely something worth pursuing. Becca draw blood from Helen and take some cells from her liver so we can compare them."

"One step ahead of you, Roger, Becca responded. "I've already entered them into Gene. I saved the results, but I haven't studied them." She hesitated for a moment and then said, "Are you ready to bring Helen back to life?"

The words jolted me like someone had shoved me from behind, even though I still had my footing. I suddenly felt extremely weak at my knees.

What if it didn't work? Would God let Helen die as punishment for me having an affair?

I'm afraid.

"Say it out loud," Roki said to Roger. Roki was the fallen angel assigned to him. The one who had placed the spirit of lust on him that enticed him to have sex with Misty. Now, Roki was bombarding Roger with doubts. A spirit of fear was ready to come on him if he spoke the words aloud.

"I'm afraid," I said aloud. "What if it doesn't work? If we turn Helen's heart machine off, she will die if the recordings don't work."

Roki jumped into action and sent the spirit of fear on Roger. He had opened the door with his words.

"Don't be afraid," Bob said. "They worked for Mark. Why wouldn't they work on Helen?"

I thought of the hotel room. I could picture myself with Misty. An overwhelming guilt flooded my soul to the point where tears filled my eyes. I remembered how horribly I treated Helen over the last few years. Would she forgive me?

"I already lost Helen once, I feel like I'm about to lose her again," I blurted out.

Becca walked over and put her arm around me and squeezed me tightly to her side.

"I understand you're scared," she said. "We're here for you. No matter what."

Bob walked over and joined the hug putting one of his arms around Becca and one around me and pulled us all together in a hug.

"Lord, we just pray for your will to be done today," Bob prayed. "On Saturn as it is in heaven."

I felt better, although the doubts were still there. I had a dire feeling that this wasn't going to work.

"Everything is ready," Becca said as we broke the embrace and walked over and stood next to Helen. She seemed so peaceful. Her lips formed a slight smile. Probably only discernible to me because I knew her so well. I had memorized every part of her face. Though I had doubts and fear, I felt an overwhelming love for her. I just wished she was alive so I could express it to her. I desperately wanted that chance.

An ear plug was placed in Helen's ear so she could hear the heartbeat. We could hear it as well. Faintly. I saw Helen's body lurch slightly when the heartbeat started. Her eyes fluttered but didn't open.

"Keep playing it," I said.

Becca started the recording again. For twenty minutes, we played it over and over again.

Bob laid his hands on Helen. He kept praying, fervently for her healing.

I went back and forth between faith and fear. I would look at Helen, thinking she was going to wake up and then when she didn't, fear overwhelmed me. And guilt. Like it was my fault she wasn't healed.

"Let's open her up," I said with urgency.

"Are you sure you want to do this?" Bob said. "Maybe it's time to let her go."

"I can't. The recordings didn't work on Mark until we did it internally. Helen is brain dead. Maybe she can't hear the heartbeat, unless it's inside her."

I was already prepped and scrubbed for surgery. So was Becca. She would assist me.

"You may want to leave the room," I said to Bob.

"I'll stay. If it's all right with you. I want to be with you for whatever happens."

I gave Helen a light sedative just in case she'd feel any pain. I then made an incision exposing her heart and the vital organs of her chest.

"What are you doing?" Becca asked.

"I'm pulling some cells from Helen's liver," I responded.

I extracted the cells and then gave the swab to Becca.

"Run these through Gene and see if the blastoma is gone."

Two minutes later, the tests popped up on the screen.

"They're gone!" Becca said. "The heartbeat healed her blastoma."

"Quick! Get the recording inside of her." My body was filled with excitement and dread at the same time. Encouraged that Helen was cured of the blastoma but confused as to why she didn't wake up.

When the recording was in place I said to Becca, "Turn off the heart machine."

She looked at me, probably thinking the same thing I was thinking. Once we turned off the machine, Helen would either wake up or be gone for good.

I nodded at Becca. "It's okay. Go ahead and turn it off."

Helen's heart suddenly stopped. My hand was holding the recording in place, and I could feel it take its last beat.

* * *

Helen's spirit lifted out of her body and began to ascend to the ceiling overlooking the room. She saw herself laying on the table. Roger was standing over her, holding her hand, tears streaming down his face. His assistant, the girl she had seen in the parking lot of his office, was looking at a machine that had a wire attached to her ear. Roger was holding something inside of her.

She had heard a heartbeat. Beautiful. Sweet like music. Coming from the machine. Every beat brought her closer to the presence of the Lord. She felt such peace until it abruptly stopped.

She suddenly knew the truth. Roger had not had an affair with his assistant.

"You shall know the truth and the truth shall set you free," she heard a voice say.

Jesus.

He was suddenly by her side. He took her hand, and they ascended out of the room and into heaven. Bright lights were everywhere. Peace. Immeasurable peace flooded every fiber of her being. She looked at her hands and feet. She had a new body. A spiritual body. There was no pain. She felt no sadness like she felt on Saturn. No anxiety, or fear. No depression. Just overwhelming joy.

"Do you want to go back to Saturn? It's still your choice," Jesus said.

"No. I want to stay with you Lord."

With those words, they flew away. Through a large gate with pearls on it. Onto a street. A street of shimmering gold.

"I have prepared a place for you," Jesus said. "Look around. There are many mansions. I wouldn't have said it on Saturn if it wasn't true. Here is your mansion. I prepared it myself. It has everything you could ever want or need in it."

A group of people came out of the mansion. Her mother and father. Grandparents. Aunts and Uncles. Two little children. She knew immediately who they were. When she and Roger were first married, she had two miscarriages. She thought she had lost the babies forever. Now, here they were. Right in front of her eyes. They bounded over to her and threw their arms around her legs. She picked them up and hugged and kissed them. They called her mommy.

Helen looked back at Jesus who had a huge and satisfying smile on his face. In a moment, he was back on a large throne that she could see in a distance, seated at the right hand of the father.

The things of Saturn had grown strangely dim.

47

"Why wasn't Helen healed?" I asked Bob, choking back the tears. The coroner had just come and taken Helen's body away. I sewed her chest back up and prepared her body for his arrival. Becca was busily working on Gene, saving all the data, preparing it for moving back to my office. The machine was delicate and had to be handled with great care. I suddenly realized that we didn't have a backup to the information. Something I needed to take care of right away.

Bob and I sat in a corner of the operating room, talking. He was trying to console me. Losing Helen had hit me like a semi-truck.

Chaz, Roki, and Livid were all watching from the portal in the heavenlies. Boor was there as well, giving them instructions. Chaz was the fallen angel assigned to Helen. Roki to Roger and Livid to Becca. They were a powerful trio of fallen angels who had ascended to the realm of rulers.

"Helen is dead," Chaz said to Boor, the one in charge of his principality. "I have accomplished the goal you set for me."

"Your work is not finished," Boor said. "We will not stop until Roger is dead, and the information on that artby is destroyed. The Nohelim chones are nearly ready to be unleashed on Saturn. We only need a few more days, and they will be on the battlefield. Nothing can stop them, except Forrester and his heartbeat machine. The Christians will be annihilated off the face of Saturn if we can stop him. I need each of you to continue to work to destroy Roger. A plan is in place. Devised by the evil one himself. He will hold each of you personally responsible for its failure."

The last words were threatening and were said in a loud, commanding voice. Even though Chaz, Roki, and Livid were rulers, they were shaking, overcome with fear at the thought of letting down the evil one himself.

"Just tell me what to do," Roki said. "And I'll do it."

"Me too," Livid chimed in.

Livid was in charge of Becca, so he didn't think there was anything for him to do with Roger. With Helen dead, Chaz thought he could move on to another subject with a possible promotion.

Boor backhanded Livid with a quick strike. "You already let Ed, the Nohelim die without getting him to mix his seed with Becca. You have already let the great one down. This is your chance to redeem yourself. All three of you stick with Roger for now. Make sure he feels as much grief and guilt as possible for the death of his wife."

Boor suddenly disappeared.

Chaz, Roki, and Livid turned their attention to Roger who was sitting in the operating room talking to the Christian pastor, Bob who had his own legion of fallen angels around him. Even with that many, they hadn't had much success hurting him. Bob was using his power and words to bring comfort to Roger. There was nothing they could do at the moment except sit back and watch. They would attack Roger once he was away from the pastor.

"Some things with God are a mystery we won't know the answer to until we get to heaven," Bob said gently.

"We did everything the same," I said. "Why was Mark healed and Helen wasn't?"

"I've laid hands on many people over the years," Bob countered. "Some were healed, and some weren't. To be honest, most weren't. The Bible says they should be."

"What does it say?" I asked.

"It says that God desires above all things that we prosper and be in good health. It says that we were healed when Jesus took the stripes on his back. We know that all of God's grace is accessed by faith."

"I don't understand then. You have enough faith. Was it me? I admit that I had doubts. Is it my fault that Helen wasn't healed? Did I do something wrong?" The thoughts of Misty popped into my mind.

Roki sent Roger that image.

"Could it be my sin that caused her to die?" I asked as the pain of that possibility shot through me like a knife. I was worried beforehand that God might be punishing me for my sin, and because of that, Helen wouldn't get healed. Now my worst fears were realized.

A spirit of guilt had come upon him, courtesy of Roki.

"We just don't know why people aren't healed," Bob said a little stronger, reaching out his hand and grasping mine. "Remember how it didn't work right away on Mark? I think sometimes we don't say the right words. Sometimes, we don't have enough faith. The Bible says if you doubt, then you are double-minded, and you shouldn't expect anything from God. I'm sure there are times when our sin blocks the healing. But God no longer punishes us for sin, because Christ took our punishment. But sometimes we can get in the way of what God is doing."

Bob moved his hand from clasping mine to my shoulder as I slumped over with my elbows on my knees and my head in my hands, no longer able to hold back the tears.

"I don't think you should beat yourself up over it. Especially when you can never know the answer. Helen might not have wanted to come back. Maybe she was ready to go on and be with Jesus. There's no way of knowing. So, it's okay to grieve, but just don't blame yourself."

I knew he was right, but I was going to need time. The thought of having lost Helen forever was almost more than I could bear. Becca quit working on Gene and walked over to us. She wiped away tears from underneath eyes as well.

"I know it's no consolation," Becca said, "but we got a lot of new information from Helen's cells."

I just shook my head in agreement unable to speak words at the moment.

Becca knelt down on her knees in front of me, put her hands on my hand and looked up at me with reassurance in her eyes and tone.

"Did you realize that Helen was healed from blastoma just from hearing the heartbeat?" Becca said. "Do you know what this means?"

I did know.

"That means we can create recordings of heartbeats and send them to hospitals everywhere. All they have to do is play those recordings in their patient's ears, and they will be healed."

"That's what you need to focus on now, Roger," Bob said. "Helen did not die in vain. Her death, while tragic, is going to save lives."

"And we now know how to kill the Nohelims in the battlefield," Becca said. "You did it, Roger. These discoveries are going to save Saturn from the Satite chones. We need to get to work on it right away."

I felt renewed strength. They were right. We needed to get this discovery into a workable form right away. Regardless of the grief, I had to set it aside and get to work. More Nohelims were showing up on the battlefield every day.

"Is Gene ready to move?" I asked.

"Yes," Becca said. "I've saved all the data to the hard drive. I ran more tests. I'm excited to show you the results."

"This has been a very emotional day for everyone. Go home and get some sleep, and I'll meet you back at my office in the morning. I'll take Gene with me. I'll take it to the office tonight so it's safe."

That had become a concern to me. I wanted to take it to the office and back up all the information. The data and software were too valuable to risk losing. The data from the chones couldn't be replicated without new subjects. If anything happened to Gene or to me, we risked losing all the information, and Becca wouldn't know how to reconstruct it.

We left the operating room and took the elevator down to the lobby.

"I'm parked this way," Bob said pointing to the parking garage.

"Me, too," Becca said as she wrapped her arms around me into a hug.

"I'm parked out front. In the doctor's spaces," I said. "Let's meet in the morning at nine. Is that too early?"

"That works for me," Bob said.

"I don't think I'm going to get much sleep tonight anyway," Becca said with a shrug of the shoulders.

I realized how traumatic a day it had been for her as well. She had lost Ed. Or at least the dream of Ed. I'm sure she was wondering about her own sin of having fallen for him and being deceived.

We said our goodbyes, and I walked out the large double doors from the front entrance onto a large sidewalk. My airmobile was just on the other side of the parking barriers.

"Dr. Forrester," Detective Stone said. "You're just the man I'm looking to see."

My heart sank at the familiar voice. Had he been waiting for me. "Now's not a good time detective."

I was too tired and emotionally drained to feel scared at all. Didn't really feel anything at that moment. I was just numb.

Another man was with him. He had a badge on his lapel, so I assumed he was a detective as well. He was younger. Fit. Slightly taller than me. Probably an assistant I assumed because Stone seemed to be in charge.

"Dr. Forrester, you are under arrest for the attempted murder of your wife, Helen Forrester."

"My wife Helen actually died tonight."

"In that case, let me rephrase what I just said. You are under arrest for the *murder* of your wife, Helen Forrester."

The other detective seized my arm before I could react, and he put it in an armbar behind my back. Gene was on a roller and clanged to the ground when he grabbed my other arm and then tied my arms together behind me.

Stone patted me down, took my caller out of my pocket and put it in his. He then grabbed me by the elbow and started making me walk with him in the direction he had come from. The younger man picked Gene up off the ground.

"Be careful with that," I said. "It has valuable information."

I looked back over my shoulder, straining to see what he was doing with Gene. I saw him walking the other direction with Gene in tow. Panic was shooting through my veins like an electric current. More from what might happen to Gene than what might happen to me.

One call to the First Minister and I would be set free immediately. Gene was another matter. I couldn't lose that information. That data wasn't backed up. The fate of Saturn was in Gene.

"You're making a big mistake," I said. "I didn't kill my wife."

"I don't care," he said. "You can tell that to the judge tomorrow morning."

Tomorrow morning.

I was supposed to meet Bob and Becca in the morning.

PART THREE

The ends don't always justify the ends.

48

The wheels of injustice move swiftly on Saturn. The next morning, I was in front of a judge who would decide my fate that morning. No witnesses would be called. I wasn't allowed representation, but I was given the opportunity to provide a two-sentence rebuttal to every accusation.

The prosecutor, Detective Hick Stone, who acted as the accuser would present a piece of evidence, I would respond with whatever argument I had to contradict the evidence, and then the judge would make his ruling. As it turned out, *her* ruling, as Judge Emily Watkins walked in the courtroom and took her place behind the large wooden stately throne that sat at least ten feet above me.

The penalty on Saturn for murder was death. An eye for an eye was the legal theory that came from an Old Testament verse. I could even be put to death for adultery, but that rarely happened, and only when a criminal act was associated with it. I didn't know if a woman judge was good or bad for me. I'd never been in the legal system before.

Judge Emily Watkins peered over her glasses and did a double take when she saw me in the witness box. She probably knew of my reputation.

"I'm surprised to see you here, Dr. Forrester," she said. She wore a black robe and her hair was short and perfectly styled. Her face was thin, and she looked tired, even though mine was the first case of the day.

"I'm surprised to be here, your Honor," I replied. "I am innocent of all of these charges," I declared confidently.

"Everybody that comes before me is innocent, right Detective Stone?" Judge Watkins said smugly. I had a sudden concern that I'd discovered her bad side first thing. "With all due respect, Dr. Forrester, you are only innocent if I declare you so. It's like in a ball game. If the umpire calls you out, you're out whether you really were or not. My job is to be the umpire. To hear the evidence and pass judgment. You may think because you are a famous doctor that you can come in here and just profess your innocence, and I'll let you go without hearing the evidence. It doesn't work that way. If you are indeed innocent, I'll know it and will rule accordingly. In the meantime, stick to the evidence and not your own professions of guilt or innocence."

A little bit of steam flew out of my confidence. I knew they had no evidence, but I wondered if I would get a fair trial. She might look skeptically at a rich doctor with a dead wife. I had asked to make a call to the First Minister, but no contact with the outside world was allowed. By the clock on the wall, Becca and Bob would be arriving at the office in a few minutes. They would have no idea where I was or why Gene wasn't there. The artby was still my biggest concern. I needed to get that data to them as soon as possible. The only way to do that was to convince the judge of my innocence.

"What's the charge, Detective Stone," the Judge asked.

"Murder. Doctor Forrester murdered his wife, Helen Forrester."

The judge said something under her breath, but I couldn't hear it.

I wondered why he was allowed to declare my guilt, but she took exception to my declaring my innocence. Apparently two sets of rules applied to the proceedings. The judge stared at me, looking me up and down, sizing me up as if she could decide my guilt by her perceptions of me. I thought it best not to say anything.

"You may proceed with your evidence, Detective."

We were both standing—he on the left side of the judge, and I on the right. My hands were free. We were both wearing suits, although mine probably cost twice as much, and I'd been wearing mine since the morning before.

"Dr. Forrester had an affair with Misty Erikson. He met her at the Hotel Segera that morning."

The court officer explained to me that the accuser would make a short statement and then I could respond. The detective had obviously found Misty and questioned her. No telling what she said.

"That's true," I answered. I figured no reason to lie in these proceedings. "Although I wouldn't call it an affair. We only had sex once."

"She said three times," Stone said, thumbing through his papers.

I just shrugged.

"I asked her if she helped Dr. Forrester kill his wife," Stone said. "I was wearing a voice lie detector on my lapel. Her answer was no, which was truthful, but she did say that she wouldn't put it past him to do such a thing."

I shifted my weight back and forth on my feet nervously. Stone must've been wearing a lie detector when he questioned me. I tried to scroll through our conversations in my mind to see what I had lied about. Before I could, he was on to the next accusation.

"Helen Forrester was lying on the floor of their bedroom, near death. Dr. Forrester was the last person to see her alive."

"That's true."

"She had twelve pills in her stomach. Pedroxin. A lethal dose for a woman her size and weight. Dr. Forrester's DNA was found in the back of her mouth. That was from when he shoved the pills down her throat."

The whole scene flashed back before my eyes. The whole terrifying moment was in my mind in living color.

"That's not true," I said with my body shaking. "I put my hand in her mouth to induce vomiting."

The judge was writing something on a pad in front of her. She hadn't looked up from the pad since the detective started presenting his case.

"Helen had a large gash on her head. The doctor who attended to Mrs. Forrester at the hospital said a large object probably caused the blunt force trauma that gave her a concussion and knocked her unconscious. That's when Dr. Forrester shoved the pills down her throat."

Stone was good. Methodical. He called her Helen to make her more a real person to the judge. His thick drawl made him sound like a good ole' boy. Believable. Things were not going well.

"She likely hit her head on the edge of the nightstand," I countered.

"That could've been easily confirmed by checking for blood on the nightstand. Unfortunately, Dr. Forrester instructed his maid to come in and clean up the entire scene before I could inspect it."

I didn't instruct the maid to clean! I wanted to shout at the top of my lungs. I couldn't rebut every point. The judge had no way of knowing if I instructed the maid to clean up the scene or not. I decided to argue the things that would make a difference.

"Did you find the so-called weapon? The large object I supposedly hit her with?" I asked Stone with a hint of sarcasm in my voice. The Judge looked up from her desk and looked at Stone. It was an important question.

"We never recovered the weapon. We presume he disposed of it before I had a chance to inspect the house. I asked Dr. Forrester if he'd ever killed anyone, and the lie detector showed deception."

This was the most damning evidence. How could I rebut it without getting the First Minister in trouble? That's why I needed to call him. He would cover this up immediately if just to protect himself and the program. An idea came in my head.

"You didn't ask me if I killed my wife," I rebutted. "Why not? That's the question before this court."

"You answered no, about killing someone, which was a lie. You could've said that you didn't kill your wife and then the lie detector would've registered your guilt or innocence. I wish you had answered the question."

"Ask me now then," I said. "I'll answer the question. The lie detector will show that I didn't kill my wife."

"The law doesn't allow it in the courtroom," the judge said. "It's only allowed to be used in investigations and then presented as evidence."

"You mean he can use it as evidence to prove my guilt, but I can't use it to prove my innocence?"

"That's the law, Doctor. I don't make the laws. I just judge guilt or innocence."

"Well, I'm innocent, and I want the record to reflect that I was willing to take the lie detector test to prove it. That should speak volumes about my innocence."

"I'll consider it."

"The next day," Stone continued, "I asked Dr. Forrester the same question. He said that he hadn't killed anyone that day. That was a lie. We never found a body, but we have every reason to believe that Dr. Forrester killed his wife and then killed someone else the next day. Probably an accomplice who could implicate him in the crime."

"That's total speculation, your Honor. I don't hear Detective Stone presenting evidence. I hear him giving his perceptions and his presumptions. What if that lie detector is wrong? What if it's malfunctioning? Are you going to convict an innocent man on circumstantial evidence?"

The Judge tapped her writing instrument on her paper. I had scored some points, I thought. My arguments were persuasive.

"Have you ever killed anyone, Dr. Forrester?" the judge asked.

"I can't answer that, your Honor. I wish I could. But I didn't kill my wife."

The program was more important than this hearing. We had to get the heartbeats into a weapon to use on the battlefield against the Satites. Whatever the judge decided, I could get it overturned by the First Minister. We could work this all out later. If I revealed the program in this courtroom, a huge firestorm would erupt. The better course of action was just to maintain my innocence and hope the judge did the right thing. If not, I'd let the powers that be get me out of it. Out of the courtroom, I could take a lie detector and prove my innocence.

"Continue, Detective Stone," the judge said soberly as if she had already made her decision.

"Last night, Dr. Forrester asked the hospital to move Helen to an operating room in the hospital. He insisted that no hospital personnel be permitted in the area. A few hours later, his wife was dead."

"She was on life support," I said as tears welled up. "I was trying to save her life. That's why I took her off life support."

"She needed the life support to survive," Stone said accusingly, raising his voice. "You took her off of the life support so you could finish the job."

"That's not true. I was trying a procedure that I thought might save her."

"You didn't want her waking up and telling the world that you had tried to kill her."

"That's not true!"

"You're a murderer, Forrester. You murdered your wife. You murdered someone else the next day. You covered it up. You lied here today. You are a murderer!"

His words echoed through the courtroom.

"It's not true," I said as I started sobbing.

Stone held a picture of Helen high in the air.

"You took this poor woman's life! You had an affair! Then you killed her! You are the one who deserves to die!"

Tears filled my eyes so I couldn't even see. I doubled over in pain. He was right. I did have an affair. I did kill the Satite. I killed Ed.

I did lie to the detective. The guilt and shame overwhelmed me. My knees buckled. I collapsed to the floor. Sobbing.

Chaz, Riki, and Livid were looking on, adding their vitriol to Stone's words. The devil is the accuser of the brethren. This was when they were in their element. When they were accusing Christians. Didn't matter that it was all a lie. They had been accusing Christians for centuries and on many planets. Many times, they deserved to be accused. Sometimes they didn't. It didn't matter to them.

"I've heard enough," the judge said. "I'm ready to rule. Bailiff, lift Dr. Forrester to his feet."

Roki loved when Christians were before a secular judge. The Bible even said to stay out of courtrooms. How can the unrighteous judge a saint? Roki himself knew he would someday be judged by Christians like Roger in heaven. For now, he could use the ungodly judge to pass judgment on the righteous. He was confident in what she would do.

"Dr. Forrester stand to your feet and take your punishment like a man," she said as her voice shook in anger. "I find you guilty of the murder of your wife. I sentence you to die by lethal injection this afternoon."

"This afternoon?"

"That's right. You profess to be a Christian. Then you can die like Jesus died. He was tried in the morning and killed in the afternoon. Not that you are anything like Jesus. God have mercy on your soul."

I collapsed to the floor again.

49

"Where could Roger possibly be?" Becca asked Bob.

They were sitting in Becca's office in the lab the next morning at the scheduled time. Becca had stopped and picked up coffee and pastries from *Joe's Coffee* and had Roger's favorite ready for him, but he hadn't shown up. Becca tried to call him, but it went straight to voicemail. They were starting to fear the worst.

"I don't know," Bob said. "Maybe he overslept. He had a very eventful day yesterday."

"He specifically said he was bringing Gene to the office last night. Roger almost always does exactly what he says he's going to do."

The artby was nowhere to be found.

"I have a bad feeling," Becca said. "What if Roger was kidnapped by the Satites? That Ed guy was a chone sent to try and kill me. What if the Satites have the artby? That has all of our data. I won't be able to replicate it."

Bob nodded although staring out the window to the office, lost in thought. "I think you're right," he said. "I just sense it in my spirit. Something has happened to him. I just don't know what it is."

"I'm not going to sit here waiting to find out." Becca started gathering her things.

"What are you going to do?"

"I'm going to go find him."

* * *

I was led out of the courtroom and into a confinement room. Detective Stone followed me into the room, more to gloat than anything.

"I didn't kill my wife."

"Tell that to God," he said tersely.

"He already knows," I retorted. "You're making a big mistake."

"It won't be my first and won't be my last," Stone said smugly. "But I know a killer when I meet one."

"Yeah. But it's my life you're making a mistake with. More importantly, what you are doing has great ramifications for Saturn. I need for you to call Elijah Lee. Talk to him. He will clear all of this up."

"The First Minister of Saturn?" Stone said incredulously. "Don't make me laugh. You're a dead man barely walking, grasping at straws. Do you really think the First Minister is going to give you a pardon for killing your wife? You're dreaming."

"It's bigger than that. The national security of Saturn depends on me staying alive. Call Elijah. He'll clear this up."

"Are you on a first name basis with the First Minister now?" he said sarcastically. "Why don't you clear it up? Tell me who else you killed before we send you to meet your maker."

"I can't. But the First Minister can. Write down this number. 555-282-5555."

Stone didn't move.

"You're not writing it down!"

"I don't have time to go on a wild goose chase for you," he said roughly. "What does the First Minister have to do with you killing your wife?"

"I didn't kill my wife. That's what I've been trying to tell you. Minister Lee needs to know what's going on. Please, call him."

"Forget it! The judge has already made her ruling. You're going to die in about four hours. I doubt you even know Minister Lee." He looked at the clock on the wall when he said it.

"Get the lie detector then. Ask me if I killed my wife? I'll answer no. You'll see that I'm telling the truth."

"I don't have the lie detector with me. It's back at the office."

"Go get it," I insisted. "You have to hurry, though. I only have four hours. Also call this number." I gave him the First Minister's number again. "Call him. Tell him you're calling about Dr. Forrester. He'll know what to do."

Stone seemed unmoved. "I don't believe you."

"Please."

He seemed unpersuaded.

"Do it for Helen. Don't you want to know the truth? Wouldn't you like to know if you're sending an innocent man to his death? Go get the lie detector. Do the right thing. Call the First Minister. If I'm lying, then all you did was waste time making a phone call. Isn't Helen's life worth one phone call?"

"All right." he said reluctantly, frowning at me. "I'll go get the lie detector. If you're still lying, I'll make sure they put the poison in your body real slow... Make you suffer. Like you did Helen. If you're telling the truth, I'll talk to the judge."

"Thank you," I said. "Please, hurry."

* * *

Stone went straight back to his office to get the lie detector. When he arrived, he looked everywhere for it but couldn't find it. He stuck his head in his Assistant Detective's office.

"Jim, have you seen the lie detector?"

"Willowby has it. He's working on a case."

"When will he be back?"

Jim shrugged his shoulders.

Stone went back to his office and called Willowby, but the call went to voicemail. He pulled the number for the First Minister, Elijah Lee.

"How is that lowlife Forrester on a first name basis with the First Minister?" he muttered to himself under his breath.

He stared at the number. Then laid it back down on his desk. Then picked it up again.

He was curious. Forrester had been so insistent he was innocent. Most people were, so that wasn't unusual. What was strange was that he kept pushing him to do things that were easily verifiable. The lie detector, for instance. Why would Forrester push for him to get it and bring it back to his confinement cell? It would prove he was guilty. No way Forrester could beat the test. Why would he insist unless he was innocent?

Same with the First Minister. There must be something there or he wouldn't put so much pressure on him to call.

"I'll look like a fool, if I call the First Minister's office," he said to himself.

Although...

He sat back in his chair, thinking. Thirty minutes had passed since he left Forrester in confinement. He only had a little over three hours until he would die. Not much time, but enough to prove his guilt or innocence one way or the other. What did it hurt to find out for sure?

Also, how did Forrester have the First Minister's number?

Maybe there was something to it after all, he decided. If nothing else, his curiosity was raised. He also wondered what trouble he might get into if Forrester was right and the national security of Saturn was at stake.

He picked up his caller and dialed the number. A woman answered.

"Office of Minister Lee," she said.

A jolt of adrenaline went through him. The number was real. He was talking to the office of the First Minister of Saturn. The most important man in the free world. He suddenly felt very nervous.

"I'm calling for Minister Lee. My name is Detective Stone of the Westminster Police Department."

"Minister Lee is in a conference."

That was probably her standard line for every caller unless she knew who it was or had specific instructions to put the call through.

"It's about Dr. Roger Forrester. It's urgent."

"Leave me your number, and I will get him the message."

Stone gave her his number and then hung up, thinking maybe it was legitimate and Forrester wasn't lying. For the first time, he wondered if he might actually be innocent.

50

An emergency meeting of the National Security Council had been called. Tension filled the room as word that more Satite chones had entered the battlefield yesterday. The meeting didn't begin until Elijah Lee, First Minister of Saturn, arrived and sat down at the head of the large conference table.

"What's the latest assessment?" Minister Lee said.

"More than three thousand chones entered the battlefield yesterday," Langston Murray, the Minister of Information said.

"Are these giants like the others?" Lee asked, afraid of the answer he knew was about to come.

The entire room collectively looked Murray's way.

"Bigger," Minister of Defense Josiah Matthews said.

All heads turned toward Mathews with various looks ranging from shock to disbelief.

"Some of them are between nine-and-ten-feet tall. They weigh about five hundred pounds of sheer muscle."

A loud gasp went through the room.

"They are killing our men at a rate of eight hundred an hour. Our armies are fighting valiantly but are no match for them."

"Are these Nohelim like Dr. Forrester said?" Murray asked.

"We think so," he answered nervously. "They have no knowledge of good and evil. They seem programmed to kill. Like they don't have a mind of their own. They are killing everyone indiscriminately. Men, women, and children."

"They are killing children?" Lee asked.

"Yes. They attacked a whole village last night. Slaughtered everyone in the village. And then burned the entire town to the ground. There are no survivors."

Lee asked the next obvious question. "Is there anything you can do to stop them?"

Matthews shook his head no. They spent more than an hour going through various plans and possible defense strategies. They finally determined they had no ideas that would work against such lethal force.

"What about Dr. Forrester?" Ralph Jones the Minister of Information spoke up. "Has he come up with a way to stop them?"

"He called me yesterday." Lee answered. "He left a message. I haven't listened to it yet."

Lee scrolled through his caller until he came to the message. He hit play and turned on the speaker.

"Minister Lee, this is Dr. Forrester. We have a weapon we know will work against the Satites. It will be ready for the battlefield tomorrow. My wife is in the hospital. So, I'm heading there now. The doctors don't think she's going to make it. Call me when you get this message."

"I'm sorry to hear about his wife," Lee said sincerely. "But it sounds like he has a weapon that will work."

The mood of the room had suddenly improved considerably.

"I'm sorry, too," Matthews said, "but we're running out of time. We can only hold them off for so long. Within a week, they'll be in Westminster. I don't think we can stop them unless this weapon Forrester has works. We need to get in touch with him as soon as possible."

Lee pulled out his phone and dialed Roger's number. It went to voicemail.

"Dr. Forrester, this is Elijah. Call me back. I got your message. There are new developments. We need that weapon now."

Elijah Lee hung up the caller and then stood to his feet and said, "Wait here for a minute. I'm going to ask my secretary if she's heard from Roger. Ralph call the hospital. See if Roger is there. We have to get in touch with him."

He walked out of the conference room, down a long hall, and to the desk of his secretary.

"Meg, have we heard from Dr. Forrester?" he asked.

"No sir. Not since yesterday. But you did get a call from a detective from the Westminster Police Department saying he was calling about something relating to Dr. Forrester. He said it was urgent."

"A detective? That's strange. Why wasn't I told about it?"

"You said you didn't want to be disturbed while the Council was meeting."

"I don't want to be disturbed unless it has to do with Dr. Forrester," he said emphatically. "Get the detective on the line and patch him through to the conference room."

"Right away, sir."

Elijah walked back to the room and sat back down in his chair.

"Did you find out anything, Ralph?"

"Dr. Forrester's wife died last night. He left the hospital shortly thereafter. They don't know where he is."

Elijah didn't speak at first as he tried to process the information. "I'm so sorry to hear that," he finally said. "Get someone over to his house. And his office. He probably turned off his caller. He's obviously in mourning."

The phone on the conference table rang. Minister Lee hit the button with the blinking light. He hit the speaker button at the same time so the conversation could be heard through the entire room.

"I have Detective Stone from the Westminster Police Department on the line," his secretary said.

"Put him through." There was silence on the line until he heard a click and breathing on the other end.

"Detective Stone, this is Minister Lee. You called me with information about Dr. Forrester."

"Yes sir."

"Do you know how I can get in touch with him? It's urgent," the First Minister said.

"Dr. Forrester is dead. He was executed by lethal injection just a few minutes ago."

A murmur went through the conference room.

"Executed! For what!"

"For the murder of his wife, Helen Forrester."

"Dr. Forrester didn't murder his wife. I've known the man for twenty years."

"A judge found him guilty this morning and sentenced him to death this afternoon. He claimed he was innocent and asked me to call you. Which I did."

Elijah looked at the clock. It was only eleven thirty.

"It's not afternoon yet."

"I guess it was a slow day at the executioner's office. They carried it out a few hours early."

"You've made a big mistake Detective Stone! A big mistake!"

He hung up on him.

"What do we do now?" Lee said.

*　*　*

Detective Stone hung up the phone slowly.

What did he mean I made a big mistake?

Stone obviously knew the First Minister. Elijah Lee seemed mad at him. What did he do? He was just doing his job. It's not his fault they executed him early. He was trying to find out the truth.

A knock on the door interrupted his thoughts.

Jim.

He had a large artby in his arms.

"I have Forrester's artby here. What do you want me to do with it?"

Stone didn't answer. He was almost in shock.

"Saturn to Stone..." Jim said playfully.

"Erase the hard drive," Stone said roughly. "Get rid of everything on it. Then destroy it. I don't want to see it around here again."

"Whatever you say, boss."

Was that the right thing to do? Was he destroying evidence? Evidence of what? Standard procedure was to destroy or sell whatever was confiscated from a criminal.

Another knock on the door jolted him back to reality.

Willowby.

"Here's the lie detector. Jim said you wanted it."

"Yeah," Stone said, still distracted. Not sure what had just happened with the First Minister. Was his job in jeopardy? Did he do something wrong? He called the First Minister like Forrester had asked.

"Just sit it on my desk," Stone said, not even looking up. The lie detector wouldn't do Stone any good now.

"Also, one of your conversations was on there," Willowby added. "I printed out the results for you."

Conversations?

What conversation would be on there? He suddenly remembered. He had the lie detector on his lapel when he arrested Forrester the night before.

He picked up the results slowly and began reading with his mouth agape.

"I didn't kill my wife," Forrester had said.

"I don't care," Stone retorted.

Results: Truthful.

51

My spirit left my body and ascended rapidly into the heavenlies where I immediately saw a bright light coming toward me like a train in a tunnel. The brightest light I'd ever seen. In a moment, in the twinkling of an eye, Jesus suddenly appeared. I bowed my knee to worship him. He lifted my head. and I could see in his eyes. All I saw was love, peace, and kindness. No judgment at all. He took my hand and raised me up to my feet.

I suddenly had a new body. A spiritual body. It seemed perfect in every way. I had new skills as well. I could fly. We flew away toward a huge city filled with bright lights and a kaleidoscope of colors. Bright colors, everywhere. There were flowers, trees, birds singing, children playing, and music. Lots of music filled the air.

Jesus stopped in front of a mansion.

"Is this mine?" I asked. The mansion was huge. Not the biggest on the street but bigger than anything I'd ever seen before or imagined could be mine.

"This is my father's house," Jesus said, waving his arms toward all of heaven. "There are many mansions. I told you, Roger, that it would be so. I left Saturn so I could prepare a place for you. For where I am, there you may be also. For an eternity. Here is the house that I prepared just for you."

Suddenly, the door to my mansion flew open. Out came Helen and two small children. A boy and a girl. The two children started running toward me. Then they went airborne and flew to me, into my arms, hugging me, kissing me, calling me Daddy.

Helen was right behind them and greeted me just as enthusiastically.

"Are these our kids?" I asked Helen.

"Yes, Roger. Aren't they beautiful?" she said.

Helen kissed me on both cheeks with a holy kiss. Nothing awkward. The difficulties between us on Saturn were not there anymore. Barely even a memory. There was no marriage in heaven, but Helen and I had an inseparable bond. Something special. Impossible to put into words. One flesh on earth; one heart in heaven.

I no longer regretted having left Saturn early, other than that my work wasn't done. I hadn't been able to save the world from the Nohelim, which was my biggest regret. The realization became even more apparent when the Christians began arriving in heaven from Saturn in droves. At first a few hundred. Then a few thousand. Eventually, every Christian was wiped off the face of Saturn by the Nohelim.

Becca and Bob arrived with the masses. They explained what had happened.

"I went looking for you," Becca said. "You weren't at your home. I finally found your airmobile at the hospital. Then we learned you were executed for the murder of your wife."

"That was not true," I said. "I didn't kill her."

"We knew it wasn't true," Bob said.

"We never found Gene, the artby," Becca said. "I don't know what happened to it."

"The police took it from me when I was arrested."

"They probably destroyed it or put it in an evidence room," Bob said. "Who knows?"

"Doesn't matter now," I replied with a shrug. "What happened with the Nohelim?"

"They attacked the Christians and wiped them off the face of Saturn," Bob said. "There was only a remnant of us left. Then God sent a huge fire down and completely destroyed the Nohelim. All life on Saturn was completely destroyed shortly thereafter."

"I only wished we could've saved everyone," I said. "Satan destroyed our plans."

As we were talking, an angel of the Lord appeared. "Roger, go and get Helen," he proclaimed, and meet me in the square. "Becca, come with me," he said, taking her by the hand.

I left and told Helen the angel of the Lord wanted to meet us. We went to the square immediately. Becca and the angel were already there.

The angel took us to a big room. It had the shape of a courtroom. We were told to sit in the front of the room where a judge would sit. The three of us were on a judgement seat. About ten feet above where an accused would stand. It looked very similar to the courtroom I was tried in.

"The Lord said in the Bible that humans would stand in judgment over angels," the angel proclaimed in a loud voice. "Bring in the unrighteous angels."

A door opened and three demons appeared. Their names were announced. Chaz, Roki, and Livid were demons assigned to us on Saturn. They were bound. Hissing. Cursing. Spitting evil words like fire out of their mouths.

I had no fear of them. They couldn't hurt us. We were well protected by a legion of good angels.

"These three were the fallen angels assigned to each of you on Saturn by the evil one," the angel of the Lord began. "Chaz lied to Helen and falsely accused her husband of having an affair with Becca. He deceived Helen into killing herself over it. Livid lied to Becca and put a spirit of lust over her and tried to get her to mix her seed with the Nohelim chone. Then the Nohelim tried to kill her in the lab. He actually tried to kill all of you.

Roki, you deceived Roger. You put spirits of lust over him and manipulated circumstances so he would meet the temptress, Misty.

You blinded his eyes so she would seem attractive to him. Then you falsely accused him of murdering his wife and had him executed for a crime he didn't commit."

"You should know that God hates the shedding of innocent blood. It is an abomination to him." The angel was shouting now in a large and commanding voice.

The three fallen angels were cowering as the truth and magnitude of their deceit was revealed.

"None of this had to happen. God's plan to destroy the Nohelim and reveal a cure for blastoma was all thwarted by the work of the evil one and his minions. Helen, you are the judge of Chaz. What do you pronounce over him? Guilty or Not Guilty."

"He is guilty," Helen said emphatically.

"Becca. What do you pronounce over Livid?"

"Guilty," she said strongly.

"Roger. What say you about Roki?"

"He is guilty as charged!" I declared in a loud voice. So loud the three of them began shaking uncontrollably.

"You have been found guilty by your judges," the angel said to Chaz, Livid, and Roki. "I command that you all be thrown out of heaven and into the lake of fire, and you will have nothing more to do with any other planets. You will no longer torment any of God's creation again. Be gone!"

The three were seized by angels and dragged out of the courtroom, their screams of torment heard as they were cast out of heaven into the lake of fire.

We stepped down from behind the throne, completely satisfied that justice was finally done. At the same time, we each had a keen sense of awareness of what was lost on Saturn. Our part in letting the deception happen didn't escape us. So much of what God wanted to do through us never happened because we allowed Satan's fallen angels to trick and deceive us and keep us from doing God's work.

The Nohelim could've been defeated. Saturn could've had a different fate. Yet, so much turned on our inability to overcome the flesh and the enemy and trust in the Word of God. While we felt no more shame, guilt, or condemnation, we were aware of how different things could've been.

The angel of the Lord came up to us and said in a comforting manner, "Justice is done. Forget the past. Think of the hope of your future and an eternity with God. You will never see those fallen angels again. Now, Becca and Roger come with me."

"Where are we going?" I asked.

"To Earth," he said.

"What is earth?"

"That is a new planet God created."

"What will we be doing on earth?"

"You'll see when we get there," he said with a broad smile.

52

The angel of the Lord lifted us in the air and transported us into the heavenlies and out into deep outer space. The journey was spectacular as we traversed galaxies and planets and flew at a high rate of speed past a number of stars, nova, and supernovas.

We slowed down when we passed Saturn. I looked at Becca, and we both felt the sense of loss as our once-thriving planet was now desolate. A cold vast expanse of nothingness. The only thing remaining that was familiar were the rings, which still maintained their glorious color and majestic shape around Saturn.

"Let's keep going. We're almost there," the angel said.

The angel pointed out the names of planets as we passed them. Next was Jupiter. We could see Jupiter from Saturn sometimes at night. Next was a large red planet. The angel called it Mars. It was beautiful, but as desolate as Saturn and Jupiter had been. The angel explained that they once had life on them. God had made man on each planet. And a garden of Eden. They had all eaten of the fruit and brought sin to the world. All had a different story to tell.

"Now when you meet someone from Jupiter or Mars in heaven, you will know more about their planet, having seen it firsthand." The angel suddenly pointed. "Look at that," he said.

Right in front of us a magnificent planet came into view. It had a blue glow. Different from the other planets in that its atmosphere had color and life to it. We arrived at the portal between the spiritual and the physical. Earth was filled with life that we could see through the portal. The view was unbelievable. Blue skies. Deep blue and green bodies of water. Green trees. Bright flowers. The sun radi-

TERRY TOLER

ated off of the atmosphere and was almost blinding except for the cover of the portal.

"Earth is like Saturn in many ways," the angel began speaking. "God made man in his image. Man and woman, he created them. They sinned and brought death to the world. Christ came to redeem them and offer a sacrifice for their sins just like he did on Saturn."

He paused to let that sink in. I still didn't know why we were there.

"Many years ago, Satan mixed his seed with virgin women. They were called Nephilim."

"Hey. That's like our Nohelim," I said.

"Most of the planets take on the same languages," the angel explained. "With some minor differences."

"God destroyed the earth with a flood and killed all of the Nephilim," the angel continued to explain.

"Same as Saturn," Becca said.

"The Nephilim are about to be revived on earth. Man has learned how to clone—you called them chones on Saturn—a human being. It's only a matter of time until the Iranians discover a Nephilim skeleton and learn to clone the evil seed."

"Do they know about the heartbeat?" I asked. "The heartbeat can kill the Nephilim."

"No," the angel said. "They also don't really know the truth about light matter either. They know a little bit, like Saturn, but they don't know the whole truth. They call it dark matter."

"Hey! That's what we called it on Saturn," Becca said. "What's wrong with people? It should be called light matter."

"A plague has also hit the earthlings," the angel continued in a more somber voice.

"What kind of plague?" I asked.

"Cancer."

"What's cancer?"

"It's like blastoma on Saturn. It attacks the body and kills the good cells."

"The heartbeat will cure that," Becca said.

"Except they don't know about it," I added. "Is that why we're here?"

"Yes, Roger. I want you to bring the revelation of light matter and the heartbeat to Earth. We regret that you were never able to finish the job you were called to do on Saturn."

I felt excitement rising up inside of me. "You mean we get to go to earth and become human again?"

"No," the angel said chuckling. "That's not the plan. You are spirit beings now with a new spiritual body. You will work out of the heavenlies, just like all the angels. Beware, though. Boor and others are here and will fight against you."

"What are we supposed to do?" Becca asked.

"I'll show you."

We walked through the portal and saw thousands of humans pass by us until we stopped at one particular place.

"Look down there," the angel said.

We looked through the portal into a small room. A man was sitting at an artby, typing.

"What's he typing?" I asked.

"He's writing a book. A fictional account of Saturn. Only it's not going to be fictional. I mean, he won't know it's not, but it's going to be very real."

"You want us to tell him our story," I said.

"Yes! Tell him everything. The good and the bad. Everything you did right and everything you did wrong. Don't leave anything out."

"This is so exciting," Becca said. "Do you know what this means, Roger? We can help earthlings discover the heartbeat and defeat the Nephilim. We can help them find a cure for cancer."

"Where do we start?" I asked the angel.

"At the beginning." That was the last thing the angel said as he suddenly disappeared.

Becca and I were alone, staring down into the portal.

"What do we do?" she asked.

"Let's listen in," I responded.

A woman had just walked into the room. Probably the writer's wife.

"I'm starting a new book," the man said.

"What planet are you writing about now?" she asked.

"Saturn."

"That's exciting. I can't wait to read it."

"What's the title?" she asked.

The man paused.

"Call it *The Eden Experiment*," I said to him.

"I think I'll call it *The Eden Experiment*," he echoed the thought I had put in his head.

"I like that," she said with a warm and beautiful smile.

The man started typing on the first page.

Saturn: The Eden Experiment.

"Let's get to work, Becca," I said. "This could take a while."

About the Author

TERRY TOLER is the best-selling and award-winning author of *The Eden Stories* series, along with the Alex Halee and Jamie Austen book series along with seventeen nonfiction books. He is a minister, public speaker, counselor, and retired entrepreneur. Impacting the lives of people worldwide through storytelling has become one of his passions in life. He can be followed at terrytoler.com.

GET YOUR FREE GIFT

As a thank you for finishing my book, I want to give you a free ebook. Go to terrytoler.com and sign up for my mailing list and I'll give you a free copy of *The Launch*. A Jamie Austen novella.

Terrytoler.com

THE EDEN STORIES

THE LONGEST DAY

WINNER 2020 BEST BOOK AWARD FOR RELIGIOUS FICTION

BEHOLDINGS PUBLISHING

Follow Terry at terrytoler.com.